I0671817

By DIANA COPLAND

David, Renewed

Published by DREAMSPINNER PRESS
www.dreamspinnerpress.com

David,
Renewed

DIANA COPLAND

Published by
DREAMSPINNER PRESS

5032 Capital Circle SW, Suite 2, PMB# 279, Tallahassee, FL 32305-7886 USA
www.dreamspinnerpress.com

David, Renewed
© 2016 Diana Copland.

Cover Art
© 2016 Anne Cain.
annecain.art@gmail.com
Cover content is for illustrative purposes only and any person depicted on the cover is a model.

ISBN: 978-1-63477-727-8
Digital ISBN: 978-1-63477-728-5
Library of Congress Control Number: 2016907096
Published September 2016
v. 1.0

Printed in the United States of America

This paper meets the requirements of
ANSI/NISO Z39.48-1992 (Permanence of Paper).

For Brandon, Dunkyn, and Dolan,
because your boys are why Boots and Scooter exist.

Acknowledgments

To Saritza Alicia Hernandez, who never gave up. To Elizabeth North, for giving these boys a home. To Betsy, who must be getting tired of saying "I told you so." To Rick R. Reed, for your unwavering support and encouragement. And to Becky Condit, who loved them from the beginning.

To all of you, thank you, from the bottom of my heart.

CHAPTER ONE

DAVID SNYDER didn't think he could take much more.

On a whim born of desperation, he'd purchased the cute, craftsman-style house on the street where he grew up, but if one more thing went wrong, he was ready to pour gasoline around the foundation and light a match.

The little old lady he bought the house from seemed so sincere. During his initial walk-through, David was charmed by the original hardwood floors and the built-in cabinets around the fireplace in the living room. He could imagine sitting near a roaring fire in a comfortable chair, reading a book, and sipping a cup of hot tea on a cold night. The homey image appealed to him, especially now, when everything had been ripped out from under him. He was lost and hurt and had no business buying a house.

He'd thought the worst he would have to contend with was some truly hideous floral wallpaper in one of the bedrooms and a blue tile floor in the bathroom. He'd even looked forward to tearing it all out, painting the walls, and refinishing the beautiful hardwood trim around the doors and windows. He would be a weekend contractor, he decided, as amusing as his friends would find that.

He agreed to a thirty-day escrow because he couldn't stand living in a hotel even one more day. The condo he'd purchased with Trevor was certainly no longer an option. Every time David thought of the high-end condo on the river, he saw his partner of five years leaning back in their black leather sofa, a blissful expression on his face as he was being blown by a young guy with a mop of thick blond hair and broad shoulders like a swimmer. He'd never forget the sight of his lover's cock in someone else's mouth. When Trevor spotted him standing just inside their front door, the flush on his cheeks spread down his neck and he scrambled to push the blond's head from his lap and to do up his fly.

"You're supposed to be in Seattle."

"It was canceled."

1

"But—"

David walked away.

He'd come home to surprise Trevor; he was supposedly home with a cold, and David had planned to make him soup, fluff his pillows. The fluff Trevor was experiencing had nothing to do with pillows, and he was surprised all right.

David had been so glad the trip was canceled, feeling the need to be home with his lover anyway. David's beloved dad had died the month before, and Trevor felt a bit neglected while David dealt with his family obligations. He'd wanted to try to make it up to him; the idea that Trevor would cheat on him then, when he was already so raw, made bile hit the back of David's throat.

"What are you doing?" Trevor came to stand in the doorway, hands on his narrow hips. David didn't answer. "David." He took two steps into the room and reached for him, but the glare David sent his way stopped Trevor cold.

"Don't touch me." David's voice was trembling, but his resolve was clear.

Trevor looked hurt. "You know I wouldn't, not that way."

But David didn't know it. There had been bruises on his wrist once, the back of his neck another time. Hiding them with long sleeves and a turtleneck had felt like lying to his friends and family. And Trevor's last boyfriend had cornered David in a men's room not long after they got together, and told him Trevor had "a tendency to get physical" when things didn't go his way. He'd never hit him, but even after five years, his anger scared David.

"Just… back away, Trevor. I mean it."

Trevor reluctantly took a step back, crossing his arms over his chest. "Jesus, David. It didn't mean anything."

"It didn't mean anything?" His voice came low and raw. "It certainly looked like it meant something."

"It was just a blow job. Christ, you always overreact."

Swamped in hurt, David continued to cram his belongings into the bag. He'd always wondered what someone who looked like Trevor saw in him. He was an effeminate nerd with carefully combed blond hair and rectangular designer glasses that mostly hid his green eyes. His body was nothing to write home about either. He'd maintained his youthful thinness, but even a concentrated six-month stint at a gym had failed to add muscles, and so he gave up. When drop-dead gorgeous Trevor first hit on him in a bar, he thought it was a joke. The man was all black hair and large brown eyes, with broad shoulders and narrow hips, and David couldn't imagine what he saw in him of all people. But Trevor was persistent, David was flattered and thrilled, and they'd been together for five years. He'd been willing to overlook the occasional rages because Trevor was always so apologetic afterward. He thought they were on the same page about fidelity after all that time too. He even planned to propose at Christmas, just three months away; the platinum band he knew would look elegant on Trevor's long, slender finger was already on hold at the jeweler.

David turned away, took as deep a breath as the constriction around his chest would allow, and resumed his packing. He was no longer frantic but methodical, placing his clothes in his suitcase with care, afraid if he started to throw things again he might fly apart in a million pieces. Despite Trevor's protests and halfhearted apologies, David moved out that afternoon and into an Embassy Suites near his downtown office. Two nights on the stiff sheets, listening to people wander up and down the halls at all hours, convinced him he had to do something else quickly.

David had been extremely careful with money during his seven years climbing the corporate ladder at A.F. Interiors. He advanced to an executive-level position, and his hard-earned savings were comfortably into five figures. Trevor even teased that he had the hardest time parting with a dollar of anyone he'd ever known. Then in one impulsive afternoon, David tossed his common sense in the garbage and completely ignored all the advice columns that cautioned not to make big decisions after a traumatic life event. He saw the charming house for sale just down the block and across the street from his mother's, and something inside of him simply said, "Mine."

Now it was his all right.

After a mere thirty days, he was in his new home. He didn't have much; Trevor was determined to be as big an ass as possible and claimed the couch and chairs David purchased when they moved in to the condo. He even kept the bedroom set David's parents bought when he graduated from college. Too hurt and humiliated to fight him, David had bought a queen-sized mattress and box springs and was using a cardboard box as a nightstand. His mom donated a truly ugly recliner for his living room, and he hauled in a cinder block from beside the garage for a side table. He bought a lamp at Target, and that was the extent of the furnishings in the two-thousand-square-foot house. He planned to shop for more the first Saturday after escrow closed. But then things began to go wrong.

First there was the shower he took the second morning after he moved in. It started off fine but turned very cold halfway through. He yelped like a little girl, then realized something must be wrong with the ancient water heater in the basement. It was annoying but not terribly surprising. He'd buy one from someplace that would install the new one and haul the old one away. David knew his strengths, and installing a water heater wasn't one of them. After he managed some toaster waffles for breakfast while standing at his kitchen counter, he opened the dishwasher to put in his plate and the door fell off. He leaned it against the wall and realized he needed to start an actual list of things that were wrong. There were already several.

When he got home from work that evening, he noticed the garage door was hanging awkwardly. He'd been parking his new red Toyota Yaris in the driveway because the real estate agent told him the remote for the garage door was missing. He planned to have someone come out, bring him a new remote, and program in a new code. Then it dawned on him he'd never even bothered to look in the garage.

Charmed again by the beautiful flower beds and verdant green lawn, he walked around the side of the small structure. The spreading maple tree that kept the entire rear yard in shade most of the day had been a huge selling point, and he realized that once he'd seen it and been delighted by it, the real estate agent hadn't needed much help in steering him away from the garage. He tried the doorknob for the garage's access door, and the knob came off in his hand.

"Lovely," he muttered. There was a filthy window in the door, and he tried to rub a place clean enough to peer through. Muted light filtered through the walls and ceiling, just enough to show him that the entire unit to open the garage door was gone. He gave the side of the garage one halfhearted, ineffectual punch and added it to his list of things to do.

Even as tired and irritated as he was, when he walked through the front door he still loved the room. Late afternoon light filtered in through the windows and shadows of wind-stirred leaves on the two large trees in his front yard fell across the hardwood floor, calming him. He changed out of his work clothes and into Levi's and an old Dolly Parton hoodie. It was faded purple, and there was a rhinestone crown nestled in her huge blonde curls. His dad had bought it for him in a vintage store and the shirt made him smile. He used to wear it all the time, but Trevor hated it, so he stopped. He looked down, smile fading to a slight frown. That shit would never happen again.

His plan was to make himself a microwave dinner and drink a cold Diet Coke, but when he opened the refrigerator door, the light didn't come on, and the contents were room temperature. He checked to make sure it was plugged in, but clearly no power was going to the appliance. His heart sinking, he got his tablet from his briefcase. It was time for that list. He made himself a sandwich with mayonnaise and turkey he was going to have to throw out, before popping open a room-temperature soft drink.

The hideous recliner was an eyesore, but it was soft. He gave himself a moment to enjoy its comforting give. Shadows played in the room now, and he turned on the lamp sitting on the cement block. It came on, but almost immediately it gave a loud pop, and the light went off again.

"That didn't sound good." He put his dinner on the floor and tried the lamp again with zero results. He got up with effort and tried the porch light, but it didn't come on either. Moving through the rapidly darkening house, he found all the switches ineffectual until he arrived in the kitchen. Ironically the overhead light came on in there. The electrical panel hung on the service-porch wall, so he walked through to the small room and opened the metal door on the wall.

One whole side of the fuse box was blackened as if there'd been a fire. Even he knew that couldn't be good. He'd known when he opted out of the inspection it was a mistake, but it was going to add two weeks to his escrow and he hadn't wanted to wait. Now he was wondering what he should do when there was another loud pop right in front of him, accompanied by a shower of sparks. He squeaked, jumping back. His heart was pounding when the light in the kitchen went out.

"Oh, holy hell."

He had no idea what to do, but he'd heard all the light switches should be in the off position. He was able to accomplish that at least.

Grumbling, he detoured back into the living room, grabbed up his pad, pencil, and food, then stalked out onto the front porch.

It was a mild evening. David sat on the top step, taking another swig of his room-temperature soda. It took a few minutes, but the gentle breeze and the neighborhood, with its abundant mature trees and beautiful green lawns, soothed him, reminding him why he'd bought the place. The flower beds bordering the steps and around the foundation were in riotous bloom, purple impatiens and pansies in every color of the rainbow. Heavy, round heads of a white hydrangea bobbed in the breeze, and dark pink clematis climbed a trellis by the steps. Late-blooming yellow lilies hugged the river-rock foundation, and their sweet scent drifted over to him. The house was a true craftsman home with the stark, elegant lines, offset by the dark angular rock that was indigenous to the area. David wasn't crazy about the flat gray paint, but he liked the rich burgundy trim. The house had great bones. Much like his failed relationship, he thought with a grimace: it looked great from the outside, but the inside was a mess.

A young couple walked by on the sidewalk pushing a stroller and leading a happy, bright-eyed corgi on a leash. They waved, giving him a friendly smile. He hoped what he returned looked more enthusiastic than it felt. They paused.

"Did you buy the house from Mrs. Howser?" the young woman asked.

"I did."

"We're the Yosts. We live two doors down."

"I'm David Snyder. I guess we're neighbors." David produced a smile for the little dog, who gave him a doggy grin and wagged his little butt where a tail would have been. He was cute as hell.

"Did she tell you about the sewer?" the young man asked.

"What about the sewer?" David frowned.

"Her main sewer line between the house and the street has a break in it. At least that's what one of those Roto-Rooter guys told her. Sorry, man, but I think you should know. That real estate lady of Evelyn's told her not to tell anyone, but that's shady."

David agreed, but what could he do now?

"According to the plumber, it's gonna cost about six grand to fix it. That's one of the reasons she sold the place."

The news hit him like a truck. Clearly passing on the inspection was a dumbass maneuver and he was going to pay for it.

"But it's a beautiful house," the wife said quickly. "I love the floors and the built-ins in the dining room."

"So do I," David agreed weakly.

"Well, nice to meet you." She pulled on her husband's sleeve. "We need to get home and get the baby to bed."

"Yeah, nice to meet you too." David waved, watching until they turned into the driveway two doors down.

"I see you're making friends with the neighbors."

David jerked his head around, startled. His sister, Beth, was walking across his lawn and he hadn't even noticed her.

"Jesus." He spread his hand on his chest, over his pounding heart. "You scared the crap out of me."

"You were too busy flirting with the neighbor's dog to notice me." She smiled.

"What are you doing here?"

"Dropped by to see Mom." She came up the steps and sat next to him. Beth was six years older, but they'd always been close. "I drive over to bring her dinner a couple of times a week. If I don't, she eats toast and that's it. She's lost twenty pounds since Daddy died."

Beth lived clear across town and David felt a twinge of guilt. Even when he'd been in the condo, he'd lived closer to their mother than Beth did.

"I hadn't noticed," David murmured.

"She hides it pretty well." She leaned against his shoulder. "Don't beat yourself up. You've had your own shit to deal with."

"Not until this week."

She gave him a pointed look. "I don't mean the asshole Trevor. Although may he get hit by a bus." A reluctant grin tugged at the corner of David's lips. "It's been tough on you," she went on. "Losing Dad."

David swallowed against the sudden tightness in his throat. There was no point in denying it; Beth always knew when he was lying anyway. He and his dad had been close. Their relationship hadn't been damaged when

7

he came out, which he'd lived in terror of from the moment he realized he was gay. When he told their dad, he just looked at him and said, "So, a son-in-law instead of a daughter-in-law. I can work with that." David didn't think he'd ever love anyone as much as he had his dad in that moment.

"It's been tough for all of us." He looked down at his tired white tennis shoes. Anything not to look into Beth's eyes and see the quiet sorrow that mirrored his own.

"But seriously." Beth pressed her hand to his forearm and thankfully changed the subject. "How's the house? I've always loved this place." Her expression was wistful as she gazed around the wide porch that ran the length of the front. "This is the perfect porch for a swing. I wonder why she never had one."

"Probably because she was afraid the roof would cave in." His tone was dark, and she looked at him, a question in the green eyes that were so like his own. "Let's just say I shouldn't have skipped the inspection."

She grimaced. "I wondered. But you seemed so sure…. How bad is it?"

"Well, according to the neighbor, there's a break in the main sewer line, which is going to cost about six grand. Add that to the water heater that doesn't work, the missing garage door opener, and the dishwasher door that fell off. Oh, and the fridge doesn't work. And the power in half of the house is out, and the breaker panel looks like there's been a fire recently." Her face grew horrified as he spoke.

"Oh my God, Davy. It's *The Money Pit*."

He'd watched the movie with Beth when they were kids. It featured Tom Hanks and Shelley Long, and they'd bought an old mansion where everything possible was wrong with it. He chuckled reluctantly.

"Except for the size, it really is." He ran his hand through his hair. "Shit. Dad would have kicked my ass for skipping the inspection."

She wrapped her arm around his shoulders, and her hair, the same honey blonde as his, brushed his cheek in the breeze. "Yeah, he would have. So, what are you going to do?"

He shrugged. "Fix it, I guess. Go through my savings."

"Isn't having two mortgage payments already doing that?" He didn't respond. She scowled. "Is Asshole going to start paying to live in your condo?"

"He's on the mortgage too."

"The only reason he isn't making the payments himself is that he knows you're the one with the credit rating worth saving." She growled. "God, I really hate that guy."

David gave her a wry look. "You never liked him."

"No, but now I hate him. Did you eat?"

"I had a sandwich."

She scowled. "I asked if you ate dinner, not if you had a snack. You've dropped enough weight already."

Beth had put on at least thirty pounds as she aged, and she wore a comfortable layer of padding around her petite frame. As a result, she always thought he was too thin and should eat. He'd never admit it to her, but he had noticed his slacks were getting too big at the waist.

She stood, brushing off the seat of her denim capris. "Come on. I brought Mom half a pot roast and veggies, and she won't eat it all."

Pot roast sounded wonderful, but it was the principal of the thing. He loved his sister, but she nagged him more than he liked. "I already ate."

"Stop arguing with me. Lock up your dark house and come visit with your family." He gave her an exasperated look. "What are you going to do? Sit out here until it's completely dark, then sit in the dark in there? Do you even have any candles?" He didn't respond, but she no doubt knew the answer. "Get off your butt and lock the place." She went down the stairs. "I'll tell Mom you're coming over and see if she's got some candles."

"Beth, for God's sakes, I'm not a kid."

"Then stop acting like one." She grinned. "Come on, Mom and I can fuss over you. It'll be fun."

David grimaced. He wasn't sure how fun it would be, but he couldn't claim he had other plans. He rose and gathered his plate and tablet. Beth was still standing at the base of the stairs, smiling faintly, and he gave her a quizzical look. "What?"

"It's nice to see Dolly back." She gestured toward his shirt. "I thought she was long gone."

Trevor was very vocal about the more flamboyant pieces of David's wardrobe and hadn't made any secret of hating them. Desperate to please him, David banished not just Dolly but all the brightly colored clothes he loved to the spare bedroom. He was glad he remembered to take them when he left, and ran his hand fondly over the faded picture.

"I thought she was too. I found her in the back of the closet in the guest room."

Beth's smile ripened. "No one should put Dolly in a closet." She batted her lashes, and he rolled his eyes when she giggled. Giving up, he put the tablet and plate inside the door, then locked the house and jogged down the stairs. When he joined her, Beth smiled, linked her arm through his, and they crossed his lawn, kicking at the first of the fall leaves, the setting sun making the rhinestones in Dolly's hair sparkle.

CHAPTER TWO

WHEN HIS phone alarm went off, David blinked awake, rolled to his back, and stared up at the ceiling. Cold air brushed his face, but the pale early morning sun painted the room in soft, mellow light. He enjoyed the beautiful wood trim and the soft butter color on the walls, thinking it was the only room in the house that didn't need to be painted. His alarm beeped again, and David sighed and swiped his finger over the screen, shutting it off.

He'd returned from his mom's with a flashlight, a bag full of candles and matches, and a ziplock baggie full of homemade chocolate chip cookies. She'd tried to get him to stay in his old bedroom, but he'd insisted he'd be fine. Now he pushed up and crawled out of the sleeping bag he'd owned since his Cub Scout days, and gooseflesh broke out above the neck of his sweatshirt. He shivered, wrapping his arms around himself, and started for the bathroom. It was damned cold in the house and he didn't look forward to climbing into a freezing shower. He longed for a cup of hot coffee and chided himself for not accepting his mom's invitation.

"You're an ass," he muttered. And stubborn. He'd wanted to stay in his house, dammit, even if it meant his dick shriveled up to the size of a vienna sausage when he stepped under the arctic blast in his shower.

Thirty minutes later he was still shivering, even fully dressed. Making his way quickly through the house, he paused at the built-ins in the dining room to pick up his keys, and his gaze fell on a lone business card, the ecru cardstock pale against the dark wood. His mother handed it to him when he was sitting at her table the night before. He'd put away more of his sister's roast than he cared to admit and was enjoying a slice of his mom's chocolate cake.

"What's this?" He wiped his mouth and read the neat, even print on the card. "Jackson Henry, Handyman." Handyman? His lips twisted. "What does that even mean?"

"A man who's handy," Beth quipped. "Which much as I love you, dear brother of mine, you are not." He shot her a dark look. "Okay, big guy, how

11

do you plan to fix your little power problem? Hire an electrician? That'll only cost you a hundred dollars an hour. Why don't you give this guy a call?"

"Shut up," he muttered, but she had him. He could decorate a home beautifully, but fix wiring? Not so much.

"Besides," she went on, a sly smile on her face. "You won't be sorry."

"Elizabeth." There was no way to miss the quelling look their mother shot his sister. Beth snapped her mouth closed and pinched her lips together, looking the other way.

"That was subtle," he drawled. "What? Does he have two heads or something?"

"Well…." Beth's lips quirked.

"Elizabeth Anne!" their mother scolded, but a laugh lingered in her eyes. "Behave yourself!"

"All right, you two are being weird." David pushed his chair back. "And when that starts, I know it's time for my exit."

"If you won't stay the night, at least come back for breakfast," his mother said as he stood. "You won't even be able to make coffee over there."

She was right. His elite edition Keurig machine was sitting on the counter in the condo across town. With Trevor. "I'll run by Starbucks, Mom." He bent and kissed her cheek. The softness of her skin and her floral perfume filled his senses, swamping him with nostalgia; she'd worn the same fragrance for all his life. Youth-Dew, by Estee Lauder. His dad bought it for her every Christmas. Feeling a pang of loss, he realized he'd be the one making a trip to Macy's this year. "I'll be fine."

He started to throw the business card back on the cabinet. His mother and sister acted far too weird and that was never a good thing. But at the last moment, he'd thought better of it and slipped the card into his slacks pocket as he headed out the door.

BY THE time David pulled back into his driveway, the sun was slanting low over the trees and the streetlights had come on. It was nearly seven, and he was tired and irritated after spending the day dealing with a manufacturer who was holding up a large installation in Boise. Six months into the project, the furniture supplier suddenly decided he didn't like the terms of his contract. Add in an infuriating phone call from someone claiming to be Trevor's lawyer, threatening legal action if he didn't make the upcoming mortgage payment on the condo, and it made for a Friday from hell.

He stared at the lopsided garage door, lips pursed. The idea of walking into the cold, dark house held no appeal whatsoever. Glowering at his front porch David shoved his hand into his pocket and pulled out the business card. Jackson Henry. It brought to mind a burly straight guy with a beard, wearing a flannel shirt over a dirty ribbed tank top, low slung Levi's and a tool belt. And a healthy butt crack when he bent over. David grimaced. He'd been called too picky more than once in his life, and he supposed he could concede the point, but he liked his men lean and clean-shaven with at least a passing acquaintance with style. Like Trevor, his mind provided unhelpfully. It was one of the things that had drawn David to him in the beginning, the way Trevor was always so beautifully put together. But he needed someone to fix his water heater, not a date.

Flicking the card against the steering wheel as he stared thoughtfully at the listing garage door, he grabbed his cell phone out of the holder on the dash and punched in the phone number before he could talk himself out of it. It rang four times, and David was about to hang up when it was answered abruptly.

"Henry, here."

David blinked. The voice was deep and smooth, and sent a little fissure of pleasure down David's spine.

"Uhm, hi," he managed. And then he wasn't sure what to say. Silence lengthened awkwardly.

"Hi," the guy said finally. "And as fascinating as this is, I'm kind of in the middle of something. Who is this?"

Heat filled David's face. If he had sounded like a jerk, he probably would have hung up. But actually, he sounded… amused.

"My name is David Snyder." David finally managed to pull himself together. "I was given your business card by my mother." He grimaced.

"Who's your mom?"

David heard the sound of rustling coming through the phone, as if Henry had gone back to work on something.

"Beverley Snyder. She lives on Sixteenth on the south side."

"Oh sure, Mrs. Snyder. Nice lady. What can I do for you?"

"I bought a house in the same neighborhood, and I'm discovering that what people say about old houses is true."

"Lots of little things," Jackson said, his tone knowing.

"Well, and some big ones, I'm afraid." David swallowed, forcing himself to push forward. "I was wondering if you might have some time to stop by and take a look at the issues?"

"One second." There were more rustling sounds; then the voice returned, slightly out of breath. "Does tomorrow morning work for you?"

He couldn't imagine starting another week with no lights and a cold shower. "Absolutely. What time is good for you?"

A soft chuckle came through the line, and gooseflesh broke out over his shoulders. David couldn't remember ever having such a visceral reaction to a voice. If the man matched that sexy laughter…. *No.* He couldn't think that way. There was no way this guy was gay. Besides, his last choice had been such a disaster he needed to stay single for a while. A long while. Maybe forever.

"How about nine?" Jackson Henry pulled David's focus back to his phone. "I usually start about seven, but it's Saturday, and I could use an extra couple of hours' sleep."

"That's fine."

David gave him the address to the house and hung up, hoping his mother knew what she was talking about. After the week he'd had he just wanted something, anything to go right. He put the card back in his pocket, retrieved his messenger bag, and got out of the car. His stomach gurgled loudly as he walked up onto his porch, and he wished he'd stopped at a damned drive-thru on the way home.

God, he hoped this guy could fix stuff.

CHAPTER THREE

DAVID GOT up at eight the next morning and decided to pass on the cold shower. His hair looked okay, and the light covering of pale beard seemed more stylish than "homeless man behind a dumpster." *What do I care, anyway?* He studied his face in the bathroom mirror. It wasn't a date for God's sakes. He combed his hair, straightened the collar on his very bright green polo shirt, another refugee he'd found while packing, and walked out of the bathroom.

It was so fucking cold in the house, he'd bet there was frost out front on the grass. It wasn't uncommon in late October. He'd tried the thermostat but there was no sound of the heater kicking on. The real estate agent had told him about the unit when she showed him the house, but he couldn't recall exactly what she'd said. He hunched his shoulders and crossed his arms over his chest, but it didn't help. The Dolly shirt hung on the back of the bathroom door and he retrieved it, yanking it on over his head. So what if between the neon polo and the lavender, rhinestone-encrusted sweatshirt he might as well be wearing a sign that said Nellie Queen? At least he'd be warm. Ish.

He walked into the nearly empty living room, arms crossed tight over his chest, going to look out at the neighborhood through the huge picture window. A couple of kids bundled up against the cold rode by on bikes, and white smoke rose gracefully from the chimney on the house across the street. David watched it, then looked at his own fireplace. It was situated on the wall to his right between two long windows, a beautiful mantle above it. The inside of the dark firebox was scrupulously clean, the grate empty. And he'd seen a pile of firewood against the side of the garage.

He didn't even pause for second thoughts. The fireplace in the condo was gas, but the one he'd grown up with was wood burning, and his dad taught him how to make a fire when he was a kid. He unlocked the front door and hurried down the steps, his breath rushing out in a cloud when the cold air hit his face, reinforcing his decision. He had a newspaper in the house on the kitchen counter, and he grabbed a handful of smaller twigs, then three medium-sized logs. The wood felt dry in his hands, which he knew was critical for a clean-burning fire. Once he had it started, he could come back out for a larger log. He needed to get his hands warm. They were so cold, they ached.

Back in the house, he dumped the armload of wood on the hearth and went for the paper. Coming back and lowering himself to sit cross-legged on the floor, he made sure the mesh metal fireplace screen was pushed all the way back on each side. After balling up the paper, he shoved it under the grate, put the twigs on top, and used the lighter from his mom's emergency supplies to ignite the paper. It lit instantly and the dry twigs began to burn with a satisfying pop. Holding his hands toward the flames, David sighed in relief when he felt the warmth start to reach out toward him. Wanting more of the blissful heat, he placed two of the split logs on the merrily burning twigs, thinking it was a fire even his dad would have been proud of.

Then it began to smoke.

"Oh, shit." Dirty, gray smoke filtered into the room. He hadn't checked the flue.

Grimacing, he got to his knees, keeping his eye on the flames and reaching up into the fireplace. He found the cast-iron handle of the flue and pulled on it, and it moved forward with a dull clunk. Cold air brushed his hand, and with a whoosh the smoke pulled back into the fireplace and disappeared.

"Thank God." David sat heavily on the hardwood floor, brushing soot from his fingers.

His relief was short-lived.

Within moments the smoke was coming back into the room. Only instead of an anemic trickle, as the log caught fire, it rolled into the room like a noxious cloud.

David pushed to his feet, trying to remember if his dad had ever said anything about a smoking fire. He dimly thought he'd heard something about cracking a window open if a fire smelled smoky, so he rushed into the kitchen and opened the window over the sink. But when he went back into the living room, the smoke was getting worse and his throat and eyes started to burn.

This wasn't good. The fire burned brightly now, but it felt like none of the smoke was going up the chimney. He rushed through the room, opening the windows, coughing, then into the dining room to do the same. A sinister thought went through his mind: what if he pulled the burning logs into the middle of the room and let the damned place burn to the ground? He knew it was far more likely he'd end up with third-degree burns and in jail for insurance fraud. What the hell had he been thinking when he bought the place?

He hadn't, he reminded himself, leaning into the open window and taking in a deep breath of icy cold air. He'd been hurt and angry, and he'd bought the house in an effort to replace the home he'd lost. He blinked quickly, and he didn't know if it was the smoke or if his emotions had finally gotten the better of him, but he was about to have a good cry. He'd been so numb from the loss of his dad that he hadn't cried once over the death of his relationship, but he was afraid he was about to. Tears slipped from beneath his lashes and his chest grew tighter and tighter until it felt like there was a vise around it.

The doorbell rang and David huffed out a desperate laugh. "Perfect." Awesome. He was about to meet the handyman with his eyes red from crying. He hoped he could pass it off as being a result of the smoke. He yanked off his glasses and rubbed his face with his sleeve as he rushed through the smoke-shrouded house to open the front door.

When he did smoke rushed out through the opening onto the porch.

He had a fleeting impression of a guy about his height with dark brown hair and startled blue eyes.

"Jesus, is it on fire?" He pushed past David into the living room and went straight for the fireplace. David could scarcely see him through the thick haze but was able to make out him reaching into the fireplace for the handle to the flue.

"I already opened it," David called, coughing. The man came back, an image appearing out of the fog, and he grabbed David's arm. He yanked him out through the open front door and over the porch, pulling him stumbling down the steps to the lawn beyond. David gasped at the manhandling and inhaled a lungful of acrid smoke for his effort. It closed his throat and he coughed, bent at the waist.

Behind him something metallic clanged. With his hands on his knees, David peered up in time to see a very fit man in worn Levi's and a beat-up black denim jacket pass him carrying a long aluminum ladder. He laid it on the lawn, extending it with a tug, then stood it up and leaned it against the roof's edge. David was going to offer to hold it but couldn't quit coughing, and it wouldn't have mattered anyway. The guy scampered up the ladder like a squirrel climbing a tree. And even though he was still coughing and bent double, David couldn't help but notice the strong thighs and very nice ass that climbed out of his sight.

Weakened and feeling like a complete idiot, David dropped heavily to his ass on the lawn, his head between his knees. Loud banging came from his roof, and even though he couldn't see the chimney from his vantage point, he could tell several minutes later when the smoke stopped pouring out through the open front door. Now it lifted from the house toward the sky in an innocuous, puffy spiral.

Instead of it being a relief, the sight made David feel even more of an idiot. What the hell had he been thinking, skipping the inspection? He didn't know the first thing about home repairs other than they were liable to cost him a small fortune.

Even steps came down the rungs of the ladder, and David glanced up as the man stepped onto the lawn, but the sun was in eyes that still hurt, and all he got was an impression of windblown dark hair. Footsteps moved past him.

A few minutes later when a soft touch fell on his shoulder, he nearly jumped out of his skin. He let out a startled cry, which started him coughing all over again.

"Sorry," a deep voice said above his head. "I didn't mean to scare you."

"No, it's okay." David blinked rapidly.

"Here."

A hand appeared in his line of vision, holding a frosted water bottle. David took it.

"Thanks." He unscrewed the cap and took a deep drink. The cold water felt like heaven on his raw throat and he sighed.

"Do you think you need to be seen for smoke inhalation?"

David frowned and shook his head.

"It's nothing to be messed with, man. Smoke inhalation can play hell with your lungs. Even lead to pneumonia."

"No, really." David struggled to push up from the grass, feeling even more like a damsel in distress when he couldn't seem to get his feet under him. A strong hand appeared before his face and David took in the broad palm, the callouses on the long fingers, and the wide leather bracelet around a tanned wrist. David hesitated a moment, then took the offered hand and was lifted easily to his feet. "Thanks. I'm"—he finally looked up into the man's face and his mouth went dry—"fine."

"I'm Jackson Henry. And I'm assuming you're David Snyder?"

David nodded.

Damn, the man would have to look like a model for the cover of *Handyman's Monthly Magazine*. David didn't know if there was such a thing, but if there were, this was their guy. They were about the same height, but that's where any similarity between them ended. Jackson Henry had high, sharp cheekbones and a square jaw darkened by the shadow of a heavy beard. His eyes were piercing and the same pale blue as the patches of fall sky that showed between the branches of the trees above. His nose was straight and strong, but for a slight hook that showed it had been broken once, and his mahogany-colored hair lifted in the cold breeze. He had a strong upper body and narrow hips, and he was holding a clipboard and pencil in his free hand. His arched black brows were furrowed in concern as he studied David's face.

"You're sure you're okay?" His deep voice moved over David's raw nerves like warm molasses. It would have been soothing, if David weren't so damned humiliated.

"Yeah. Thanks." He held up the bottle. "This helped."

"Good." Jackson continued to look at David as if afraid he'd keel over any second.

"So, um." David shifted uneasily under the steady gaze of his keen eyes. "What happened? I opened the flue, even felt a rush of air when I did."

"There was a cap on the chimney. I think originally it was to keep pinecones from those big firs from falling down into the opening." He gestured toward the three towering evergreen trees next to the side of the house. "But I'd be willing to bet it's been years since anyone checked it. It was completely blocked with pine needles."

"How did you get it cleared?"

A smile pulled at the corner of Jackson's full lips. "I yanked the cap. When I pulled on it, it was so corroded, it broke off in my hands." He shrugged one square shoulder. "You'd be better off with a screen, at any rate." He looked down at the clipboard and made a quick note in jagged handwriting.

"Thanks." When Jackson looked up, David tried for a smile, not sure he succeeded. "I guess that means you're hired."

Jackson snorted softly. "Why don't we do a walk-through before you commit yourself?"

"Oh, sure." Once again David felt like an idiot, but he led Jackson back up onto the porch and through the open front door.

The house still smelled of smoke but the acrid cloud was gone. Jackson paused and looked around the room with clear appreciation. "Have you any idea who the architect was?"

David blinked at the unexpected question. "No idea, but I imagine I can find out. Why?"

"It looks like one of Andrej Janic's homes." He moved to the built-ins near the fireplace, reaching out to touch the leaded glass facing the cabinets almost reverently. He ran a broad palm over the smooth wood of the mantle, and David saw he had beautiful hands, the fingers long and the nails neat and clean. For some reason they weren't what David expected a handyman's hands to look like.

"The name sounds familiar." The way Jackson ran his palm over the wood was almost… seductive.

"He was a Dutch immigrant who moved here in the last part of the nineteenth century. He worked for Langdon and Sons Architects."

"That's a name I recognize," David said. They'd designed city hall, and the only five-star hotel downtown. It was a grand old building, full of Victorian details and stained glass. A little heavy on the rococo for David's taste, but beautiful nonetheless.

"He worked there until 1914, then went out on his own. Most of the craftsman-style homes in town are his or copies of them." Jackson continued through into the dining room, his step deceptively light considering the heavy work boots he wore. He made a delighted sound when he saw the dining room built-ins and the amber-colored glass sconces on the walls. Pausing, he studied the small rectangular chandelier in the middle of the room, a masculine combination of wrought iron arms topped with more amber glass lampshades. He touched it lightly. "If this is original to the house, it's probably worth five grand."

David looked up at the fixture. He'd thought it was cool but assumed it was a reproduction. "Damn." He rubbed his jaw. "I do interiors, and I had no idea."

Jackson looked at him with a raised brow. "You do interiors?" With a wry smirk, he glanced meaningfully at the ratty recliner and the lamp on the cinder block. "I mean, I've seen minimalist before, but this might be pushing it."

David felt his face color. "Bad breakup."

"Ah." Jackson nodded sagely. "I take it the other party took custody of the furniture."

David snorted. "He got custody of... well, pretty much everything."

He held his breath, waiting to see how the contractor would react to the *he* comment, but Jackson grunted softly and continued on into the kitchen, David behind him. He took in the fifties-era appliances with a pleased expression, opening the massive oven in the white enameled range. He glanced at the old Philco refrigerator with the heavy chrome handle on the outside, then crossed to the dishwasher door leaning against the wall.

"This isn't good." He bent and looked at the hinges. "Looks rotted out. Might be cheaper to replace it."

"I wondered." David didn't like the baby-pink dishwasher anyway. The old white enameled refrigerator and range were cool if they could be made to work, but that pink monstrosity had to go. He liked the butcher-block counters and the subway-style backsplash in brilliant white, and the heavy farm-style sink looked to be original too. "The fridge isn't working, but I'm hoping it's because the power's out."

Jackson looked over at David. "How long has the power been out?"

"Two days. The breaker box is on the service porch."

"Did you call Inland Power?"

David felt his cheeks heat. It was one of the problems with being as fair as he was; everything he thought ended up in a blush on his face. "I didn't even think to."

Jackson grunted softly and David grimaced. He led Jackson onto the service porch, then stood back as he found the gray box and opened the door.

"Oh, holy shit." A mixture of wonder and concern colored his voice. "When did they last update the wiring?"

"No idea."

"Looks like the 1950s." His gaze followed a line of soot up to where the ceiling was discolored with water damage. "That doesn't look good." He started making quick notes on his clipboard as he studied the box and the discolored wall above it.

"Can it be fixed?" David looked over his shoulder at the old-fashioned glass fuses.

"Anything can be fixed," Jackson answered, still surveying the damage. "It depends on how much you want to spend. First thing, this panel needs to be replaced, transferred from fuses to breakers."

"Can you do that?"

"I'm licensed. First we need to figure out what's going on with the roof. You've got a leak." He used the pencil to point at the large brownish stain on the ceiling. "We also need to check inside this wall for mold."

The word made David cringe. "Any idea how much?"

Jackson chewed on the corner of his lower lip as he studied the fire-damaged box. "The box shouldn't be too bad, depending on the wiring. Five, six hundred. I'll know more when I get a look at the roof. That needs to happen before bad weather rolls in. But if you've got mold...." He shook his head. "Mold eradication is pricey, and I don't do it. You'd need a professional team for that."

David's heart sank. "The heater isn't working either. I tried to turn it on this morning, and nothing. The Realtor told me it was replaced in 2006, and the unit looks sound." He was relieved he remembered that much.

"Gas or electric?" Jackson looked at the venting near the ceiling.

"Forced air gas."

"Where's your thermostat?"

David led him back through the kitchen and down the hall, and showed him the small plastic box on the wall. "There's your problem," Jackson said, making another note on his clipboard. "Electric thermostat, gas heater. At least that's what I'm going to bet. We won't know for sure until the power is back on."

"Okay. Any idea how long...?"

"A couple of days."

"Oh." Disappointment swamped David. A couple of days? He supposed that meant returning to the hotel or taking his old room at his mom's, and either option felt like failure.

Jackson looked at him, brows arched. "Problem?"

David swallowed and shook his head. The motion of his throat walls sent up a warning shot of pain, and he took another drink from the bottle of water in his hand. "No," he said when he realized Jackson was still looking at him. "That's fine. Uhm, there's an issue with the water heater too."

"Okay. Where is that?"

"Basement."

David led the way.

BY THE time they trooped back up the stairs, David knew two things: he'd probably need a second mortgage to cover all the repairs, and Jackson Henry was going to drive him insane.

The area in the basement where the water heater was located was tight, between the large tank and the boxy heater unit. Jackson glanced at the latter and said the pilot was lit and it looked okay, the first bit of good news David had, but then he amended the statement by saying he wouldn't really know until the power was back on. He also thought the water heater was probably a lost cause.

He'd crouched down to look under it, and while there was no butt crack, there had been a couple of inches of firm, tan skin above jeans and a thin band of dark briefs that looked like it would be smooth to the touch. David could also see part of a tattoo on the right side of his back above the belt line, some lines and a splash of dark pink, disappearing beneath the waistline of his jeans. Most of the shape was hidden, and David was instantly intrigued. The small space also forced David within touching distance, and since the basement was the only place that didn't smell like smoke, he was able to smell Jackson for the first time.

The scent of tangy cologne on a clean man was David's kryptonite and he knew it. Jackson smelled like a clear, crisp fall morning combined with cedar, and the scent went straight to David's dick. He tried to take a step back but the space was too small, and he was grateful the oversized

23

hoodie he wore fell past his hips because he was pretty sure he was more than half-mast. More and more nervous in the man's presence, he didn't take another deep breath until they came back up the rickety basement stairs, which Jackson said should probably be replaced too. David lost track of the climbing repairs, and he lost what was left of his mind when he followed Jackson up to the first floor and was at eye level with the shifting muscles in Jackson's ass. Never before in his life had David wanted to sink his teeth into someone's butt, but he did then.

WHEN THEY were once again standing in the living room, Jackson surveyed his list silently for several minutes, so long that David's frayed nerves felt like someone twanged them with a tuning fork.

"Well," he said finally, "the most pressing things are probably getting the power back on, checking that roof, making sure there's no mold in the wall between the kitchen and the back porch, and replacing the water heater. The less important things, like the dishwasher and the basement stairs, can be done over the next few months. That way it won't be such a big hit to the bank account at once. We have a small window with the roof. We shouldn't start to see snow for another six weeks, but weather is weather, so you never know. I should also tell you that if the roof is a complete loss, I don't do that. But I do know a guy who'll be fair."

"Oh, I forgot." David cringed. "A neighbor mentioned there might be a problem with the plumbing."

"Like?"

"He said the previous homeowner was told there was a break in the main sewer line between the house and the curb."

Jackson whistled softly between his teeth. "If that's true, it's pricey. I don't do that either. But again, I know a guy."

"That's fine." David felt a little faint. What was money, anyway? He could always take a cardboard sign, write Bankrupted by Home Repairs, and stand on a corner during his lunch hour. He fought down a slightly hysterical giggle. "That all sounds fine," David finally managed to choke out, then fought spiraling alarm. He had no idea how much he'd committed to when he usually knew how much he planned to spend at the grocery store before he walked in the door.

Jackson seemed to recognize his panic.

"Look, I know this is a bit overwhelming, particularly when you just bought the place." He paused. "Did you have an inspection? Because I find it hard to believe that back porch passed."

David shook his head miserably. "And I knew better." He scrubbed his hand over his head, pushing his fingers through his hair. "I acted impulsively. I was living in a hotel, and I saw the sign...." He shrugged. "I grew up in this neighborhood. It seemed like a good idea at the time." He knew he sounded foolish, but Jackson smiled faintly.

"Did you even look at the porch?"

David sighed. "Long enough to know I'd have to buy a washer and dryer."

Jackson's smile deepened enough for a dimple near his mouth to pop into view. God, on top of everything, the man had dimples. David stifled another sigh.

"I know it's none of my business," Jackson said, tentative for the first time. "But do you mind my asking what you paid for it?"

David cringed. "A hundred and sixty-five?" He wished a hole would swallow him up.

One of Jackson's brows shot up, but David didn't know him well enough to know if that was a good or a bad thing. "Well, if it helps, if this is one of Janic's houses, it's probably worth a whole lot more than that." He looked down at his expansive list. "Okay, I can bill you one job at a time if that would be helpful. Not to sound like a jerk, but I won't pad the labor costs and I'm good."

David felt his face heat and he hoped like hell he wasn't telegraphing what his traitorous imagination pictured Jackson being good at. He was going to have to get past this attraction; he'd just gotten out of a five-year relationship. It was too soon for him to be drooling over some guy like a teenager. If the man was going to be around for a while he could enjoy the scenery, but that was it.

"Would you like a chance to think about this?" Jackson's brow furrowed when David's thoughts spun out longer than they should have.

"I... no," he finally answered, knowing he was blushing. Again. With the amount of times the blood had rushed to his face in the last hour, he was surprised he didn't pass out. "No, like I said, that all sounds fine. When can you start?"

"Well—" Jackson glanced at the watch on his wrist. "—I can work for a few hours today if you like. I'll have to leave by four, but that should at least give me time to diagnose the issue with the breaker box. And I can order a new water heater."

"That would be great," David said emphatically. "The sooner the better."

Jackson nodded. "All right, then. I'll go get my tools and be right back."

"Perfect."

David watched him walk out through the front door, then collapsed into the ugly recliner in the middle of the room, his hands on his head. He couldn't remember the last time he had been so intensely aware of a man's presence. He glanced out the front window. Jackson was leaning into an open toolbox behind the cab of his truck and as he moved his jacket rode up his long body.

David was really curious about the rest of that tattoo.

WHILE MYSTERIOUS bangs and clanks came from his service porch, interspersed with long silences, David threw down an old blanket to protect the living room floors, then hauled in two more cinder blocks and a piece of shelving wood he found in the garage. After balancing the wood on the blocks, he made himself a makeshift desk in front of the recliner. It was awkward, the wood below the level of his knees, but it would have to make do. It was time to get realistic about his finances, especially if he was going to have to hire a lawyer. Going through his statements and monthly bills, cataloging them in stacks on the floor around the chair, David realized he was going to have to outfit an office. He missed the file cabinet and desk at the condo, but he was surprised he didn't really miss anything else. Including Trevor.

Leaning back in the chair and staring pensively through the window, he let that reality flow over him. He didn't miss the condominium near the river, or the furniture Trevor picked out to furnish it. None of it was David's style. The black leather couch and the expensive modern art on the walls, the chrome tables and the glass coffee table—it was all pretentious, nothing he'd have selected. He liked wood and fabric and warmth. He liked a home that felt like a home and not a showroom floor. He'd decorated high-end corporate headquarters that had more personality than his own condo, and he wondered again if he'd really been so eager to please Trevor that he'd simply gone along, subjugating his own taste in an effort to please him. With a sinking sensation in his chest, he knew he had.

He'd met Trevor straight out of college in a gay bar downtown. Shy and painfully insecure, David hadn't believed it when smooth, handsome Trevor Blankenship had zeroed in on him. He'd been so damned thrilled with the glamorous man's attention he'd have done just about anything to keep it. Including turning into his doormat.

"Never again," he muttered. "Never fucking again."

The sun slanted through the front window at a low angle, turning the room golden. Footsteps sounded behind him and David turned to see Jackson looking around the room, the denim jacket draped over his arm and his blue-and-brown plaid button-down shirt rolled up on his forearms. They were thick and sprinkled with dark hair, and David forced himself not to stare. He had a thing for men's forearms.

"This room is really beautiful." Jackson's face softened, and the transformation on his handsome features was dramatic. It made him seem more approachable.

"Yeah," David looked around. "I love the wood."

"Me too." Jackson shrugged into his jacket. "Well, I have some good news." He freed the collar of his shirt from the dark denim. "The wiring is all copper, not aluminum, so I can change out the box without too much trouble. I'll pick one up on Monday. And I yanked out some of the drywall. The best news of the day is I didn't see any mold."

"Oh, thank God." The rush of relief made David almost light-headed.

"Yeah," Jackson agreed. "You lucked out there. The drywall was still damp, so I have a feeling the leak isn't very old, which is also good news. It means it hasn't been going on for years and compromising the structure. I have a feeling the only reason the fuse box didn't set the house on fire was the wall above it was still wet."

David felt a chill run the length of his spine. God, the house could have burned down while he was sleeping. There wasn't a single smoke alarm in the place, something else that would have shown up with an inspection.

"The leak might have happened during that last bad storm," Jackson went on. There had been a violent thunderstorm right after David bought the house, with soaking rains and wind gusts upward of sixty miles an hour. He'd been glad none of the massive old trees on the side of the house had ripped out of the ground and come down on the roof. Other places in town hadn't been so lucky. "I'll know more on Monday when I get up on the roof."

"Okay." David gave him a slight smile.

They stared at each other, and then Jackson cleared his throat. "I hate to ask, but… I'm going to need a deposit if I'm buying stuff."

"Oh God, of course you are." David moved some papers and found his checkbook, grabbing a pen from the top of his makeshift work station. "How much do you need?" He looked up at Jackson expectantly.

"Three hundred should do it for now. I'll let you know Monday how much the water heater is going to be."

David wrote a check for eight hundred instead, ripped it from the pad, and held it out.

Jackson tucked the check into a pocket. "Thank you."

"If you need more money, tell me."

"Sure thing. What time do you leave for work in the morning?"

The question startled David and he blinked in surprise. "About seven thirty usually. Why?"

"Well, unless you want to give me a key to your house, I need to be here before you go." He shrugged a bit self-consciously. "So, I'll see you about seven thirty on Monday."

"Okay. I'll see you then."

Jackson gave him a tight nod, then walked out.

David stared after him, thinking however long it took for the repairs on the house to be complete, it wasn't going to be long enough for him to get tired of that view.

CHAPTER FOUR

AFTER GOING over all his financial information, David decided he could get everything done on the house without cashing in any of his retirement fund, as long as he economized everywhere else. Well, and as long as Trevor paid the mortgage on the condo. As a result, he decided staying with his mom until he had power and hot water was the best way to go. She welcomed him with open arms and wouldn't even hear of him helping pay for groceries. He knew his dad left her well taken care of, but decided he'd start taking her out to dinner once a week if she was determined not to let him contribute. Plus, as he slept in his old room and sat at her table, he was reminded how much he enjoyed her company. The relationship between his family and Trevor had always been cool, and he hadn't wanted to spend any more time with them than he'd had to on Thanksgiving and Christmas.

Come Monday he'd have to find a lawyer. He had to separate his finances from Trevor's. Trevor had a decent job as a salesman for a high-end liquor distributor; he could afford the payment on the condo—he'd just never had to make it, and pretty clearly he didn't want to. David had received several texts from him in the last couple of days, all with the same theme: you know it didn't mean anything, you know I love you. With a spurt of anger, David decided Trevor had pretty much proved the opposite, and if he wouldn't make the payments on the condo, then it would be sold.

He had breakfast with his mom Sunday morning at the same kitchen table he'd eaten his morning cereal at as a kid. He watched her moving around the kitchen, refusing his help, making him pancakes while he nursed a cup of coffee. No one made better coffee than his mom, not even the Keurig he'd lost custody of.

She set a plate in front of him and got a cup of coffee for herself before pulling out a chair and sitting on the other side of the table.

"Aren't you going to eat?" he asked as he poured syrup over his pancakes. His mom had the good kind, in a little jug straight from Vermont.

"I ate earlier," she answered.

"Toast?" He arched an eyebrow. She gave him a withering look.

"You've been listening to your sister."

"Toast isn't enough for breakfast, Mom. You've told me that for years."

"I had a carton of yogurt too. Don't fuss." She fixed him with a level look. "So, what do you think of Jackson?"

That was certainly an effective way of changing the subject. David picked up his knife and fork, then cut into the soft pancakes. The smell that lifted from them made his stomach grumble. "Well, he's gorgeous," he said finally.

"Isn't he?" His mom gave him a mischievous smile over her coffee cup.

"I hope he's as good at what he does as he is at filling out those Levi's."

She chuckled. "Well, he seemed very efficient when he was here."

"What did you have him do?" David took a bite of his pancakes and rolled his eyes in bliss. They melted on his tongue and were his childhood Christmas mornings in one bite. Warmth swamped him, along with the realization he hadn't spent enough time with his mother for the last five years. "These are amazing, Mom," he said when he'd swallowed. "Thank you."

"You're welcome. And in answer to your question, the garage door stopped working about six months ago." The offhand comment reminded David of his own missing garage door opener, and that he meant to tell Jackson. "Your dad wasn't feeling up to bothering with it, and I'd heard about Jackson, so I called him. He got it working again in an hour and didn't even charge me." Her smile ripened. "I baked him cookies." David grinned and she shrugged. "You aren't the only one who enjoys eye candy, my dear."

He laughed. "Where did you hear about him?"

"I know his mother. She's in my garden club." Beverley took another sip of coffee. "She has the most beautiful rose garden, which I believe Jackson helped her install. You should ask him about it. Rose bushes would look lovely down the side of your driveway."

They might be a bit high maintenance for someone who worked as much as he did, but he didn't say that.

"He's gay, by the way."

David choked on his pancake. She patted him on the back while he sputtered and took a drink of his coffee.

"How do you know that?" His voice came out a bit ragged.

"I know his mom. We talk."

"About your sons' sex lives?" David felt heat rush up his face and feared his voice sounded like he hadn't reached puberty yet.

"No." His mother gave him a pointed look. "But we do talk about our children, including what our sons do for a living."

"That's why you and Beth were so weird the other night, because he's gay." David sighed. "Well, he's very professional. I didn't pick up on it at all. He didn't cruise me even once." He took a bite of his breakfast. "Dammit," he said around a mouthful of pancake. He was teasing, but the thought actually was disappointing. She smiled, but it faded and she looked troubled for a moment.

"What's that face about?"

She sighed softly. "Did you wonder why he's a handyman, why he works alone?"

"Not really. Some people like to work alone." He studied her pensive face. "But I have a feeling there's a story."

"There is. He moved here to help take care of his mom. She was diagnosed with MS recently." She sighed. "It's such a shame. Sometimes she's fine, but...." She shrugged one shoulder.

"That's hard," he murmured. He couldn't imagine, actually. After watching his dad die slowly, the idea of his mom being diagnosed with something debilitating made him feel cold clear through.

"She has two other children and they live locally, but they're busy." Beverley sniffed, letting David know what she thought of that. "As if Jackson isn't. He is the only one who doesn't have kids of his own, however. He'd been living on the coast, but the moment his mom said she needed help, he moved right back here. Over there he worked with a large construction company, and he made really good money. But here...."

David frowned. "There is construction done here. I see crews working downtown all the time. Isn't he in the union?"

She nodded. "But he doesn't hide, Davy. Not who he is, not anything."

Now David understood. "Ahh." David grimaced. "The good old straight-boys network."

The town had over four hundred thousand people in it, but the predominant attitude was very small town and conservative. Not particularly gay friendly. He should know; he'd grown up being the butt of every gay joke and prejudiced expletive imaginable. Good old straight boys raised children just like them.

"He couldn't get hired. Then one night someone took a baseball bat to his truck as it sat in the alley behind his mom's house. Broke out every bit of glass, slashed the tires. Spray-painted 'faggot' on the side. It was awful. And very expensive to fix."

A slow, simmering anger filled him. David only had a dim recollection of a pickup truck in the driveway, but he could imagine what it cost to replace all the glass and tires. He'd been called faggot from the time he'd been in the fifth grade and all the way through high school, but it hadn't figured in his professional life. Of course he worked in an industry where his sexual orientation wasn't an issue, and since he was the head of his department, if anyone did have a problem they were smart enough to keep it to themselves. But for Jackson….

"That's a hate crime. Did he call the police?"

Beverley nodded. "They took a report, but there wasn't a whole lot they could do. There were no witnesses. It was a lousy welcome home for him."

"No shit," David growled. She gave him a scolding look, but he didn't care. He shook his head slowly. "This is wrong on so many levels." He pushed the plate away. He'd eaten about half of the pancakes, but his appetite had faded. "Why didn't you tell me about Jackson before?"

Beverley looked at the tabletop and worried the edges of a paper towel with her fingernail. After a lengthy pause, she looked up into David's eyes. "I wanted you to meet him first and hire him if you thought he could help you with the house. I didn't think he'd want the main reason to be because he's gay."

David thought about the man he'd spent hours with the day before. He pursed his lips, then nodded. She was right. But then, she usually was.

AT SEVEN thirty Monday morning, David stepped out of his mother's house and began the short walk to the craftsman a block over. It was chilly and he was glad he'd slipped into his long black wool overcoat and wrapped a scarf around his throat. A soft breeze picked up his bangs and stirred the brilliant fall leaves that made a canopy over the street. He loved fall, and he closed his eyes and inhaled the scents of wood smoke and the late-blooming lilies. A school bus passed him, stirring a small flurry of dried leaves, and he checked both ways before striding out to cross the street.

A silver pickup truck with ladders hanging on each side sat in front of his house, Jackson sitting behind the wheel, sipping from a cup of something hot. Steam rose, curling around his head. David waved and Jackson nodded in response before he stepped out of the truck as David reached him.

"Good morning." David glanced at the late model GMC, saw how spotlessly clean it was, and recalled what his mom had told him about the vandalism. The whole thing upset David all over again.

"Morning." Jackson studied him, a slight frown growing. "Everything all right?"

David forced his irritation down. He never had been able to hide anything, his emotions crossing over his face the moment he thought them. "Oh, everything's fine. Just... Monday," David improvised, and Jackson nodded slowly, but David could see he wasn't quite buying it. "So, I'll let you in." He started around the front of the truck.

"What time do you usually get home?" Jackson fell into step beside him.

"It varies." David dug his keys out of the pocket of his slacks as they crossed the lawn. "Why?"

"I was able to chase down a water heater at a really good price, but I'll need to go pick it up. And I need to go get the new breaker panel. I didn't think you'd want me to leave the house unlocked."

David chuckled. "God forbid they take that recliner."

Jackson's lips curved in a smile. "You don't want to lose any of the fixtures or hardware, though."

David chewed his lower lip thoughtfully. After a moment he began to work his house key off his key ring.

"Here, this way you won't have to worry about whether I'm here or not." Jackson stared at the key, an odd expression on his face. "What?"

"You're sure you want to do this?"

David angled his head to one side. "Yeah. I'm sure."

"You're pretty trusting. How do you know I don't have designs on that dining room fixture?"

David studied the handsome face and the vivid blue eyes. "My mom is a pretty good judge of character and she likes you. I'll risk it."

A slow smile curled Jackson's lips and a corresponding heat began to fill David's chest.

"Well, I have to admit—" Jackson took David's key, and when their fingers brushed, David fought to hide a resulting shiver. "—I do sort of covet that recliner."

David laughed. "If I ever get anything else to sit on, I'll give it to you as a bonus." Heat filled his cheeks when Jackson arched an ironic eyebrow. Had he sounded like a jackass? He wasn't sure.

"Throw in the cardboard box and the lamp and you might have a deal," Jackson drawled. David gave a small, relieved chuckle.

"Do you want me to leave this?" Jackson held up the key. "I could return it to your mom."

"No, keep it until the job is done. I've got another one, and this way you can set your own hours."

Jackson nodded. "Thanks. Sometimes I have to take off unexpectedly, and that helps."

Jackson's mom's condition came to mind. "Sure."

They separated at the porch steps, and David allowed himself the luxury of watching Jackson climb them before he walked around the house, unlocking and climbing into his cold car. Shuddering, because no matter how many layers he wore the leather seats were always cold, he switched on the heater. He backed down the driveway and braked at the street for a passing car, glancing absently at the back of Jackson's truck. There were two bumper stickers on the heavy black bumper. One was a small rainbow heart, and the other was black-and-white and featured a line drawing of an irritated Jesus next to block script that read, "OMG, I said I hate *figs*."

David laughed out loud, and his smile lingered almost all the way to work.

CHAPTER FIVE

By the time David was back in his car and headed up the hill toward home, he was exhausted. Mondays were always hard, and this one was no exception. In fact, it was probably worse than normal.

When he entered the office that morning, his assistant, Michael, had met him at the door, an irritated scowl on his face.

David met Michael Crane two years before when he came in for a job interview, and now David didn't know what he'd do without him. Michael knew his schedule better than David did, and he ran interference when there were clients who had worn his patience down to a nub. An attractive young guy, he tended toward oversized sweaters, bulky scarves, and skinny jeans, but the look fit his slender frame. He gelled his dark hair into a modified fauxhawk, and he wore clunky black glasses that did nothing to detract from his fine, regular features. Michael was also his friend, and the thundercloud currently furrowing his brow didn't bode well.

"What's wrong?"

Michael took David's messenger bag, hanging it over his own shoulder, shaking his head slightly, and gesturing toward a small group of women who stood nearby. David understood, leading the way to his office. Once the door was closed behind them, he turned to Michael.

"What?" David unwound the scarf from around his throat, hanging it on a coatrack inside the door.

Michael hung the bag next to his scarf. "Trevor was here earlier."

David paused in the act of pulling off his gloves. "When?"

"He was here when I got here at seven thirty." Michael looked meaningfully toward David's desk. "In here. He was going through your desk."

David's eyes widened. There was nothing personal in his desk, and the current contracts were in a locked file cabinet, but Trevor had no business being in his office at all. David crossed to the desk, checking the surface carefully. He wasn't really concerned about business; he never left anything on his desk, and he cleared it off completely when he left each day. Still, his heart pounded at the base of his throat and he felt somehow violated.

"I told him to get out or I'd call security."

David looked up at his assistant, who was standing in front of the desk with his arms crossed, his lips pinched.

"What did he say?"

Michael angled his head. "Not much. He asked me for your new address, and I told him no. He then told me to fuck off."

David's heart sank. "I'm sorry, Michael."

Michael gave him an irritated look. "Don't you apologize for that asshole, David. You didn't do anything wrong. I did make sure security was aware of the breach, and they promised it wouldn't happen again." Michael's look was direct. "David, I know you don't want to, but you need to hire a lawyer. I think you should also consider reporting this to the police." David frowned, sitting heavily in the chair.

"Do you think that's necessary?"

"I think he doesn't understand boundaries at all. He was in your office. Where you work. That isn't okay."

David sighed, letting his head fall back. "No, it isn't. Let me make sure nothing is missing. And I'll think about it."

Michael didn't seem satisfied with that, but he didn't nag. He gave David his messages and left the office, but David knew that wasn't the end of it with Michael either. He'd be asking again.

David leaned on his desk and stared at the closed door. He hated the idea that Trevor had been in his office without his knowing, but did he really want to report him to the police?

Later that morning he did what he hadn't wanted and hired an attorney. After interviewing two on the phone and nearly gagging at the two hundred and fifty dollar an hour price tag, he gave the name of Trevor's lawyer to Karen Ridgeway, his new attorney-at-law. After he filled her in on what was going on, she told him she knew the other lawyer and that she'd make a polite phone call before she got out the brass knuckles. She also suggested that David consider a restraining order, but the decision was ultimately up to him. He hung up, liking her more by the moment.

By the time he walked out of the door of his office building, he was exhausted. Driving through rush hour traffic on the surface streets leading to his neighborhood, he wondered if Jackson would still be at the house. Not only would the sight of the man in his shirtsleeves lift David's mood because he was lovely to look at, the one thing he truly missed was having someone to go home to. Having Jackson there wasn't like coming home to someone who loved him, but it was better than an empty house. Maybe he'd get a dog, perhaps a corgi like that cute one two doors down. The homeowners' association at the condo complex had forbidden dogs, saying they made a mess on the property. Now that he owned a house, he could have a dog if he wanted one. The idea made him smile, and it widened when he pulled onto his street and saw Jackson's truck still parked out front.

He pulled into the driveway behind two sawhorses with a sheet of plywood across them, and some sort of large saw clamped to the top. Jackson was bent over the makeshift table, goggles protecting his eyes as he used the noisy saw, sawdust in his hair and a pencil gripped between his teeth. Was it odd that he envied the pencil? He got out of the car. Jackson looked up, and the loud whine of the saw abruptly faded. He took the pencil from between his lips and shoved the goggles up into his hair.

"Hey." David's spirits lifted at the sight of him. His jacket was gone, and today he was wearing a fitted gray Henley. There were some impressive muscles on display beneath the snug fabric, and David was glad his own bulky jacket hid the fact he didn't have an equal build to display. He was an interior decorator who spent long hours on his job and maybe one day a month at the gym, and it showed. He didn't have any extra weight on his slender frame—in fact, Beth was probably right, he was too thin—but he knew his muscle tone wasn't terribly impressive. What had always worked for David had been his boyishness. There wasn't one thing about Jackson Henry that was boyish.

"Hey." Jackson smiled and a lot of David's fatigue melted. "I've got something to show you."

Jackson's grin was infectious and David grinned back.

Jackson led him into his house. They stepped over scrap drywall, and Jackson gestured toward the gunmetal-gray power panel on the wall. David looked at it, then looked back at Jackson, clearly not getting it.

Jackson's grin widened and he flipped a switch on the wall to his right. Not until the overhead light shut off did David understand. Then Jackson flipped the switch again, flooding the small service porch with light.

"Oh my God," David breathed. "You fixed it!"

"It is my job." Jackson gave him a wry grin. "I rewired it, replaced the fuses with breakers. Come here, there's something else." He walked through the kitchen and into the hall, and he paused. "What do you feel?"

David looked around, his brow slightly furrowed. The temperature inside the house was pleasant, not varying on arctic the way it had been the last two times he'd been inside, and he realized what Jackson was getting at. "The heater!"

"It was that the power was out. Like I told you, the thermostat wouldn't function without the electricity being on. There's nothing wrong with the heater."

Relief made David's knees weak. He'd been so afraid he was going to have to replace the whole unit, and a little bit of Internet research the night before into pricing had left him in a cold sweat. "Jackson, I could kiss you."

Jackson looked startled. It was only when he stiffened that David realized what he'd said.

"Oh. I'm sorry. That was…." His voice trailed off and he wished he could disappear in a puff of smoke.

"Flattering." Jackson gave him a small smile. "Don't worry about it." David felt abruptly breathless. "And did you want me to include your garage door in my bid? Because you might want a place to park that cute little car before the snow flies."

Effortlessly, Jackson smoothed over the awkwardness.

David's desire to kiss him grew even more.

NOW THAT his lights were back on, it was warm in the house and the refrigerator was cold, another fear put to rest on the "not having to replace a major appliance" front, David prepared to make a run to the grocery store. He asked Jackson if he wanted anything. Jackson shook his head and thanked him.

He was surprised when he returned and Jackson's truck was still there. It looked like he was finishing up for the night, though. The heavy saw was gone from the makeshift work center in the driveway, and the scrap wood and drywall were gone from the lawn. David popped his trunk as he got out of the car, and Jackson came out through the back door, shrugging into his jacket.

"You work some long hours, man," David said, taking three plastic bags out of his trunk. "You make me feel like a slacker."

"Anyone who leaves his house at seven forty-five and doesn't get home until after six is hardly a slacker," Jackson said. "And I usually take a couple of hours for lunch in the middle of the day, so it balances out. I wanted to let you know I'm picking up the water heater tomorrow. I'll install it and haul the old one to the dump for you."

"Do you need more money?" David asked.

"No, I'm good." Jackson slipped his hands into his jacket pockets. "I checked out the roof today, and from what I can see, it's only that one spot that looks bad. I also spoke with a friend who's a plumber about your pipe, and he can't get out here for about another week. Would you like me to try to line someone else up?"

"Is there a problem with me using the shower?"

Jackson gave him a wry look. "Not as long as you don't have sewage backing up over your toes."

"Ew." David shuddered. "Maybe I should shower at Mom's."

"Might be a good idea, as long as she's so close."

It wasn't what he wanted to hear, but it wasn't that inconvenient. David shut the trunk and held up one of the bags. "You sure I can't buy you a Coke?"

"No, I need to get home. I'll see you tomorrow."

David watched him go until he disappeared, admiring the shifting muscles of Jackson's ass. Yeah, that view was never going to get old.

CHAPTER SIX

DAVID MOVED his car to his mom's and didn't go by his house the next morning. He felt like a bit of an idiot for blurting the "I could kiss you" comment and he didn't want Jackson to think he was some mad queen, stalking him. Jackson's truck was already in the driveway, the sound of the saw whining as he drove by.

Tuesday was another of those days when his job seemed to be more trouble than it was worth. The suppliers were flaky, and even though the most recent recession seemed to be behind them, the purse strings at corporations were being held as tight. They wanted four hundred-room hotels decorated and furnished, but they didn't want to pay for it. His position had become as much about finessing the clients as it was about supervising decor for their spaces. At least when you did someone's house you could see their pleasure at the end. There was very little positive feedback involved in what he did anymore, and it made him tired. Really, really tired.

When he got home that evening, Jackson's truck was still there. Butterflies fluttering in his stomach, David climbed out of the car and trudged across the lawn, pausing to look around the neighborhood. The slight breeze that picked up every evening carried the scent of wood smoke from someone's fireplace tonight, and streetlamps cast mottled shadows on the asphalt. He shivered with unease. It might have been a leftover from Trevor breaking into his office, but he didn't know. Rubbing at the uncomfortable gooseflesh that rose on his arms, David started to head into the house when a rapid clicking sound neared him. Moments later a stubby-legged little dog with a big happy grin and ears like a bat ran toward him through the shadows.

David crouched down, sinking his fingers into the corgi's thick, soft fur. "What are you doing out here, buddy, huh?" The little dog licked his hand and gave him another doggy grin, and David chuckled. "God, you're really so adorable." He scratched under the corgi's chin, and the pudgy dog rolled over onto his back, his square miniature feet with their white socks in the air. David's chuckle evolved into laughter and he happily scratched the furry belly. "What are you doing over here? I'm sure someone has to be missing you."

As the words left his mouth, the porch light two doors down came on and the front door opened.

"Oh, you're in trouble now." The little dog didn't seem to care. He nudged David's hand with his nose and licked his wrist.

"Bootsy?" his female neighbor called, and David grimaced.

"Bootsy? Good God, no wonder you're running away from home." He looked toward his neighbor's house. "He's here," he called. She stepped out onto the porch, crossing her arms, and he stood up, patting his leg as he walked toward her. Bootsy rolled to his feet and followed, tongue lolling out of his smiling mouth, panting merrily. The neighbor watched him approach, her dog on his heels.

"Thank you for bringing him home. He's been restless and whining all evening." She looked down at the little dog. "Walking the streets now, are you?"

David laughed. "Well, he made a nice little welcoming committee for me just now. I've had a lousy day, and he's a cutie."

"He's also a bit of an attention whore."

"I noticed that." The dog sat next to David's feet and leaned against his calf, looking up at him.

David felt the woman's eyes on him. She was studying him and David began to feel awkward beneath her gaze.

Finally she uncrossed her arms and came down the steps. "You're Beverley's son, aren't you?" She stared at him.

"That's me." His tone was bright, but he felt a crawling sensation between his shoulder blades. He thought he knew where this was headed.

Oh, here it comes. Beverley's "queer" son.

At the condo there had been several gay couples, but he was pretty sure he was the only one here in middle-class suburbia. His caution was instinctive. She hesitated another moment, then held out her hand. David stared at it.

"Hi, I'm Jordyn."

"David," he replied.

Her tentative smile allowed the tension to drain from his shoulders, relief flooding in to take its place. He supposed his adolescent scars stayed with him and made him wary. He took the offered hand.

"It really is very nice to meet you," Jordyn said after giving his hand a squeeze. "Once you're settled, we'd love to have you over for dinner. You and your mom."

"Thank you. I know she'd enjoy that." Boots—David couldn't think of the poor dog as Bootsy—let out a hearty sigh and David laughed. He bent and scratched his head. "I'm sorry, are we ignoring you?"

Jordyn watched them with an indulgent smile. "Told you. Total whore."

"Well, if you ever need anyone to dog-sit, let me know."

"I may take you up on that."

Growing stronger, the breeze ruffled David's hair and he saw Jordyn shiver. "You should go in. It's getting really cold."

"It is. Come on, Bootsy."

Boots got up and went to her, and David liked to think it was reluctantly. They climbed the steps and she opened the door for him. With a wiggle of his little butt, Boots trotted inside, and she glanced back at David. "Welcome back to the neighborhood, David."

"Thanks."

He felt pleasure well in his chest, and he walked back to his own house. It was funny how a few friendly words could undo the knots his day had tied in his shoulders. He was also considering trying to find an adult dog at the local shelter, although he'd really love to get a little corgi. He'd have to mull it over; he worked too many hours for him to have time for a puppy. He started up his steps, noticing his porch light was gleaming, something he'd missed when he pulled in the driveway. The sight lifted his spirits. He was tired but not as emotionally drained as he'd been before, and he unlocked his front door. The only light inside seemed to be coming from the service porch at the back of the house, and David flicked on the lamp next to the recliner in passing.

Once inside he went straight to the kitchen. Noise came from the back and he glanced through the window over the sink. The light was on in the garage and the top of Jackson's head was visible through the dirty window in the garage side door. He glanced at his watch. Seven forty-five.

Jackson was certainly working late. For a moment he considered going out and saying hello, but David still felt a little weird about the whole I-could-kiss-you thing. He grabbed a Diet Coke from the refrigerator before returning to the living room to flop into the ugly recliner.

He popped the top and took a drink, savoring the fizz and the taste, easing into the back of the chair and closing his eyes.

The doorbell echoed through the empty house, and sighing in irritation, David set the soda pop on the floor.

When he opened the door, it took everything he had not to slam it again.

"So this is where you are." Trevor gave him a scowl. "That little queen who works for you wouldn't tell me anything."

David went back to his chair. "The 'little queen's' name is Michael." He sank into the recliner and reclaimed his drink. "And he didn't give you any information because I told him not to."

"Nice, David. And Diet Coke?" His supercilious expression encouraged David to salute him with the can. "You know aspartame is bad for you."

David's lips twisted. "That which does not kill us and all that." Trevor gave him a derisive look and came into the living room uninvited, standing with his hands on his hips, looking around with distaste.

"This is lovely, really. What do you call it? Ghetto chic?"

David glared at him. "How did you find me?"

Trevor looked at him like he was an idiot. "How do you think? I followed you."

"You followed me?" David gave him an incredulous look. The idea that Trevor followed him home, then sat in the dark watching him while he talked to his neighbor, sent a chill down David's spine. "And you're in my office, going through my desk. Stalker, much?"

Trevor crossed his arms over his chest. "Well, if you'd stop acting like a child and answer my texts or take my calls, it wouldn't be necessary."

David stared at the man he'd lived with for five years and thought he'd loved. He took in his slick dark hair and patrician profile, his expensive clothes and designer shoes, and wondered if he'd ever known him at all. Somehow he didn't think he had. "Fuck you."

Trevor's tweezed brows lifted. "Charming. Developed a new vocabulary? And that's hardly like you."

"I don't think you know the first thing about what I'm like. And I believe I began developing a new vocabulary the day I came home to find you getting your prick sucked by someone in my living room."

Trevor sighed. "You're never going to let that go, are you?"

David took another drink of his pop. "No, I don't believe I am. I know you don't see it the same way I do. But to me, getting head from someone other than me constitutes you cheating. And it makes me wonder how many times it happened before." Trevor gave him a baleful stare. "Are you going to stand there and tell me that was the first time?"

"Yes." It was said without hesitation, but David studied his face and knew he was lying. Trevor had probably been cheating on him for years, and he'd gone blithely on, thinking they were in love. He'd even convinced himself that Trevor's insistence they always use condoms was a personal idiosyncrasy, that he'd wanted to be sure. He "didn't trust the tests."

Suddenly too tired and heartsore to spar, David set the pop can carefully on the floor near his foot. "Why are you here, Trevor?"

"I'm here," he said, his voice glacial, "because my lawyer apparently heard from your lawyer. I didn't know you had one."

David shrugged, his shoulders shifting against the ancient upholstery. "You didn't leave me much of a choice."

"It didn't have to be this confrontational. That's your doing."

David eyed him balefully. "So, I should ignore what I walked in on and blithely go on paying the bills?"

"You chose to leave." David huffed out a bitter laugh and Trevor's jaw hardened. "I will not agree to sell the condo."

"I didn't instruct my attorney to ask you to sell the condo," David replied. "I told her to tell your lawyer that if you wanted to stay, you can refinance it and take over the payments."

"You know I can't afford to do that."

Anger broke through David's exhaustion. "You can if you stop eating out and buying expensive wine. Not to mention those five-hundred-dollar shoes."

"I won't change my lifestyle and I won't be forced out of my home." He took a threatening step forward and David felt a jolt of fear, but wouldn't allow himself to back down.

"Then refinance the mortgage and take my name off the deed. I'll let you have the furniture and everything else I paid for. But I'm not going to make payments on a place where I'm not living."

"This whole tired wronged-party routine you're playing is getting really old, David. You know that when the condo is eventually sold, you'll clear a decent profit."

"So because I'll *eventually* see a profit you want me to pay your way now?" David shook his head. "No, Trevor, I won't do it." Trevor looked startled. He took a step toward David, who stiffened. "That's close enough. I won't explain bruises away for you, ever again. Touch me, and I call the police."

Trevor stayed where he was as if testing David's resolve. Finally he retreated, and it was all David could do not to sag in relief.

"I'll take you to court."

"And say what? That after you fucked around on me I refused to pay your bills? We aren't married. You don't get alimony."

"My lawyer might disagree with you. There is a little thing called domestic partnership."

"So because we lived together, you think that argument is going to work? We never registered as domestic partners." David sighed in exasperation and leaned over, snatching up his soda. "Your lawyer can talk to my lawyer. Let's let them sort it out. That's the civilized way to do it, isn't it?" He held the can up and saluted Trevor. "By all means, let's be civilized."

"When did you turn into an asshole?"

David huffed out an incredulous, bitter laugh. "I'd say it probably coincides with realizing I'd lived with one for five years. Finding you with your pants around your ankles and a kid attached to your cock was the icing on the cake."

"I won't even dignify that with a response." Trevor turned toward the door.

"Oh, I'm sorry," David said to the back of his head. "Were we going for dignified? Hate to break it to you, but I think that ship has sailed." God, the words felt liberating. He could scarcely believe he had the nerve to say them.

Trevor didn't respond. He stomped out through the front door, leaving it standing open behind him. David watched him walk away and was surprised by how little he felt other than weariness. There went five years of his life, and all he felt was... empty.

"That the ex?"

The voice startled him and David turned as Trevor roared off down the street in his Mini Cooper. Another luxury David helped pay for. Apparently his level of gullibility knew no bounds.

Jackson was in the kitchen doorway, staring out through the front door. He was wearing a tight T-shirt, this one black, and worn Levi's with a tool belt slung low on his hips. His protective clear goggles were pushed up into his sawdusted hair.

"Yep," David said finally. He could feel Jackson's gaze even though he tried to avoid looking at him. "Trevor Blankenship."

"He's kind of a jerk, isn't he?"

Jackson crossed through the dining room and walked past him, closing the front door almost carefully, stopping the cold air that was drifting through the room. He leaned against it, crossing his arms and surveying David.

"I didn't mean to eavesdrop," he said. "But I heard voices...."

"It's all right." David blew out a breath and let his head fall against the headrest. "We weren't exactly quiet."

There was a long silence. "David," Jackson said finally, "can I say something, even though this is really none of my business?"

David looked up to find clear blue eyes steady on his face. "Sure."

Jackson's hand curled around his own bicep, long fingers pressing into his arm. "I don't know you very well, but everything I've seen tells me you're a nice guy. A bit impulsive, maybe, but I think I get why you bought the house the way you did now. But you're a good person. No one deserves to have their partner cheat on them. And no one deserves to have their partner put hands on them. No one." After a wave of embarrassed heat surged to his face, David stared at him, feeling sadness roll off him in quiet waves.

"Speaking from experience?" For some reason the idea of Jackson feeling anything like he did made David's throat tight.

"No one has ever touched me in anger, but let's say I can commiserate." His gaze lifted and David felt the kind, direct stare like a caress. "Remember something: this isn't something you did. This is on him."

47

"I know. I keep telling myself that. But I thought…." He shook his head. "I guess it doesn't matter what I thought, but it's certainly made me question my judgment." He gestured wryly around the room. "About everything."

"Well, this particular decision might actually work out for you." Jackson stepped away from the door and reached into the back pocket of his jeans. "I did some research." He withdrew a small square of paper and unfolded it. "This is a list of all the houses Andrej Janic designed here in town." He handed it to David. "Fourth down."

Sure enough, fourth from the top was a small black-and-white picture of his house, along with the address. "Where did you find this?"

"Online at the local historical society."

"What does it mean?"

"Well, considering that almost everything inside of it is still original, all of the woodwork and everything, I'd say it's probably worth about three hundred and fifty thousand."

"Seriously?"

"That's conservative, actually. One not far from here sold for closer to four last year."

David felt a giddy laugh building. "That's… amazing."

"It certainly ought to make you feel better about buying it. And when you finish doing the necessary upgrades, it'll be worth even more."

David grimaced, rubbing his lower lip. "Now I wonder if I cheated the old lady I bought it from."

Jackson laughed. It was a wonderful sound, a deep rolling chuckle that raised gooseflesh over David's shoulders.

"What?"

"Haven't you been thinking you paid too much for it?"

"Well, yes, but…." David felt his face fill with heat. "She was nice."

"And she left you a mess to deal with. I doubt she could afford the upgrades necessary, and the value would have continued to decrease the longer she owned it. You did her a favor."

David looked at the built-ins he loved and the beautiful hardwood and he smiled slowly. He already felt more at home in the house than he ever had in the condo. "No, I think she did me one. Now I just need to buy an entire house full of furniture. No big deal." He laughed wryly.

Jackson hooked his thumbs in his tool belt. "There's a possibility I might be able to help you out with that too."

David arched a brow in interest. "Seriously? Who are you, Santa Claus?"

Jackson laughed again. It was a nice sound, and David wanted to hear it again and again. He pushed up from the chair. "Let me get you a Coke, and you can tell me about it." He picked up the empty can from the floor and found Jackson watching him, an odd expression on his face.

"I'm sorry," David said quickly. "You must have somewhere else you need to be—" Jackson was usually headed out the door between six and seven, and it was long past that.

David let the words dangle and waited. After what seemed a long time, Jackson slowly shook his head.

"Not tonight. And a Coke sounds great."

"Excellent!" David led the way, accompanied by the soft sound of Jackson's boots on the hardwood floor as he followed.

CHAPTER SEVEN

ON FRIDAY morning, David walked out of his house early, planning to make a stop at Starbucks for the last time. He liked their pumpkin spice lattes, but buying one every day felt indulgent at a time when he wasn't sure he could afford to be. Determined to stop at Target after work and pick up a Mr. Coffee, which he could pay for by *not* going to Starbucks for a week and a half, he pulled his scarf snug around his neck and locked the front door. After jogging down the steps, he headed toward his shiny, pomegranate-red Yaris and froze, staring at the little car he'd owned for barely two months. Cold rushed over him, like someone had drenched him with ice water.

The driver's side window was gone. Shards of tempered glass littered the driveway, gleaming in the bright morning sunlight, sparkling like diamonds. Remnants clung to the frame like sharp snaggleteeth. Scrawled on the door in white paint was the word FAGGOT, with a small symbol scribbled beneath it. It looked like an egg with a lightning bolt through it, but David couldn't make sense of it. He couldn't make sense of any of it. It didn't seem real. He was still staring at the car, hand over his mouth, when Jackson's truck pulled up out front.

The slam of a door echoed over the yard, and David watched as Jackson circled around the back of his truck.

"David, what's wrong?"

"I was going to go to Starbucks because I don't have a coffeemaker…." He realized how ridiculous he sounded. "My car…."

"What…." Jackson stopped next to him and David saw him register the damage to the door.

"Son of a bitch."

Jackson dug in his pocket and pulled out his cell phone, yanked his glove off with his teeth, and scrolled through his contacts.

"What are you doing?"

"Calling the police."

David looked back at the car, feeling dangerously close to tears. He knew it was dumb; it was just a car. But it had been years since anyone had used that word when referring to him, and looking at it made him feel like he might throw up. When Jackson wrapped his arm around his shoulders, David leaned into his hard side.

"Detective Mitchell," Jackson said into the phone. After a few moments, a faint, deep voice responded. "Jackson Henry, sir. I'm calling to report another hate crime."

David stiffened and looked at Jackson's implacable profile. This was a hate crime? His gaze went back to the defaced door and he realized that yes, it was. A shudder passed through his body and Jackson's arm around his shoulders tightened.

Jackson spoke for a few more minutes, giving the detective on the other end of the line David's address. When his call ended, he gently turned David toward the house.

David looked at him.

"Aren't you cold?"

David realized for the first time that he was trembling. Whether from delayed reaction or cold, he couldn't be sure, but going inside sounded like a great idea.

"Did you touch anything?" Jackson asked as he took out his key and opened the front door. David frowned. "On the car, David. Did you touch anything on the car?"

"Oh, no. I found it before you pulled up. I was going to go to Starbucks, and then…."

"Yeah. Come on." He steered David toward the recliner, crouching in front of him. "Do you have tea bags? Anything I can make you that's warm?"

David looked into the level blue eyes, trying to think if he did or not. "I… think so?"

Jackson rubbed David's knee, his long fingers caressing the boney cap. "I'll find something."

Jackson walked into the kitchen, and David heard cupboards opening, then water running. He stared at the front door, trying to wrap his head, once again, around the damage to his car.

Who would do that? And when had they done it when he wouldn't hear it? After Jackson left the night before, he'd nuked a frozen dinner, most of which he'd thrown in the trash. Then he'd grabbed a bag of chocolate chip cookies and retired to bed to watch *Law and Order*. He hadn't been able to concentrate on it, however. He'd probably fallen asleep about ten thirty, and even then he'd been restless. He was still too angry at Trevor to settle.

Trevor.

David stiffened. Could Trevor have done that to his car? David had to acknowledge Trevor might do anything when he didn't get his way. Yes, he could have bashed in the window of his car.

Jackson returned, holding out a mug. David took it with trembling hands, and the homey scent of hot cider lifted from it. He wrapped his hand around the hot mug gratefully.

"It's the packaged stuff." Jackson shoved his hands in his back pockets. "It was all I could find."

"Thank you. I think my mom gave me that box when she was afraid I would starve to death if left to my own devices."

"How're you doing?"

"The shock is fading. Now I'm mostly pissed off."

"Good. That's the appropriate response. You should be pissed off. I know when someone hit my truck, I was good and furious for a week."

"I'll bet. I… hate to even say this, but I wonder if it was Trevor."

Jackson's brows arched. "The ex?"

"Yeah."

"I don't know, David. I mean, he's certainly asshole enough to break the window, but he's gay. Why in the world would he write faggot on your car if he's gay too?"

David felt his face heat. Explaining would be embarrassing, but Jackson's steady gaze was compelling.

"Trevor always felt words like faggot applied more to gay men like me."

"Like you?"

David looked down into his cider. "You know, more… flamboyant."

Jackson didn't say anything for several seconds. When he did speak, his voice was stark. "And how would he describe himself, then?"

"He doesn't have a problem with gay or queer. He said, you know, words like pansy and faggot…." He shrugged awkwardly.

"I get it." Jackson's voice was clipped. "Christ, he's an idiot."

The doorbell rang and Jackson answered it, then introduced David to a tall, balding man named Detective Mitchell.

The rest of his morning was taken up with the police investigation. They took dozens of photos, opened the door and checked the connections to the engine and the electrical system. It never occurred to David that someone might have tampered with his engine, but everything appeared to be in working order. The detective seemed particularly interested in the small symbol under the scrawled slur, and he took several close-ups of it.

"It looks almost like a gang tag," he said as he crouched low, studying it.

"There was something similar on my truck," Jackson said, and David looked at him, startled.

"I remember," Mitchell said, straightening slowly. "This is clearer, probably because yours was done in spray paint and this is...." He reached out and rubbed his finger over the paint. When he applied his nail, it scratched right off. "Huh. Must be some kind of temporary paint marker." He glanced at David. "I hate to say whoever did this showed any consideration, but this is a lucky thing, Mr. Snyder. This way it should come right off and not necessitate you having to have your car painted."

"I feel like I should tell you," David finally worked up the courage to say. "I'm having issues with my ex."

"The guy really is an ass," Jackson provided. "He didn't know where David moved, so he tailed him home last night."

Mitchell withdrew a small notepad. "And what's his name?"

David gave him the pertinent information, including the fact he'd turned up in David's office and the multiple text messages. He felt torn. If it had been Trevor, he wanted him stopped. But if it hadn't been, having the police come to question him to question him might make him angrier.

The detective finally left, and David called Michael, telling him he probably wouldn't be able to make it in, but that he would explain later. He called his insurance company and arranged for his agent to meet him downtown at the Toyota dealership. Moments after he'd finished the call, Jackson appeared with a small tub of something he'd fished from the toolbox in the back of his truck. He knelt next to the door and opened the lid, then began to apply the thick paste to the door with a large sponge in brisk, scrubbing motions. After a few swipes of the paste, the letters began to disappear.

"Oh my God, Jackson. Thank you." David had resigned himself to driving through town with "faggot" scrawled on his door, but he was relieved he didn't have to. "What is that?"

"Turtle Wax," Jackson replied as he used a small hand towel to remove the wax. All the temporary paint came with it, and relief filled David's chest. He put his hand on Jackson's shoulder.

Jackson looked up at him, and for a moment all David could do was stare at him. "Thank you," he finally managed. "For everything."

Jackson gave him a small smile, and David was sure he saw pink on his tanned cheeks. "You're welcome." He stood up and walked briskly back to his truck. When he pulled out his tool belt and strapped it around his hips, David figured that was his cue to go.

ONE OF the things his dad had always drilled into David, along with how to make a fire, was to carry sufficient car insurance in case of emergency. As a result, he only had to pay his deductible for the replacement window, and as his car was practically brand-new, the dealership had it in stock. He sat and chatted with his insurance agent, the same man who had been his dad's agent and still handled his mom's policy, while the window was replaced.

When he got back home, it was nearly three and the shadows stretched long across the front yard, an indication of the earlier fall sunsets. David flipped up the collar on his coat against the chill before stepping out of his car. Jackson was perched on a ladder in the open garage and climbed down as David exited his car.

"Window all fixed?"

"Yeah, it is. Relatively painlessly too."

"That's a good thing. There was enough pain this morning. You didn't need any more."

David gave him a weak smile, aware Jackson was studying him. "Are you okay?" he asked finally, and David shrugged.

"I'm okay. Mostly it seems like something that happened to someone else."

"I understand."

Of everyone he knew, Jackson actually did.

"But hey, I have some good news." Jackson grinned at him and picked up something from the bench along one wall, then walked outside to join David. "You're here in time for me to test it."

Jackson held a remote, and he pointed it at the garage door and pressed a button. Instantly the door slid closed almost silently. He pressed the button again and it slid easily open.

"Jackson," David gasped.

"Now you can park your car inside." He handed David the controller.

David didn't know what to say. He looked at Jackson, his heart in his throat. Finally he managed a strangled sounding "thank you."

"One less thing for you to worry about." Jackson rubbed his hands over his hips, as if he felt awkward. After a moment he took a step back. "I need to go home and shower before I take you over to Gil's. I'll be back in a bit."

David watched him go, resolved not to sigh like a twelve-year-old girl.

DAVID FIDGETED with the hem of his heavy sweater, chewing on his lower lip and staring out through the passenger window of Jackson's truck as he drove through the tree-lined streets. It was a huge vehicle, and the cab with its rear seat was easily twice as large as the interior of David's Yaris. But sitting across from Jackson, smelling a faint hint of his spicy cologne, made the space feel too small. Jackson drove easily, his left hand on the steering wheel while his right wrist rested over the top, and David couldn't help but shoot furtive glances at the tan skin of his forearm, below the rolled-up sleeve of his denim shirt. Or notice the way the muscles in his right thigh flexed every time he moved his foot from the gas to the brake. Fearful of being caught looking, David tried really, really hard not to be obvious. He was pretty sure he failed.

"Gil's dad's place is around the corner." Jackson flipped on the blinker.

"Okay."

Jackson had told David about his friend Gil the night before as they shared a soda. Gil's mom had died, and his dad was moved in to an assisted living center that specialized in treating patients with dementia, and Gil was left with a house full of furniture he didn't know what to do with. David didn't hold out a whole lot of hope he'd find something he liked; he knew he was a snob, but he had a vision for how he wanted to furnish the house. Looking at the empty rooms, he could imagine the Greene and Greene-style furniture, all rich wood and smooth, masculine lines to go with the style of the house. He wanted leather and rich upholstery, and was ready to wait in order to get what he wanted. Somehow he doubted he'd find what he was looking for in a little old man's house. Now he was afraid he was going to look like an elitist ass in front of Jackson's friend. Determined to find at least one piece he could use, even if it went in a room he rarely used, he studied the house when Jackson pulled in the driveway. There was already another truck parked there.

"Is this one of Janic's houses?"

"It is." Jackson put the truck in park and turned off the engine. "Earlier than yours, actually. Yours is 1921. This one was built in 1918."

David gave him a small smile. "You know a lot about these places, don't you?"

Jackson shrugged. "I admire his style. Craftsman houses were being built all over the country, but his have an attention to detail you don't see a lot." Jackson's blush charmed David. "And yes," he went on with an eye roll, "I am an architecture nerd."

David chuckled. "Well, I'm an interiors snob, so don't feel bad. I've been sitting here trying to figure out a way to find something in your friend's stuff and not look like a complete ass when I can't."

Jackson's smile widened. "It may surprise you."

They got out of the truck, David feeling like a bit of a princess when he couldn't step down the way Jackson did. He had to hang on to the door until at least one of his feet was on the ground. He saw Jackson glance at his midriff and pulled down his sweater self-consciously; there wasn't any six-pack on his stomach, and he'd bet there was on Jackson's.

The house resembled his quite a bit, and David studied the details as they climbed the steps. A porch light cast an amber glow over the thick planks that made up the wide porch and caught in the faceted glass of the window in the heavy oak door.

A porch swing hanging from heavy chains swayed slightly in the cool breeze. "I want one of those," he said wistfully, sinking his hands into his pockets. The swing was gleaming hardwood, all graceful lines with a padded cushion on the seat. Jackson glanced at it as he rang the bell. It echoed through the house.

"Gil might sell you that one."

"Really?" David asked brightly. Jackson nodded as footsteps approached inside the house.

The door opened and a mountain of a man stood framed in the doorway, wearing a ribbed sweatshirt and khaki cargo pants. He was completely bald, head gleaming in the golden porch light, jaw square and narrowed eyes intimidating. A fissure of alarm slid down David's spine at his stony expression. Until the man saw Jackson, and then he smiled and the difference in his expression was astonishing. When he smiled a dimple appeared in his cheek and his face brightened.

"Hey, man." He offered his hand and Jackson shook it.

"Gil. How're you doing?"

"I'm good."

When Gil held out his hand to David, he took it, relieved that his wasn't shaking. David's hand felt like a little kid's in the giant grip engulfing it. Absently he noticed there was white paint on the inside of Gil's wrist and his sleeve.

"This is David Snyder," Jackson said. "He's the man I told you about."

"Another member of the Andrej Janic fan club?" Gil gave him a crooked smile.

"Recently converted." David tried for a firm handshake even though he was afraid his palm was clammy and his grip weak.

"Come on in." Gil pushed the door wide and David stepped tentatively into a living room not unlike his own. Except it was furnished, and the furniture was exquisite.

"Oh my God." Drawn in by one of the most beautiful examples of a mission-style sofa he'd ever seen, David crossed to it. The arms were a rich, dark wood, gently sloping toward the back, slats down the sides. The cushions were thick, upholstered in deep brown leather, and when he touched them, David sighed. They were as soft as butter, and he ran his hand over them carefully. "This is gorgeous. Oh, man. So is this."

The coffee table matched the sofa except delicate carvings of branches with small blossoms ran across the top. It was covered with a sheet of glass, protecting the stunning craftsmanship. It was so beautiful David actually felt his throat grow tight. Then he noticed the simple but lovely rocking chair crafted in the same dark wood, the seat upholstered to match the couch. And there were matching end tables, lamps on top with golden, rectangular glass shades, one strip of red glass on each side to break up the amber glow. Even the large rug beneath it all was perfect, the design a muted Indian pattern in shades of burgundy and brown and black, and David knelt to test the nap. It felt thick and rich beneath his fingers.

"This is all stunning," he murmured, straightening.

"Think you'll be able to find something you like?" Jackson teased, and David shot him a narrow-eyed look.

David turned to Gil. "I'm so sorry about your dad. Mine died a month ago, but he knew who we all were until the end. I can't even imagine." Gil dropped his huge hands into his back pockets.

"It's been hard." His deep voice was solemn. "He hasn't been the same since my mom died."

"Yeah, I worry about my mom for the same reason." David and Gil shared a look of understanding. David returned his gaze to the furniture. "This stuff is beautiful, Gil. Are you sure you don't want to keep it? I mean, I'd love to buy some of it, but you should know it's worth a small fortune."

Gil shrugged. "It isn't my style."

"He uses carved bears in his decorating," Jackson quipped, then ducked aside when Gil swiped at him. It was as carefree as David had seen him, and it made him almost irresistible.

"I actually like midcentury modern," Gil said, "but this stuff was my parents' pride and joy. They used to travel all over, picking up unique finds. After Dad retired, it's what they did. This living room set came from Pennsylvania." He eyed David with speculation. "More than anything, they'd want it to go to someone who would appreciate it. Why don't we walk through, and you can let me know what you might be interested in?"

David loved it all. There was a dining room set with a long table, six chairs, and a sideboard made of three different shades of wood that glowed in the soft overhead lighting. A rolltop desk with a swivel chair and several wooden file cabinets were in one room. In another a set with a bed, vanity, and highboy with inlaid wood that looked French provincial filled the space. It was a little feminine for David's taste, but it was lovely. In another room an enameled brass bed with a white dresser and nightstands, also beautiful but not his style, gleamed in the overhead light. But in the last bedroom a complete suite of furniture, head- and footboard, two nightstands, and an armoire taller than he was, all in the stark yet beautiful craftsman-style that made David sigh, filled the room.

"It's perfect." He ran his hand over the front of the armoire. "But I know there's no way I can afford all of it."

Gil crossed his arms over his barrel chest. "I don't really have any idea what to ask for it. How much do you think it's worth?"

David pursed his lips, calculating in his mind. He knew what antiques of this vintage and quality went for.

"For everything? Conservatively you could get at least thirty grand for the craftsman-style stuff, and that's not including the French provincial set or the brass bed. You could probably get more."

Gil looked startled. "Seriously?"

"Oh, yes."

"He's an interior designer, Gil." Jackson leaned against the wall. "He'd know."

"I should have fudged and told you it was worth a lot less, but I can't do it." David liked Gil. For all his imposing appearance, he seemed like someone he could be friends with.

"Wow," Gil huffed, rubbing his rough jaw. "Well, that's a problem."

David frowned. "A problem? How?" He'd have thought it was wonderful. His own parents tended toward serviceable Sears particleboard stuff that wouldn't be worth what it cost to haul it away.

Gil sat on the foot of the bed and it creaked beneath his weight. He leaned forward, his hands linked loosely between his big square knees. "See, it's like this. I'm the executor of my parents' estate. I have two siblings, a brother and a sister, both younger, who know what the house is worth and are chomping at the bit to get their hands on the money. I, on the other hand, would like to limit what they get their hands on."

"Shouldn't all of it go for your dad's care?" David asked. "I mean, I know those places are really expensive."

"My dad was a very, very smart man. He bought long-term care insurance years ago, before anyone knew how valuable it would be. His care is paid for. Unfortunately, my siblings know that. Dad hadn't been in assisted living five hours before they were talking about how they'd spend their share of his money."

"I'm sorry," David murmured. "That's lousy."

"I've always known they were spoiled, but…." He shook his head. "You want to find out who people really are? Wait until there's money involved." He exhaled heavily and looked around the room, his expression pensive.

Once he'd gotten over Gil's size, David saw a gentle giant, handsome in his own way. He had a ready smile, and his eyes were kind. His huge hands were careful as they touched the footboard.

"My brother and sister aren't going to have any more idea than I did of what this stuff is worth, and they don't want any of it. As far as they're concerned, it's a bunch of old junk. They just want his money. And that's the last thing I care about." Gil looked around at the furniture. "I'll sell you the lot for four grand."

David's mouth dropped open. "All of it?" Gil nodded, his expression satisfied. "Gil, I can't let you do that. It's worth too much more."

Gil shrugged. "I don't have the time to parse it out and sell it a piece at a time. And frankly, Jackson likes you. He says you're a decent guy who needs furniture." David looked over at Jackson, who pointedly looked the other way, his arms crossed over his chest. "So, what do you say, David? Want it?"

David rubbed his hand over his mouth. "I can't let you sell it to me for four thousand dollars. It's not enough, Gil."

Gil rolled his eyes and shot a look at Jackson, who shrugged. "Fine. Five. But that's my final offer. You take it, or it's going to Goodwill."

David quickly reached out and shook Gil's hand. "To save it from Goodwill, it's a deal."

Gil grinned, and David's heart began to beat quickly in excitement. The furniture was spectacular; it would be gorgeous in his house. Finally he'd have a home that reflected his taste. The thought sent a shaft of warmth through his core.

Gil stood. "You available tomorrow, Jackson? I can bring the box truck and we can probably do it in one load."

"Wait, what?" David looked between them. "You don't have to move it. I can take care of that."

"Listen, I want it out of here ASAP. That way I can get the Realtor to list the place."

"You don't want to... wait?" The moment the words were out of his mouth, David regretted them, but Gil smiled sadly.

"For what? He's never coming back home, and if I sell the house I can at least get my idiot siblings off my back. Besides, why pay to have the furniture moved when we can do it for you?" He clapped Jackson on his shoulder. "You got other plans?"

"No, I'm good." Jackson led the way out of the bedroom.

"I'll get Manny too."

David saw Jackson pause and glance at Gil over his shoulder, his expression cautious. "You think Manny's up for that?"

Gil nodded. "He's okay."

Jackson didn't look convinced, but he didn't say anything more.

"Gil, seriously." David followed them. "I can hire...." He felt like the caboose on a fast-moving train trying to keep up.

Gil glanced at him over his broad shoulder. "You want to trust regular moving guys with this stuff?"

That made David pause. The last time he'd hired movers, they dented both his washer and dryer and took a chunk out of his black lacquer headboard. Dealing with their customer service department afterward, trying to get them to refund some of his fee, had been a nightmare. He nervously chewed the corner of his lower lip. As they walked into the living room, he looked at the beautiful old sofa. "If you're sure...."

"Ah, shut up, David." Gil sat in the rocker with a good-natured grin. "Line up some more muscle."

David blinked. Compared to Jackson and Gil, he wasn't sure anyone he knew could be considered "muscle."

DAVID WAVED to Gil through the window of Jackson's cab. He looked enormous standing silhouetted in the doorway.

"What a nice man." David watched Gil as Jackson pulled off down the block.

"He is. A really nice man."

"I feel like I'm stealing that furniture. Don't get me wrong—I'm thrilled. But he could get so much more for it."

"He doesn't want more. He wants it to go to someplace where it will be appreciated." Jackson's voice sounded deep, and the darkened cab created a sense of intimacy. David studied his profile and the way the streetlights cast it in sharp relief. He was so handsome, he took David's breath. "He wasn't kidding when he said his brother and sister are only in it for the money," Jackson went on, unaware of his effect on David. "And trust me, they don't need another thirty grand to fight over."

"You know them?"

Jackson nodded. "I met them at Gil's mother's memorial service. Let's say I can see why the three of them have never really gotten on." He turned at the corner, and his hands moved on the steering wheel, bringing David's attention to the wide leather band that circled his wrist. He didn't know why, but he found it incredibly sexy.

"Were they jerks or something?" David asked.

Jackson snorted softly. "You could say that. His brother has a Ted Cruz bumper sticker on his Beamer."

David recoiled slightly. "Oh, that's not good."

"He and Gil don't have a whole lot in common. And I think both of his siblings resent the fact his parents made the queer their executor."

David frowned. He knew how lucky he was his family accepted him. He had good friends whose families didn't. He thought of the funny, friendly man he'd met and felt a sinking sadness. "That's awful."

"It is," Jackson agreed. There was something in his voice, something that made David think he was intimately acquainted with that kind of pain too, but he wasn't comfortable asking. Something else popped into his mind.

"Can I ask you something?"

Jackson glanced at him. "Sure."

"Who's Manny?"

Jackson was silent for several seconds. He did that, David noticed. Thought before he spoke. But the silence made David nervous.

"I'm sorry." He feared he'd overstepped. "It's none of my business."

"No, it's okay. I'm trying to decide what to say." Jackson's thumb bounced on his steering wheel, the only outward indication that he might be uncomfortable. "Manny is a friend of ours. In fact, he's the guy I mentioned that could help out with the plumbing at your place. He knows his stuff. He had this boyfriend named George." His lip curled when he said the name. "I never liked him. He treated Manny like shit. We tried to tell him, but he thought he was in love…."

David knew what that was like. Beth had never liked Trevor. In fact, several of David's friends, including his best friend, had been very cool to Trevor, making excuses not to spend time with them. Trevor was a snob, and he hadn't liked the people who worked for David either, telling him he "shouldn't socialize with the employees." Yeah, David had been there.

"I was always concerned that George's nasty disposition was going to be a problem, but even I didn't see it coming. One weekend, Manny got tired of George pushing him around and told him to knock it off. George went into their garage and came back with a baseball bat."

David's stomach rolled. "Oh God," he murmured. Jackson stared through the windshield, his jaw hard.

"He beat the shit out of Manny. By the time he was done, he'd broken his arm and several ribs, and given him a skull fracture. He needed plastic surgery to repair his face. I think if Manny hadn't managed to dial 911 on his cell while George was in the bathroom, he'd have killed him. The cops came and arrested the bastard, and Manny spent the next six weeks in the hospital."

Horror made David cold clear through. Something he'd read months before came back to him. "Oh my God, Jackson, there was a trial, wasn't there?"

"Yeah. It was the top story on local media for months. 'Gay lovers' spat results in attempted murder charge,'" Jackson sneered. "They called it a *spat*. Manny was nearly beaten to death, and then he had to dodge the goddamn snotty press at every turn. George was convicted and sentenced to twenty-five to life."

"That's horrible."

Jackson nodded again. "Yeah, it really was. I hope Gil's right about Manny being okay. The last time I saw him, he still looked pretty rough."

David's heart ached for the man he'd yet to meet. The mood in the truck felt heavy and sad. In an effort to lighten it, David reached for something, anything to change the subject. "So, does Gil have a significant other?"

Jackson shot him a sharp look, his brow furrowed. "No, but you really aren't his type."

David's mouth dropped open on a startled laugh. "I wasn't asking because I'm interested. I was curious. He's a nice person."

Jackson's jaw relaxed. "He is. One of the best I've ever known." He smiled almost reluctantly. "However, he has… singular taste in men."

Intrigued, David shifted until he faced Jackson. "What does that mean? Is he some kind of leather daddy or something?"

Jackson smirked. "No, he likes twinks. The twinkier, the better."

David stared, disbelieving. "You're lying."

Jackson's white teeth were bright even in the darkened cab. "Swear to God. He likes 'em young and cute."

"I would think he'd terrify them. The man is huge."

"You'd be surprised. Gil has—" Jackson stopped, and he looked like he was fighting a reluctant smile. "Let's say he does all right. Although lately he's been making noise about finding someone special and settling down." Jackson took on a faintly cynical expression. "If such a thing exists."

David wanted to tell him it did, but he wasn't sure he believed it any longer. The thought made him sad.

He stared, unseeing, through the windshield.

CHAPTER EIGHT

DAVID WAS out of bed by six on Saturday morning, brewing a pot of coffee with the new drip coffeemaker he'd purchased at Target. He'd loved the Keurig, but he missed the old Mr. Coffee Trevor had gotten rid of more. The scent of the Dunkin' Donuts coffee brewing, wafting through the house, was one of the things that made him think of his dad. He'd come downstairs in the morning before school and Dad would be sipping from a cup, standing by the sink in his dress shirt and tie, half a pot still warming on the hot plate. David Snyder Sr. worked at the power company as a systems analyst for thirty years, and David Jr. never saw him heading to work without wearing a suit.

He smiled faintly as he wandered into his living room, holding a Mickey Mouse mug his mom had given him. He was coveting a set of Fiestaware he'd seen on the Macy's website the night before, but was holding out until he had a better idea what the repairs were going to end up costing. He wasn't sure four hundred dollars for dinnerware and mugs was an expense he needed when he could buy CorningWare for forty. He sighed softly. It would look so great with that awesome dining room furniture, though.

A small white car pulled up and parked at the curb, and David grinned as the slender young man climbed out from behind the wheel. He was wearing a skullcap covering his dark hair, a gray hoodie as a nod to the cold, overcast day, and skinny jeans. Even though he was twenty-five, he looked closer to high school.

David unlocked the front door and stepped onto the porch as the lithe brunet crossed the lawn, kicking up dried leaves as he walked. *Time to get out the rake*, David mused absently.

"Good morning," he called.

"Hey, David," Michael called back. "The house is so cute!"

"Thanks." He held the door open wide and let Michael in. "It will look even better with furniture in it."

Michael gave the plaid recliner a dubious look. "Wow, that's ugly."

"I guess I won't give it to you for Christmas, then," David teased. He'd been in Michael's one-bedroom apartment, and even though it was small and not in the best neighborhood, it was immaculate and the furnishings were carefully selected. He wasn't surprised when Michael shuddered.

"Perish the thought. Thanks, but I think it might be better to take it to the dump."

"Snob."

"Guilty."

"Coffee?" David held up his mug.

"That would be great, thanks."

Michael followed him into the kitchen, his eyes bright. "This is beautiful. It's so much more you than that condo." Michael accepted the mug of coffee David poured for him with murmured thanks. This one had a picture of Mount Rushmore on it.

"Sweetener in the bowl, creamer in the refrigerator door."

Michael nodded and moved about, doctoring his coffee. He ran his hand down the front of the vintage refrigerator before he grabbed the handle. "Did this come with the house?" He took the hazelnut-flavored creamer from the shelf in the door.

"It did. I'm glad it works."

"It's very retro."

"I imagine when the lady who lived here bought it, it was the latest thing."

Michael's dark brows rose. "Seriously? How old was she?"

"A hundred and twenty," David answered, his voice dry, "and very sweet as she hung me with several thousand dollars in repairs."

Michael wandered into the dining room, crossing to the built-ins. "But it will be so worth it once it's done." He opened a drawer, studying the original hardware. David followed him and leaned against the wooden cabinet next to Michael.

"I think I owe you an apology."

Michael looked up at him, frowning. "For what?"

"For Trevor. Has he been to the office more than that one time?"

"Once more." Michael shrugged. "He's all mouth. I've tried to keep him away from you."

"And I thank you for that."

Michael searched David's face. "He found you, though, didn't he?"

"He followed me home from work on Thursday."

"Why didn't you tell me?"

Now David shrugged. "I had my hands full with something else yesterday."

"Yeah, about that… what happened?"

David took a deep breath before telling Michael about his car. He reacted with horror, grabbing David's arm with a sharp gasp.

"That's terrifying, David. I'm glad you called the cops."

"Actually, Jackson called them."

"Oh, really? Do tell."

David felt his face heat. "He knew someone from when his truck was vandalized. And he was able to get the writing off my door, so that's good." David took a drink of his coffee, but he could feel Michael studying his face.

"So, do I get to meet the mysterious handyman today?"

Movement through the front window of his house caught David's attention. A silver GMC truck pulled in behind Michael's car. "As a matter of fact…." David moved to open the front door. Michael followed him, his face growing avid. "And you behave yourself," David warned. Michael's white teeth flashed, but he held up his hand, palm out.

"I'll be good."

David doubted that, but he opened the door before Jackson had a chance to ring the bell.

"Good morning."

"Hey."

"Coffee?" David offered.

"We should probably head out to Gil's dad's place. He was going to pick up the truck and then meet us there with the other guys."

"Other guys?" David wondered how many of them there were going to be. Behind Jackson's back, Michael gave him a pointed look that said, "Excuse me? I'm standing here." "Oh, I'm sorry. Jackson Henry, meet Michael Crane. He and I work together."

Jackson held out his hand, and David had to swallow a smile as Michael's eyes widened. "Nice to meet you." Jackson returned his attention to David, and Michael mouthed "holy shit" behind his back.

"What other guys?" David repeated, giving Michael a stern look.

"Gil asked his buddy Vernon. And Manny."

"And they won't let me pay them."

Jackson dropped his hands into his pockets. "Nope."

David was both flabbergasted and uncomfortable. Why would strangers do that? "Will they at least let me buy pizza and beer?"

"Pizza and beer?" Michael made a face. "Talk about a carb fest."

"I'll buy you some chicken nuggets."

Jackson snorted when Michael flipped David off.

"I'm sure pizza and beer would be welcome. And I thought we'd take my truck," Jackson said. "Some of the smaller stuff could go in the bed."

"That's fine." David took Michael's still nearly full mug and walked into the kitchen, putting both in the sink. He came back and glanced at Michael. "You ready?"

"Sure. I'm just along for the ride."

"No, dear." David held open the front door. "You're my muscle."

"Me?" Michael gave him a startled look. "Dude, if I'm your muscle, you're so screwed."

"You're what passes for muscle in my world, Michael." David clapped him on the shoulder as he passed. "You can carry the sofa cushions. And try to look studly, will you?"

"Screwed, man, I'm telling you."

Jackson clearly swallowed a laugh.

THERE WAS a white panel truck backed into the driveway at Gil's dad's, and Gil stood on the front lawn with two other men nearly as big as he was when Jackson pulled up in front of the house.

"Holy shit," Michael murmured. "That's muscle. What do they do for a living, eat small children?"

Jackson grinned. "Relax, Michael. I'll make sure they don't take any bites out of you." David covered a smile with his hand, but secretly he agreed with Michael. All the men were wearing jackets in deference to the cold, overcast weather, and it made them look bigger. Bulkier. Scarier.

"I look like a cricket compared to them," Michael whined.

"No," David countered. "But right now you sound like one."

"Oh, shut up." Michael batted him on the back of his head. Jackson was still grinning as he stepped out of the truck. "I have so much hatred for you right now," Michael muttered.

"Tough it up, big boy, and come meet the other guys." David got out of the truck and held the door open for Michael.

"So much hatred," Michael repeated as he climbed out behind him. David smirked and followed Jackson to the small crowd on the lawn.

"Hey, David," Gil called, a grin on his wide face. "Is that your muscle?" He gestured to Michael, his smile turning wry. But David also noticed the way his gaze moved over Michael's lithe form, and he thought of what Jackson had told him about Gil's taste in men. Michael was certainly his type.

"This is Michael Crane." David pulled Michael forward when he hesitated. "He's my chief design assistant. He can also lift plenty. I've seen him heft an armchair when necessary."

Michael glared and held out his hand. "He's totally lying. I'm the tablecloth-and-decorative-pillow kind of muscle."

Gil chuckled. "Hey, we've got plenty of small stuff to move too. Not everyone needs to be a gorilla."

"Nice," one of the men David hadn't met yet quipped in a deep, distinctively rough voice. He had salt-and-pepper gray hair, pulled back in a low ponytail, and a full gray mustache. He could have been anywhere from forty to sixty, his face a roadmap of lines and wrinkles, but his dark eyes were bright. "I get asked to help move shit and end up being described as a primate."

"You like it," Gil teased. "Makes you feel manly. You should thank me. Old guys like you don't get asked to be muscle much."

"Bending you over the railing and making you squeal would make me feel manly, Gilbert," he growled. He offered his hand to a wide-eyed Michael. "Vernon Dwyer. Pleased to meet you."

Michael shook his hand warily, no doubt still trying to purge what Vernon had described from his mind. David shook his hand next, noticing how crooked his fingers were, how hard his palms.

"Don't let him scare you," Gil said to Michael. "He's all talk."

"You keep telling yourself that, boy."

Gil grinned and gestured to the other man beside him. "David, Michael... this is Manny."

David had seen pictures of Emanuel Martinez when he went online to read about the trial that had put George Wilkerson in prison. Manny's injuries at the hand of his ex-lover had been described in graphic detail, and the list had been horrifying and extensive. A broken hand and arm on the right side, broken ribs on the left. One blow had fractured his skull above his right eye. In photos accompanying the articles, Manny looked pale, dark circles beneath his eyes, his hair shorn short revealing the myriad scars that made a grim patchwork of the right side of his face. The Manny standing before him now was tense, his slender body held tight, but his features had been restored by a very skilled plastic surgeon. There were scars, but he was also so beautiful David had to remind himself not to stare.

A baseball cap covered his curly black hair, but when he looked up his chestnut eyes, surrounded by thick black lashes, were arresting. There was one particularly angry scar bisecting a brow and curling around his cheekbone, but other than that, his smooth, golden brown skin was healed. He nodded in greeting but didn't offer his hand, his shoulders hunched and his hands deep in the pockets of his jacket. David ached looking at his body language, the way he held himself withdrawn even when surrounded by his friends.

"So, that gives us six guys." Gil surveyed the group, then looked back at the house.

"Actually I think David and I should only count as one." Michael gave David an irritated look.

"Speak for yourself, Mary," David shot back and the other men laughed.

"Let's start in the living room and work our way to the back, okay? I think we should load the couch first. Vern, why don't you stick with me? You, Manny, Jackson, and I can grab the heavy stuff. Michael and David, why don't you put the lamps and smaller pieces in the back of the GMC? We want to make sure they don't break."

It made David feel a bit marginalized, but he also could see Gil's point. They started toward the house and David grabbed Gil's arm, halting him. He put his hand in his jacket and pulled out a check, placing it in Gil's hand.

"Thank you," he said softly. "Really."

Gil winked at him, squeezing his hand before putting the check in his front pocket without opening it.

They spent the next three hours emptying the house of all the furniture plus a few other things. It wasn't long before the heavy outer jackets were abandoned. Jackson and Manny were whipcord lean with broad shoulders and impressive biceps, but Vernon and Gil were built along the lines of a mountain range. For an older guy, Vernon had a spectacular body, shown to advantage in a tight dark T-shirt.

"Wow, Vernon," David said the first time he saw him without the jacket. "That's… impressive."

Vernon grinned and flexed his bicep. It was bigger than David's head.

Several times over the course of the morning, people would call out "Does this rug go?" or "What about this mattress, man?" David started to answer, but Gil overrode him with "Everything goes. If David doesn't want it, he can put it on Craigslist." They systematically emptied each of the rooms, rolled up the rugs, gathered up the lamps. As more and more was placed in the box truck and the back of Jackson's pickup, David was still convinced he hadn't paid nearly enough for all of it. Even the extra five hundred dollars he'd added to the check he gave Gil didn't make up for it. When Vernon appeared on the front porch with tools and began to unscrew the bolts holding the swing in place, David stopped in the middle of the lawn, his hand over his mouth in dismay.

An arm draped over his shoulders and for a moment, David thought it was Michael. But then his sense of smell kicked in. It was Jackson with his arm around him. Heat slid down David's spine as his body registered the strength in his arm, the muscled ribcage against his side. Jackson had put his arm around him the day before, when he'd been panicked, but this was… different.

"What's the matter?" Jackson asked, his voice pitched low.

It took David a moment to remember. "The swing," he murmured, turning his head. Jackson's face was so close, his eyes on a level with David's. "It's too much."

One of Jackson's brows arched. "You don't want it?"

David inhaled deeply. "Oh, I want it. From the moment I saw it, I've wanted it. You know that."

"Then what's the problem?"

David exhaled in consternation. "I didn't pay enough for everything as it is, Jackson. Not all the different bedroom furniture and the swing…."

Jackson squeezed his upper arm and turned his mouth to David's ear. His breath brushed David's skin and gooseflesh rose on his arms. Jackson smelled like spicy cologne mixed with healthy, clean sweat and the scent went straight to David's chest, then headed south. "When Gil told you his dad had investments?" he said, so softly only David could hear. David nodded. "He didn't tell you that his dad was loaded. Seriously loaded. Let him do this, okay? He likes you."

"Okay, but it doesn't feel right to me."

Jackson's hand slid to David's nape and rested there. David fought the urge to close his eyes and lean into the calloused hand.

"So hire him to do some work at your place."

Jackson was so close, David could see the flecks of darker blue in his sky-blue eyes, and he had to grasp for what he'd been going to ask. "What does he do?" he finally managed. How silly that he didn't already know. Jackson gave him a relaxed grin.

"House painter. A good one. And that kitchen of yours is a crime against nature."

David laughed. Actually the bathrooms were worse. The tile in the bath off the master was light blue but the walls were yellow. Yeah, he could definitely hire Gil to paint. And then he might not feel so guilty about what had to be considered the deal of the century.

Vernon passed them, the swing held in one strong, misshapen hand. "Come on, lovers. There's still work to be done in there."

Jackson flipped him off casually and went back into the house, and David could feel the heat as it filled his fair skin. *Lovers?* He could only wish. The tingling ghost of the touch of Jackson's hand at his nape still lingered.

"Very subtle." Michael came to stand beside him. "You're cool as a cucumber. As long as people ignore the fact you all but humped his leg."

"I will fire you," David muttered.

"You won't. Then you'd have to do your own job."

"You're obnoxious." David elbowed him in his ribs and Michael made an aggrieved sound and rubbed the spot.

"Asshole."

"Princess."

Michael crossed his arms. He'd lost his sweatshirt at some point and he looked very young and very thin. "And what's wrong with that I'd like to know? Believe me, if I was a princess, I wouldn't be schlepping your shit around."

"Sure you would be," Gil said, walking by and patting Michael on the shoulder. He almost knocked him to the ground. "Think Cinderella. She could schlep circles around you."

Michael huffed in exaggerated outrage even as Gil closed the back of the huge box truck and slid the bolt home. "We ready to roll, girls?"

"Speak for yourself, pal." Michael pulled his hoodie back on. "I'll have you know I'm very manly."

"You keep telling yourself that," Vern teased. "Those skinny jeans are so tight I'm surprised they don't cut off circulation to that part you think makes you manly." He gave Michael a wicked grin as he blushed. "But I do want to thank you for the scenery. You have a mighty nice ass there, sweetheart."

"I...." Michael seemed at a loss. David swallowed a grin; he didn't think he'd ever seen Michael at a loss for words.

Gil grimaced. "Jesus, Vern. Leave him alone."

"What?" Vern spread his hands, looking honestly surprised. "It was a compliment."

"Just... try to stop being a jackass." Gil trudged past David and Michael, Vern winking at a still-speechless Michael as he passed.

Manny gave them a small, shy smile as he followed them.

Michael stepped closer to David's shoulder. "Okay," he murmured, "so what's Manny's story?"

"Later," David promised, pulling on his own jacket before climbing into Jackson's truck.

CHAPTER NINE

Six hours later, David sat sprawled on his living room floor, looking around at the men draped across the furniture and at the pizza boxes, empty plates, and beer bottles in various stages of completion that, very thoughtfully, mostly sat on coasters. His furniture, he thought with a low thrum of pleasure, looked as magnificent in the space as he'd known it would, even with six tired men lounging on it. And on the floor. And in the ugly recliner, which had been shoved to one side.

They were all exhausted, but they'd busted their collective asses. David's bedroom was set up, as was a guest room with the ornate French furniture, and a home office in the third. The brass bed and the white furniture were taking up temporary residence in the back of his garage, which still left room for his little car. And David hurt in places he didn't even know he had.

If he was sore, he could only assume the others had to be so much worse, but the only one bitching was Michael.

"I'm not built for manual labor," he whined from his spot in the recliner. He was so tired he'd dropped into the ugly chair without even complaining about the upholstery.

"Good thing," Vernon growled from his spot in the rocker. "Because you didn't do much."

"Hey."

"Be nice, you old bitch." Gil kicked Vernon's foot from his spot on the sofa. "He worked hard. I didn't see your sorry ass carrying a dozen lamps and throw rugs out of the house." Vern grumbled under his breath and Gil sent him a teasing smile. "If you can't be nice, I won't invite you to play with us anymore."

"Is that what you call it?" Vern grimaced. "Baby, if this was your idea of playing, it's no wonder you can't get laid."

Gil's broad face filled with embarrassed color.

"Time out." Jackson made a T with his hands from where he was sprawled on his back on the floor. He'd had at least three beers and to David's delight his usual quiet, almost pensive nature had been replaced with a loose-limbed grace and a gently ironic sense of humor. "Ten yards for excessive bitchiness."

Everyone but Vernon laughed. Vernon gave him a scowl, and to David's amusement, Jackson blew him a kiss.

David studied each of the men in turn. Gil, the gentle giant, Vernon, the crabapple with a decent heart at his core. Michael, watching Gil with surprising interest, as if trying to figure him out. David would pursue that topic later. His gaze moved on to Manny, who was sitting next to Gil on the sofa. He'd removed his baseball hat, tossing it on the coffee table, running his fingers through his damp, curly hair. The beer seemed to help him loosen up too, and he wasn't as self-conscious about his scars.

David was glad. He liked these men, even irascible Vernon, and he wanted them to be comfortable in his home. He wanted to pursue friendships with them, and it was freeing to know he wasn't going to have to listen to Trevor's bitching and snotty comments about how they weren't "on the same level" as he was. He even wondered if he could maybe reconnect with the friends he'd allowed Trevor to run off over the years.

Someone nudged his foot. Jackson's booted foot lay between his, and David followed the long line of his body up to his face. His arms were pillowed beneath his head and he watched David with a slight smile. He looked amazing, even after a day's hard labor, and David's heart lifted looking at him.

"You okay?" Jackson mouthed, dark brows lifted. David returned his smile, nodding. Jackson winked at him and closed his eyes.

A persistent buzzing sounded nearby and Jackson jerked, then rolled onto his hip to reach back and pull an iPhone out of his back pocket. He sat up, frowning before punching a button on its face and bringing it to his ear.

"Henry," he answered briskly. He listened for a few moments and the color drained from his face. "Where?" he asked, his voice hard. "I'll be right there." He disconnected the call, then sat for a moment, staring blankly at his phone.

"Jackson? Man, you okay?" Gil sat forward.

"I… it's my mom." He shoved the phone back into his pocket and pushed to his feet. "I've got to go."

"Is she okay?" David stood as well, wincing at a stab of pain in his lower back as Jackson began to pat down his pockets, apparently looking for his keys.

"I don't know," he answered faintly. "That was the neighbor. I guess she fell…." He continued to look for his keys, growing more agitated.

"I'll drive you," David offered.

A frown pulled down the corners of his mobile mouth. "No, I can…."

"You've been drinking, Jackson." David gentled his voice. "The last thing you need is to get pulled over."

"I'm fine."

"Dude, you can't even find your keys," Gil pointed out. "Let the man drive you."

"I… okay." Jackson wasn't happy about it, but he apparently didn't want to argue about it either.

"That's our cue, boys." Gil grabbed his jacket off the back of the couch and shrugged into it.

The other men were on their feet, collecting jackets and heading out the door, telling Jackson they hoped his mom was okay. Michael paused before he left, touching David's elbow.

"Call me," he said, his voice quiet, but the words were no less emphatic for their volume. David nodded, then locked the door after him.

"We'll go out through the back." David turned off the lights in the dining room as they passed. The house fell into shadow behind him. They went through the kitchen and down the step to the service porch.

The Yaris was parked in the garage, and the lights of Gil's box truck lit up the doors briefly as he backed out of the driveway. It was after five o'clock, but it got dark earlier and earlier this time of year. They went into the shadowy garage and Jackson jogged around the back of the car as David climbed in behind the steering wheel. He opened the garage door with a press of a button.

"Where am I going?" He started the car.

"Fourteenth," Jackson answered, clearly distracted as he fastened his seat belt. "Take Meadow Wood south. That's the closest route."

Other than giving terse directions when they reached intersections, Jackson didn't say anything, and David didn't try to engage him in conversation. When they turned onto the street where Jackson's mom lived, Jackson cursed under his breath. An ambulance was in a driveway halfway down the block, red and blue lights rotating, cast weird shadows on the people milling about at the curb.

"I take it that's it?" David stared in concern.

"Yeah."

Jackson was out of the car before David had pulled to a complete stop, and he ran across the lawn as David parked in front of the house.

David jogged after him, pushing between two of the neighbors in time to see paramedics emerge through the front door of the nondescript little house, a gurney between them with the head raised. An older woman with shoulder-length, wavy white hair lay on it. There was a thick bandage around her head that was already soaked with blood. Jackson was speaking to the female paramedic at the rear of the gurney when David arrived.

"…said she lost her balance and fell against a bookcase in the office," she was saying. She leaned toward him slightly. "Does your mom drink?"

Jackson shook his head. "No, she has MS." The woman nodded.

"She's pretty out of it. She couldn't even tell us what medication she's on."

"I have a list in my phone."

"Jackson?" Jackson's mom spoke, her voice wavering. She held out her hand and he took it in his, wrapping his long fingers around her small palm.

"I'm here, Mom. What happened?"

"I was paying bills, and when I stood up from my desk, I… got so dizzy." She took a deep, shuddering breath on what sounded like a sob. "I'm so sorry, honey. I couldn't remember your phone number. I'm so sorry."

"Hush." Jackson rubbed her arm. "You didn't do anything wrong. It's okay."

"The only number I could think of was Evelyn's. I'm ruining these clothes. And there's blood all over the floor…."

"Don't worry about that. I'll take care of it."

"You already have to take care of too much." Now she was crying openly, tears streaming down her cheeks, and it broke David's heart.

"Hush, Mom. It's okay." Jackson spoke to her so gently, bending his head to kiss the knuckles of the hand he held. "It's all going to be okay."

They loaded her into the open back of the ambulance and the paramedic spoke to Jackson. "We can't let you ride in the back, but we're taking her to Holy Family. If you could get her insurance and medication information and meet us there, that would be great. Does she have an advanced directive?"

David's hands curled into fists. He knew what that meant. Jackson nodded, running his hand through his hair.

"Jackson!" His mother sounded panicked, and Jackson leaned in through the ambulance door.

"It's okay, Mom. They're going to take you to Holy Family and I'll meet you there."

"You can't come with me?"

"I can't, but I'll be right behind you. I promise."

Jackson's mother subsided into the padded top of the stretcher. Jackson saw the male paramedic lean in and speak to her softly, his hand over the one clenched in her lap. Slowly her fingers relaxed.

"How bad is it?" Jackson asked as the female paramedic closed the back doors. She paused.

"It's pretty bad. Head injuries always bleed a lot, but this one is significant." She ran around the side of the ambulance, and Jackson and David stood in the street as it pulled out of the driveway, heading off with the siren blaring.

Jackson stared after it, such a lost look on his face that David's heart rolled over hard.

"Jackson." He touched his arm. "You need to get your mom's stuff together."

Jackson looked at him, then blinked and nodded. "Right, right." He went into the house and David followed.

An older lady stood inside the door. She was trembling.

"Honey, I'm so sorry," she said to Jackson. "I probably should have waited but she was bleeding so much and the cut is so awful...."

"Evelyn, you did exactly right." He squeezed her elbow. "Thank you for taking care of her." He disappeared down a shadowed hallway, and moments later David heard drawers being opened.

The woman looked up at David, her eyes wide and frightened. She had blood on her hands and some on the sleeve of her housedress.

"You're going to want to go get cleaned up." He gentled his voice. She looked down at her hands and exhaled heavily.

"I've got six children." Her voice was trembling. "I've bandaged more cuts and scrapes than I can say." She shook her head. "I've never seen anything like this."

David nodded, taking her elbow and steering her gently toward the door. "I know he really appreciates you being here."

"Are you Jackson's… boyfriend?" she asked delicately.

David shook his head. "No, a friend."

She squeezed his arm and David fought a grimace. There was blood under her nails.

"He's going to need you," she whispered. "Her head is a mess."

David nodded. "I'll stay until they're done."

She patted his shoulder. "Good boy. Ask him to call me when he gets a minute." David promised he would, and she went out into the dark.

Jackson came out of the hallway, papers in his hand.

"You ready?" David asked.

Jackson nodded and went through the front door, and David followed, pausing long enough to lock it, then jogging to keep up. Jackson was halfway in the car when he paused.

"Shit. I didn't lock the door."

"I did." David started the car, and Jackson gave him an enigmatic look before pulling in his legs and slamming the door.

The ride to Holy Family Hospital was made in tense silence. David thought of things he wanted to ask but chose not to. Words of comfort also came to mind, but David knew they'd sound hollow when he knew nothing about Jackson's mom's condition. Silence seemed the best option. Jackson was as tense as a piano wire, never really relaxing into the seat, and during the entire fifteen minutes, he curled and uncurled the papers in his hand. They were sitting at the stoplight before the left for the hospital and David finally reached over and touched his arm. Jackson jerked, his eyes very wide.

"She was conscious." David tried to give him an encouraging look. "That's a good thing."

Jackson took a deep breath and released it slowly.

David parked the car in the closest place he could find to the emergency room doors. When he started to get out of the car, Jackson caught his wrist. His palm felt cold and clammy against David's skin.

"You don't have to stay." Jackson frowned. "This could take hours."

"You don't have your truck. How do you plan to get home?"

"I could call my brother. You don't have to stay...."

David placed his hand over Jackson's and squeezed. "Don't be dumb." He spoke gently. "I'm here. I'm not leaving."

Jackson closed his eyes for a moment before he got out of the car.

David figured they wouldn't let him go into the back with Jackson. He honestly wasn't sure he wanted to. But after Jackson gave the nurse at the admitting desk his name, and she came around to lead him back into the ER, Jackson looked at David, hesitating. "Go, I'll be fine."

Jackson followed the nurse in her pink scrubs. David took a seat on one of the ugly plastic chairs near a television turned to CNN. David watched Jackson until the doors swung closed behind him. It was Saturday evening and the ER was crowded; he knew it would be a while and he settled in to wait.

Shades of blue covered the seats and floor of the large room, no doubt intended to soothe, but the chairs were uncomfortable and the florescent lighting was anything but flattering. Large plants were tucked into corners, and even though they looked healthy enough, the antiseptic smells of alcohol and disinfectant never let David forget for a moment where he was.

One by one people around him were ushered through the large electric doors to the back, and more and more filled the chairs. He watched Anderson Cooper; then the same three news stories over and over: flooding in the south, another drone strike on ISIS, a Republican primary somewhere in the Midwest. He wasn't really paying attention. His mind kept wandering to Jackson and how very much he wished he'd been able to give Jackson's neighbor a different answer to her question.

All of the arguments went through his head about why it was foolish. It was too soon for him to be looking at anyone. Jackson hadn't really shown any interest. That wasn't strictly true, though, because earlier in the day Jackson had dropped his arm around David's shoulders, then cupped his nape in his hand, and that had been before the beer. Of course those were probably just friendly gestures on his part. But his hand had lingered on the back of David's neck and it felt so good, so right. He closed his eyes, letting himself sink into the memory of the touch, the wide, warm palm, the calloused fingers. For the life of him, he couldn't imagine what a man like Jackson could see in him, but he couldn't forget how that muscled arm had felt around his shoulders. David glanced toward the large doors for at least the hundredth time, but they remained stubbornly closed.

About two hours in, a very nicely dressed couple arrived at the admitting desk. At first he was admiring the man's dark wool coat, but he stiffened slightly when he gave the nurse a name.

"Henry," the man repeated. "Shirley Henry. She's my mother."

"One moment, please." She began to type into her computer, and David watched Jackson's brother.

He had to be older. There was gray threaded through the dark hair at his temples. And if he'd looked at the face instead of the suit, he'd have known this man and Jackson were related immediately. The resemblance was pretty marked. They had the same dark hair, same square chin, and same pale blue eyes. Even the same slight widow's peak. But David realized that was where the similarities ended. This man looked rigid and self-important. He was angry that he had to wait and it showed. A muscle in his square jaw flexed and his lips were pressed into a flat, hard line. The fingers of his right hand kept a steady drumbeat on the side seam of the expensive overcoat.

"Is this going to take much longer?" he asked in a clipped voice.

"I'm sorry, sir. We're experiencing some computer problems tonight." She gave him an apologetic smile. "If you'll bear with me...."

"It might be faster if you walked back there and looked."

"Travis." The woman with him took his arm, her voice soft but emphatic. He pointedly didn't look at her. But David did.

She was very attractive, her reddish shoulder-length hair neatly styled, and her burgundy dress, short fur jacket, and black stiletto heels elegant. A gold band paired with a very large diamond solitaire graced her left ring finger.

"She's doing her job," she went on to his rigid profile. "Don't take it out on her."

"Ah, here we go," the nurse said. "There's already someone with her and we limit family members to two in the ER."

"I'll wait out here," his wife said. "You go on back."

"How about you"—he pointed at the woman behind the desk—"go tell my useless brother to come out, and then we can go in together."

David stiffened, clenching his teeth in irritation.

"Travis, I can wait out here. I don't mind."

Travis bared his teeth. "I mind." He turned back to the nurse, who was watching him warily. "Check."

She hesitated, then stood and left the desk.

"You need to calm down," Travis's wife said softly. "I know you're concerned but you can't act like this."

"I'm not concerned," he retorted. "I'm royally pissed off. I want to know why my mother is in an emergency room with a gash in her head."

"Jackson told you, Trav." She attempted to calm him by running her hand up and down his arm. "She got dizzy and fell and hit her head on a bookcase. We knew dizzy spells were likely when she was diagnosed."

"This is why he's supposed to be with her. Why wasn't he there? He has one job, Juanita, one, and that's to make sure Mom is okay. So why the hell wasn't he home?"

"I don't know why he wasn't home. Maybe he was working—"

Travis snorted.

"—maybe he wasn't. But he's entitled to a life, Travis." His nostrils flared, but she didn't seem cowed. "And what if he'd been in the living room when she fell in the office? You can't prepare against every eventuality, and you can't blame him for everything that goes wrong. Your mom is an independent lady. He is here with her now and he did call you. It's not his fault we didn't get the message until the dinner was over."

Travis leaned against the desk, crossing his arms over his chest. "You're always making excuses for him," he groused. "Sometimes I think you like him better than you do me."

"Oh, I do." Her eyes were bright with suppressed humor. "But he's gay."

David chuckled until Travis snorted. "Yeah, don't remind me," he muttered, and David's humor slipped away. He and Gil certainly had irritating siblings in common.

The nurse returned, and behind her was a tall, powerfully built man with skin the color of dark chocolate, wearing a security guard's uniform. He stopped next to the desk, his hands propped on his belt. "Your mother was adamant about having your brother remain with her," the nurse said, her back stiff, "but you're welcome to go back with Officer Bailey."

Travis gave her a scornful look. "You called security?"

The nurse faced him, her chin lifted. "Sir, it's my job to make sure the patients in this ER aren't disturbed by anything more than their own injuries or illnesses. Your decision to take issue with your brother while inside this hospital is not acceptable. I understand you're upset, and I understand that you're concerned, but those are family matters best dealt with outside of this ward. Officer Bailey is merely here to make sure that the peace is kept."

David wanted to applaud but decided it was probably a bad idea.

"Sir, I'd be happy to take you to your mother." Bailey's voice matched his appearance, and David bet not many people gave him trouble. Bailey gestured toward the electric doors and Travis looked at his wife.

"I'm fine, really. I'll catch up on the news. You go on."

The muscle that seemed to throb in concert with his irritation was moving in Travis Henry's jaw again, but he preceded the security guard through the door.

"Ma'am, I am sorry," the nurse began. Juanita Henry reached across the desk and touched her hand.

"Don't worry about it. I'm perfectly fine out here. And please allow me to apologize for my husband. He's in the middle of a congressional campaign, and the stress is making him very cranky. Even at home."

"My condolences." The nurse gave her a wry grin and Juanita laughed.

"I'll take them."

He was running for Congress, was he? David was pretty sure he knew for which party. And he hadn't done anything to garner David's vote.

Mrs. Henry crossed around the bank of chairs and sat in one two over from David. He covertly studied the expensive patterned burgundy silk, the jacket he'd bet was real fur, and the giant diamond on her hand. He recognized her elegant, strappy heels as being by designer Betsy Johnson. He wasn't as much of a clotheshorse as Trevor, but his mother had always loved shoes, and he found himself looking at department store fliers all the time. Those were in the latest Macy's ad for two hundred and ninety-nine dollars. They were also a good way to start a conversation.

"Lovely shoes," he offered, gesturing to her feet. "Betsy Johnson?"

Juanita Henry looked over at him, clearly pleased. "Why yes, they are. And thank you. I've wanted them forever, but they were finally on sale at…."

"Macy's. Two hundred and ninety-nine, down from three fifty."

"Yes." She studied him. "How nice to meet a man who knows so much about ladies' shoes."

"My mother loves shoes. It was become a convert or die of boredom every time I took her to Nordstrom."

She laughed and it was a lovely, musical sound. She held out her hand. "Hi. I'm Juanita Henry."

David took her hand and squeezed it. Her skin was very soft and her nails impeccably manicured. "David Snyder. Pleased to meet you."

"Nice to meet you too, totally disregarding the dismal surroundings." A slight frown line appeared between her brows but it was the only one. She had to be thirty-five, but there wasn't a line on her face. She leaned slightly closer. "You don't have a loved one inside do you?"

"No, I'm here with a friend. He has a loved one inside." He paused, then decided he should be completely honest. "In the interest of full disclosure, my friend is Jackson Henry."

Her face underwent an interesting transformation. She actually looked sheepish. "Oh, dear. You overheard my conversation with my husband, didn't you?"

"I wasn't trying to eavesdrop, truly."

She laughed, something he hadn't expected. "Travis wasn't exactly trying to keep his voice down either, was he?" She sighed. "I'll bet if I tell you he's actually a very nice guy, you're going to find it hard to believe."

"It's a stretch," he agreed.

She lifted her chin and fixed him with a fetching smile. "Was it the charming way he treated the nurse?"

"It was more the way he described his brother as being 'useless.' I've known many people in my life, and Jackson is the least useless of any of them."

"He didn't mean that. He was concerned and frustrated, and Jackson is an easy target."

David grinned at her. "Are you his PR person? You certainly should be."

Her brown eyes sparkled. "I've told him that, but does he listen?" She crossed her hands on top of her small black evening bag. "So, are you and Jackson just friends or…?"

David snorted softly. That was the second time this evening. "Yes, we're just friends. I met him when I hired him to do some work on a house I purchased recently. He was actually recommended by my mother."

"Some of the very best recommendations I've gotten in my life came from my mother."

David smiled. "Me too. If I'd listened to her about my last boyfriend, I'd have saved myself a world of hurt."

Juanita Henry really did have a lovely laugh, and as he watched her perfect white teeth flash, David thought under other circumstances they could be friends. He doubted he'd ever feel that way about her husband.

"So not to be nosy, even though I really am a hopeless busybody." Her eyes sparkled, and David grinned again. "Why are you here with Jackson if you aren't… dating?"

He loved the way straight people felt the need to use euphemisms with gay men. Clearly what she meant was "if you aren't screwing."

"Well, the reason he wasn't at home with his mother today was that he was helping me move an entire house full of furniture." She angled her head to one side like a curious toy poodle. "Long story."

She stretched out her lovely long leg and bumped her Betsy Johnson against his calf. "I've so many other pressing things going on here at the moment."

David could see her point and smiled. "Okay, that's fair. I bought a house full of furniture from a friend of Jackson's. His dad recently moved in to assisted living, and Jackson, because he's been doing repairs on my place, knew I was basically living with an old recliner upholstered in fabric that should be illegal and a mattress and box spring set on the floor."

"Because…."

"Because of the boyfriend my mother hated. Possession is nine-tenths of the law and he is in possession of about everything."

"He's a jackass, then," she said bluntly. David chuckled.

"Huge, enormous jackass. And apparently had me fooled for a very long time."

"Ah." She nodded sagely. "Haven't we all had at least one of those?"

"I hope he was my one," David quipped and she grinned. "Anyway, Jackson and several friends were helping me get my house furnished today. That's why he wasn't at home when his mother fell."

"You really shouldn't take what Travis said to heart. He didn't mean it, and he'll feel bad about it later."

David doubted it but he held his silence.

"Jackson needs to have days where he isn't babysitting," she went on. "Shirley is a lovely person, but they really should have someone with her all the time, and it isn't reasonable to expect him to do it. He's already sacrificed a lot by moving home to live with her."

Yes, David thought, he could really like this woman.

His cell phone sounded off in his pocket and he took it out, looking at the name on the screen. "Speaking of mothers, this is mine. Pardon me."

Juanita nodded and David pushed to his feet, paced toward the ER's outer door, and walked outside. The temperature had dropped dramatically and he shivered as he went to a cement barricade by the parking lot and leaned his hip on it.

"Hey, Mom."

"Hi, honey. Did you get the furniture moved?"

"Yeah, we did."

"Well, I promise not to be one of *those* moms, but I couldn't help but notice no one is home at your place, and…."

He heard a noise in the background. "Oh, for God's sakes, Mom." It was Beth's voice.

"Well, I'm trying not to pry."

"God!"

"Elizabeth," their mom complained. Then he heard what he was sure was the phone changing hands.

"Where are you?"

David snorted and laughed at the same time. "Hey, Beth. How are you? And is this the way my life is going to be from here on out?"

"You're the one who bought the house across the street. Where are you?"

"What if it's none of your business?"

"Then say so."

"It's none of your business."

"You're an ass."

David laughed. "And you're nosy."

"That's no news flash." Beth was unperturbed. "Mom made pie for all of you."

David sighed. "I wish she'd told me."

"Are you out to dinner?"

"No, actually." David glanced around the quiet parking lot, wondering if he should say anything. He decided he couldn't see the harm in it. "I'm at Holy Family."

There was a weighted silence. "David Wayne Snyder." Beth's voice was low and intense. "Why are you at the hospital?" None of them had good memories of this hospital. He understood.

"What?" he heard in the background. "What's wrong?"

"I don't know yet," Beth said to their mom. "Give me a minute here. David, are you hurt?"

"No, no it's not me."

"It's not him," Beth told Beverley. "So, what happened?"

"Actually it's Jackson's mom. She took a bad fall, hit her head on a bookcase, and split it open."

"Oh God, David."

"Yeah, it's pretty bad. Don't... make it sound so bad to Mom. They're friends."

"I know. I've got it covered." There was another heavy pause. "How did you end up there with him?"

"He'd had a couple of beers when we got done with the furniture and I hadn't, so I thought—"

"No, I get it," she said briskly. "Listen, come by on your way home, okay? Mom's going to worry anyway."

"I have absolutely no idea what time it will be." David looked down at his watch. It was only quarter to eight. It felt much later.

"Whenever it is, she'll fret if you don't."

David sighed softly even as he heard his mother saying "Oh, I will not" in the background. But she would.

"Okay. Tell her it might be a while."

"Will do. Love you."

"Love you too, Beth."

He rang off and walked back into the now nearly deserted ER.

As he started to sit, his phone vibrated with a text message. David rolled his eyes and Juanita laughed.

"Popular guy," she teased.

He frowned as he reached for his phone again. "Not ordinarily." He looked at the screen.

The number was Michael's. He pulled up the text.

How is Jackson's mom?

Not sure, David texted back. *He's still in the back. Hey, have you heard of Travis Henry?*

There was a pause. *The Travis Henry running for Congress?*

The very one.

He's a conservative jackass. Why?

David snorted softly. *Guess who he's related to?*

There was another pause.

NOOOOOO.

David laughed. *Yep.*

Oh, good God. Poor Jackson. That's just wrong.

I'll have to tell you how nice he was to the nurse in the ER.

That's crap, right? It's a lie. He was a total douche.

David grinned. *He was.*

Lucky for you his brother ISN'T. And speaking of the lovely Jackson, what's up there, boss man? Y'all were pretty cozy there for a minute today.

Since when does your text voice have a southern accent? David typed back. *And I noticed you checking Gil out, so watch yourself.*

GIL???????

David laughed aloud. He could almost hear Michael's screech.

He could squish me like a bug.

But you LIKE all those muscles.

Fuck you.

David let his laugh settle into a fond smile. *I will fire you.*

Oh, please. You need to stop saying that cuz everyone knows it's a big old lie. Let me know how Jackson's mom is, okay? I'm concerned.

David's smile mellowed. *I promise not to tell anyone you're actually a very nice person.*

There was another pause. *Bite me.*

David pocketed his phone, his smile lingering. He started to take the chair he'd deserted when Juanita looked past his shoulder and stood. He straightened as Jackson and Travis came through the electric doors, and neither of them looked particularly happy. Standing next to each other, the resemblance was undeniable, but their expressions couldn't be less similar. Travis still looked irritated, and Jackson looked tired and careworn. When Jackson saw David, some of the tension bled from his shoulders.

"How is she doing?" David murmured when he was close enough.

"Okay." Jackson sighed. "It took more than fifty stitches to close her head."

"Oh my God, Jackson." David reached out and touched his arm. "Are you okay?"

"Well, I never thought I'd see my mother's skull, but compared to her, I'm fine."

David grimaced, catching Jackson's hand and squeezing it. Jackson made no effort to pull away.

"She apparently hit the shelf at her hairline and it peeled the skin back. Most of the stitches are in her hair. She probably won't even have a noticeable scar."

"But that's good, isn't it?"

"Yeah. She was worried about it." He exhaled roughly. "She's in there bleeding all over the place, and all she cares about is if she'll have a scar. Oh, and that she's ruining her sweater." Jackson held up a bag David hadn't noticed. "I think I'll probably burn it."

"No, we can get the blood out of it. I'll wash it for you."

"David, you don't have to—"

"Oh, hush and give it to me." He took the bag from Jackson's limp fingers. "I'm a whiz with laundry." He remembered belatedly that he didn't currently have a washer and dryer. He'd wash it at his mom's.

Jackson gave him a weak smile. "Good to know."

"It's my one marketable skill." David squeezed his hand again. "Is she coming home?" He tried to figure out the logistics of getting her from a wheelchair into the car, but Jackson shook his head.

"They're going to keep her overnight for observation. The doctor is a little worried about a concussion even though she never lost consciousness. Not until they were all done, and then she fell asleep. I think she's exhausted."

David studied Jackson. "She isn't the only one." He took in the lines of strain around Jackson's mouth. "When will they release her?"

"He thinks they'll let her go tomorrow. It's going to depend on how steady she is on her feet."

"Is she going to be able to climb up into the cab of your truck?" David thought of the trouble he had getting into it. He couldn't imagine Shirley being able to do it.

Jackson stared at him for a long moment. "I hadn't even thought about it."

"We have a meet and greet luncheon at the Yorkshire at two," Travis said, sounding put out. "I won't be available."

"I didn't ask you, Travis." Jackson didn't even look at his brother. "I'll deal with it."

"How? If she can't get into that ridiculous truck of yours, how—"

"I can pick her up." David met Travis's eyes. "I have a Yaris, which she won't have any trouble getting into."

"Who are you?" Travis looked between Jackson and David. When his gaze landed on David's hand, which was still tucked in Jackson's, his expression flattened.

"This is David, honey." Juanita jumped in quickly. "He and Jackson are friends."

Travis glanced away from their clasped hands. "Yeah, I can see that," he muttered. "I don't suppose you could keep the PDA to a minimum, at least when you're with me where other people might see you? Christ, Jackson, does your 'friend' know I'm running for office or do you want me to lose?"

David stared at him, aghast.

"Yeah, Travis. That's my goal. I just spent two hours watching them stitch my mother's head back together, but David and I formulated a plan to make sure you'd lose your fucking election. Self-absorbed much, brother?"

Travis took a step toward Jackson and sneered. "Could you say that a little louder? I don't think they heard you in the parking lot."

Jackson didn't back away, nor did he release David's hand. "Maybe I'll just offer to do an op-ed piece for the paper: what it's like growing up the queer sibling of a conservative tight ass."

Travis's lip curled in an ugly snarl. He and Jackson were nearly nose to nose but it never occurred to David to release Jackson and get out of the way. "You self-righteous prick," Travis hissed.

"Wow, watch your language, Candidate Henry," Jackson retorted in a very similar tone. "Someone might hear you."

Sure they were within seconds of taking a swing at each other, David finally did move, stepping in front of Jackson and moving his hand to his chest. It was hard beneath his palm and he could feel his heart pounding. Behind him Juanita took hold of Travis's arm.

"I think everyone needs to calm down," she said in a soothing tone, looking between them. "Don't you?"

"I really don't blame you for wanting to take a shot at him," David whispered for Jackson's ears only. "But if you get thrown out of here tonight, how can we pick your mom up tomorrow?"

Jackson's gaze left his brother and settled on David, and David watched the fury leach out of his eyes. Shooting one more glare at Travis, Jackson took a step back. Travis's nostrils flared and he stormed away. They watched him stalk out through the ER's doors.

Juanita paused, reaching out toward Jackson, her hand coming to rest on his arm. "Thank you for getting her here. I know he's grateful."

Jackson snorted softly. "Yeah, he sure seems it. Nice try, Nita. I know how he feels about me."

She squeezed his forearm with a small, sad smile, then followed her husband out through the doors.

"Christ." Jackson stepped back and pushed the fingers of both hands roughly through his thick hair, then let his arms fall heavily to his sides. "This has been some fun for you, huh? Nothing like family drama."

David shrugged. "Beats watching reruns of *CSI*."

Jackson gave him a surprised look and snorted out a rough, startled laugh. "You wouldn't be watching CSI. If you were home, you'd be rearranging your new furniture."

David gave him a small smile. "Probably. But your sister-in-law was very entertaining."

"Nita's actually a really nice lady. What she sees in Travis I'll never know."

"It's a mystery," David agreed amiably, intentionally keeping his tone light. "You ready to get out of here?"

"Absolutely."

They walked out into the cold evening, their breath puffing out in soft clouds of steam as they crossed the lot to David's car.

CHAPTER TEN

WHEN THEY were seated in the car, David immediately cranked up the heater.

"God it's freezing." He glanced at Jackson, who stared through the windshield, his elbow on the door and his hand curled into a fist pressed to his lips. He still looked angry, and David really couldn't blame him. "So what does your brother do when he isn't running for office?" He glanced over his shoulder as he backed out.

Jackson let his hand slide wearily into his lap. "He's a lawyer." His voice was flat.

"I'm betting he doesn't do pro bono work for indigent clients."

That pulled a tired smile from Jackson. His shoulders weren't as hunched as they had been. "No. He does corporate law. Contracts, nuisance lawsuits, stuff like that." He grimaced. "His boss calls him his 'pit bull,' and it's an apt description."

"I gather he's not a Democrat, then?"

Jackson sounded like his laugh surprised even him. "Nope, not even close." He paused, his head dropping back against the leather headrest. "He's exactly like my dad. He did everything he could to mimic the old man. Dad was a lawyer, specializing in corporate law, and a fire-breathing Republican."

David winced. "That must have been fun for you."

"Oh, yeah," Jackson replied dryly. "Every holiday was a warm and fuzzy family portrait." He stared straight ahead, his expression flat. "It's why I left and went to the coast. I haven't lived at home since I was a freshman in college."

David had no frame of reference because his relationship with his own dad had been the rock he'd built his life on. The defeated tenor of Jackson's voice saddened him. "When did he pass away?"

"Two years ago. Cancer." He didn't elaborate and David didn't press. He was curious about something else, though, and he chewed his lower lip before speaking again.

"I have a question but I don't want to make you angry."

"You won't make me angry, David."

Their eyes met and held briefly before Jackson looked back through the windshield.

"If you have other siblings, why did you move back here? Couldn't they have helped out with your mom?"

The pause was so long David was afraid he'd offended Jackson, but finally he cleared his throat. "Long story."

David chanced another look at him. The colored lights on the large boulevard cast bizarre, brightly hued shadows on his face, but there was enough light to see Jackson's troubled expression.

"I'm a good listener," David offered softly.

Jackson gave him a weak smile, then looked back at the road, as if it was easier to answer if he wasn't looking at him. "I have one brother. Travis. And one sister, Michelle."

"Doesn't she live here too?"

"Yeah, she does. But Mickey is… different." His lips twisted.

"Different how?"

"Basically she's spoiled. She was Dad's little princess, and she isn't capable of dealing with what's going on with Mom. From the moment the diagnosis came in, I could see her backing away. Mom has MS. Did I tell you that?"

David shook his head. "No, my mom did."

"I keep forgetting they're friends." He scrubbed one of his hands over his head. "Anyway, anything to do with illness and Mickey is done. Even as close as they were, she did it with Dad's cancer, and she's doing it now with Mom." David bit his lower lip so that he didn't say what he was thinking, and waited for Jackson to go on if he wanted to. "I can feel the wheels turning from here, David," Jackson said with a dose of irony.

"It's none of my business, Jackson. I'm trying to be a friendly ear. I'm not entitled to an opinion about what's going on with your siblings. I just—" He forced himself to stop. He liked Jackson too much to push the issue.

"You just what? Really, I want to know."

David glanced over, but he'd have been able to feel Jackson's steady gaze even if he hadn't.

"I don't think it's fair that you had to move back to take care of your mom because your siblings are either too busy or can't deal. That's all."

Jackson's silence stretched out again and nerves made the skin on David's shoulders crawl. This man's silences discomfited him; he was used to a man who verbalized everything without a care for whom he embarrassed or hurt. He'd thought that was bad, but these weighty silences were almost worse.

"I guess I didn't explain it very well," Jackson said finally. "Don't misunderstand. My brother and sister are a pain in the ass, but I came home because I wanted to. Mom and I have always been close. Travis and Mickey were Dad's, but I was Mom's. She was the first person I told I was gay because I knew she wouldn't think less of me." He paused, then cleared his throat roughly. "She's been my rock, always. I don't have an issue with returning the favor now. And yeah, Travis is a dick and Mickey is a flake, but even if they weren't, I'd still have moved home. Wouldn't you, for your mom?"

"Yes," David agreed without a second thought. "There's a difference, though. I wouldn't be leaving a good job to come home to a bastion of conservative assholes."

Jackson snorted. "Yeah, well, that was just a side benefit." He sighed and it sounded like it came from his soul. "It was time for me to get out of there anyway."

The sad disappointment caused a deep clenching in David's gut. He recalled what Jackson had told him, how he'd commiserated with David over Trevor's betrayal. "There was... someone?"

Jackson huffed out a dark chuckle that was anything but amused. "I thought so, but we had a difference of opinion about family loyalty. And fidelity, for that matter. It didn't take long for him to find someone else."

"I'm so sorry he hurt you."

"I'll survive."

And he would, David realized. Despite what fate threw at him, Jackson was a survivor. And apparently, so was he.

"So, the bastion of conservative assholes." Jackson sounded like he was intentionally lightening his tone as he changed the subject. "You managed to build a career here in spite of them."

David's laugh was only slightly strained. "That's only because they expect someone like me to be an interior decorator. Or a florist. Or a ballet dancer." He flapped his wrist, but Jackson didn't smile.

"What does that mean, someone like you?"

"Come on, you know what I mean. I'm not exactly a pillar of masculinity."

"Who told you that? The asshole ex?" There was a crease between the arched black brows.

"Yeah, him. And about everyone I've ever met outside of my living room. I know who I am, Jackson, and I don't have a problem with it. I think people don't give me grief because I'm precisely what they expect me to be. I fit the stereotype. You, on the other hand, challenge their preconceptions about what a gay man ought to look like."

"Why, because I don't skip down the street and fart glitter?"

David laughed, but Jackson didn't.

"I hate that crap." His mouth twisted into a grimace. "The whole 'straight-acting vs. gay-acting' thing. What does that even mean? Believe me, I'm plenty gay. The fact I drive a pickup and wear a tool belt doesn't have a damned thing to do with anything other than how I make a living."

"But with the pickup and the tool belt, you look like them, and it freaks them out." Jackson frowned at him and David held up his hand. "Jackson, I'm on your side, remember?"

Jackson blew out an explosive breath. "Yeah, I know. I just think you're fine the way you are."

Warmth curled through David's belly. "Thank you. And I happen to like your tool belt, okay?"

That made Jackson laugh, and the sound warmed David clear through. He looked at David, one brow raised. "Oh, yeah?"

David nodded. "Definitely. Very sexy." He turned onto his street, slowing his speed. "Now, are you tired?"

"Exhausted," Jackson answered. David swallowed his disappointment. He'd been going to invite Jackson to his mother's for pie, but he understood how worn he must be. "It's weird, though. I'm drained, but I'm not sleepy. That doesn't really make any sense, does it?"

"It makes all kinds of sense." David glanced over at him again. "Are you hungry?"

Jackson looked thoughtful for a moment. "Yeah, actually. I am."

"Perfect." David smiled. "That I can fix."

WHEN DAVID came through the front door with Jackson, if Beverley Snyder was surprised to see him with her son, it didn't show. She hugged Jackson, rubbing his back between his shoulder blades. He stayed stiff in her arms for a moment, then lifted his hand and patted her in return.

"How's your mom, honey?" She leaned back and studied his face. "Not so good, then?"

"No, she's okay, Mrs. Snyder. I mean, she'll be okay. Right now she looks a little bit like a stitched-up rag doll."

"What happened?"

"She got dizzy. The doctors told us it could happen. She was in her office, which is really just this little room crammed full of crap. When she stood up from her desk, the closest thing was a bookshelf. She didn't quite get there and hit her head on it as she went down."

Beverley grimaced. "Oh dear. Well, then." She stepped back with a tight nod. David recognized the gesture and her expression. That was his mom's "all right, let's get on with it" face. He'd seen it when he was a kid and hadn't finished his science project. He'd seen it when Dad was diagnosed with cancer. Once her fear and grief had passed, she was all about making the best of it. He'd seen it when his dad died and there were things to be done. This was what she did; she sprang into action, and she'd apparently decided Jackson needed help.

"Are you boys hungry?"

"Yeah, we are, Mom. And I understand there's pie?"

"There is." She was clearly pleased. "You like apple pie, Jackson?"

"Love it. It's my favorite."

Her smile could have lit up downtown. She opened the cupboards above the counter and took down two dessert plates. "You like that pie à la mode?"

Jackson gave her a tired smile. "Yes, ma'am."

"Well, have a seat, and I'll warm this up."

Jackson sat on the far side of the table and David sat beside him, reaching under the cover of the cloth to touch his leg. It felt solid beneath the denim. "How're you holding up?" he asked softly while his mom cut pie and put plates in the microwave.

"I'm okay." He looked weary as he pushed his thick dark brown hair off his forehead.

David noticed that his beard looked darker beneath his pallor. There were tight lines around his mouth, but he smiled at Beverley when she set a plate in front of him. On it was a huge slice of pie, vanilla ice cream melting on the sugary top crust. She set an equally enormous piece in front of David, and he groaned. "Mom, that's too much!"

"If you can't finish it, I can." Jackson dug into his slice. He lifted the bite, dripping with cinnamon and vanilla ice cream, into his mouth and groaned. "Mrs. Snyder, this is amazing."

"Thank you, Jackson." She wiped crumbs off her counter, then brought out an uncut pie, covered it with aluminum foil, and set it on the table in front of Jackson. "Now, you take that home with you, and you and your mom can share it."

Jackson stared at the covered plate. "Thank you, ma'am. I know she'll enjoy that."

"You're welcome." She wiped her hands briskly. "Now, you boys take your time and enjoy that, and I'm going to go watch the news and make a shopping list. I'll throw some things together that you can heat up for quick dinners. David and I will bring them over tomorrow."

"You don't have to do that."

"If I thought I had to, I probably wouldn't." She rubbed his shoulder in passing, smiling gently. "You'll have enough on your hands, honey. Let me do this."

Reluctantly he nodded, and she beamed as she left the room.

Jackson stared after her. "Is she always like that?"

David chuckled. "That was pretty laid-back, actually. She's a force of nature."

"She's amazing." Now Jackson reached over, and he caught David's hand, looking into his eyes. "You're amazing."

David's face felt hot. "I'm glad you think so, but I didn't do that much."

Jackson shook his head. "Don't downplay it. You drove me to the ER, sat there all evening, and kept me from decking my asshole brother. Then you brought me back here for the best apple pie I've ever eaten in my life."

"I can't take credit for the pie."

"I don't think you take credit for much of anything."

David always hated how much he blushed, but never as much as he did right then.

Jackson smiled slowly. "You're blushing. You do that a lot."

David looked away. "God, I know. It's embarrassing."

Jackson slipped his fingers between David's and squeezed his hand. He leaned close, until his mouth was inches from David's ear. "I like it," he whispered. "Almost as much as I like you."

David bit his lip, his heart pounding. "I like you too."

Jackson ran his thumb over the side of David's index finger. "Good."

Yes, David thought. It certainly was.

THE STREETLIGHTS cast mottled shadows on the ground as light filtered through the canopy of branches that met over the street. There were enough leaves still on the trees that the shadows shifted in the light breeze, making a soft rustling sound. Jackson's truck was still backed into David's driveway, so David parked in front of his house. They got out, Jackson balancing an entire apple pie on his hand.

"Your mom didn't have to do this." He held up the covered dish.

"You could go back and tell her," David teased and Jackson chuckled.

"Yeah, I don't think so."

"And prepare yourself for more tomorrow."

"I sort of got that." Jackson smiled. "She's a nice lady."

"Yeah," David agreed, "she is."

They were crossing over the sidewalk when the sound of rustling seemed to intensify, and David knew exactly what he was hearing. He grinned.

Bootsy ran up to them and went up onto his back legs, balancing and dancing, a happy smile on his little dog face.

"Well, hello." Jackson looked down at the little corgi, his smile spreading to include his eyes for the first time since they left the hospital.

"Hey, Bootsy." David bent and scratched behind his large, pointed ears. "Making another break for it?"

"Bootsy?" Jackson made a face. "That's just wrong."

"Yeah. The poor guy has to be embarrassed by it." David straightened as Jordyn called for the dog from her front porch. Bootsy ignored her, looking up at the two men, his tongue lolling out of his mouth. "You'd better go before you get both you and me in trouble, buddy."

Almost as if he understood, Bootsy glanced over his furry shoulder. When Jordyn called him again with more force than the first time, he sighed and grudgingly trotted back home.

Jackson chuckled. "Friend of yours?"

"Oh yeah, we're tight." David grinned after him. "If there was any way in the world I could get away with it, I'd steal him."

"This close to his house, they'd probably figure it out. He's cute as hell, though." Jackson looked over at David as they continued across the lawn. "He likes you."

"The feeling is entirely mutual."

Jackson unlocked his truck and opened the door, placing the pie on the passenger seat. Slipping his hands into his jacket pockets, he stayed within the protection of the open door and studied David's face for what felt like a long time. "So, you already know I like you too." Jackson's voice was soft, but David heard the words clearly. He smiled slowly even as his heart kicked hard against his ribs.

"That feeling is entirely mutual too."

"Come here."

Jackson's voice dropped into a deeper timbre and it sent a shiver across David's shoulders. He stepped closer and Jackson reached out, putting his hands around David's ribs before pulling him into a tight hug. David wished he would kiss him but chose to take what he could get from the embrace. The feel of Jackson's hard chest against his and the strong arms around him swept everything from his mind but pleasure.

"Thank you, David," Jackson whispered against his ear, his voice hoarse. "For being there tonight. And for your mom."

"You're welcome." He slipped his arms around Jackson and returned the embrace, relishing the feel of his slender waist and the strong muscles along his spine. David closed his eyes, inhaling Jackson's scent: the faint, woodsy cologne, soap, and the reminder of hard work lingering beneath it all on his skin. David's cock began to fill instantly. Startled, he abruptly tried to angle his hips back and away.

Jackson leaned back without releasing David and looked into his eyes. "Where are you going?"

"Uhm...." David knew his face was as red as it was hot, and prayed it was dark enough it didn't show. His capacity to form a sentence apparently deserted him, and he faltered.

Jackson studied him, another of those weighted silences stretching out. Finally he slid an open palm down David's back, continuing past his waist to the base of his spine. He pulled David in snug, pressing his hips forward, and David caught his breath when he felt an answering hardness behind Jackson's fly.

"Oh."

"Yeah, oh. It was damned inconvenient when I got hard sitting at your mom's kitchen table, watching your tongue every time you licked your fork."

"I did? I... uh... you did?"

"Yes."

"Why?"

Jackson was startled. "Why? What kind of question is that?"

"I... I mean, you're... you, and I'm...." David faltered.

Jackson's eyes narrowed. He lifted a hand and cupped David's jaw, his calloused thumb moving slowly beneath his lower lip. For the first time in his life, David understood what it meant to be breathless.

"I don't know what the voice in your head is saying," Jackson murmured, "or who you're hearing, but you need to ignore it." His thumb pressed into the softness of David's lips, and they parted under the delicate pressure. "I find you very sexy, David Snyder. Very, very sexy."

Jackson couldn't have said anything that would have shocked David more. When his hand slid around David's nape and he speared his fingers into David's hair above his collar, David softened into his touch. Jackson pulled David forward while angling his head and David tipped his in counterpoint. Jackson leaned in, then paused when their lips were barely an inch apart. His hot breath on David's lips caused chills to break out down his back. "I'm going to kiss you now, okay?"

"Oh my God, yes," David gasped. "Please."

Jackson's mouth curled in a soft smile before he closed the distance between them, pressing his lips to David's, and David realized you truly could feel someone smile against your mouth. It was gentle and so tender, perhaps the sweetest kiss David had ever received, and it made his toes curl in his shoes. He clutched Jackson's jacket and whimpered a bit when Jackson's tongue fleetingly touched his upper lip. David opened his mouth, desperate to feel Jackson's tongue filling it, but instead Jackson pulled back, sighing softly.

"Much as I hate to, I have to go," he whispered. "I have to get to the house and clean up that rug. It can't look like that when she gets home."

David managed not to sigh in disappointment, but it was a near thing. "Of course. I understand." His cock didn't, but it was going to have to get over it.

"I'd rather stay, believe me." Jackson slid his hand farther down and pressed in with his fingers along the cleft in David's ass, curling them unerringly over his tailbone. A shudder passed through David's body. He bit his lower lip when Jackson rolled his hips forward in a slow movement, putting pressure against David's groin. Abruptly Jackson stopped and took a step back, his hands lingering for a moment before slowly sliding from David's body.

"I have to go," Jackson said, almost as if he was attempting to convince himself. "I really do."

"I know." David forced himself to take a step back, and then another to leave the security of the open door. Jackson closed it at his back. He looked at David and the regret was clear on his face.

"Call me tomorrow when they give you a time she's being released," David said. "I'll be there."

Jackson nodded and walked around the back of the big truck, opening the driver's door before he paused again. "Thanks." His voice was soft and deep, carrying in the quiet evening.

"Of course. I'll see you tomorrow."

Jackson gave him a fleeting smile, then climbed up into the truck. David backed up, wrapping his arms across his waist as the big engine roared to life and Jackson pulled out into the street.

David watched him all the way to the corner, taillights growing smaller in the distance until the truck turned the corner. When he climbed his porch steps with a soft sigh, he prayed fervently Jackson didn't have a change of heart before he saw him again.

There was a sharp snap behind him and David whirled, his hand on his doorknob. He stared into the shadows dappling his lawn and the near blackness of the neighbor's driveway as it curved behind their house, the memory rushing back—Trevor sitting out there somewhere in the dark, watching him and his smashed car window. Nothing moved, but he knew how exposed he was, standing under the porch light.

His hands trembled as he unlocked his door, and he didn't feel safe until he was inside, the door once again securely locked behind him and his blinds down, blocking the view into his house.

It took a long time for his pulse to return to normal.

CHAPTER ELEVEN

"JESUS, MOM, there's enough food here for a small army."

David loaded another casserole in its padded carrying case into the back of his car. There were three already loaded, along with a picnic hamper full of rolls, brownies, and a cobbler. There was also a small igloo holding a container of potato salad.

"When did you have time to do all of this?" He took a Crock-Pot out of her hands.

"Last night and this morning." David caught a whiff of what he held, and the aroma made his mouth water.

"This is the italian wedding soup, isn't it?" He paused to take another deep sniff.

"I thought that would be easier for tonight." She locked her back door. "That poor boy has already got his hands full."

David placed the Crock-Pot in the car and closed the hatch, sighing. That was the understatement of the century.

Too tired the night before and too busy reliving every moment of the most amazing first kiss he'd ever had, David had spent the morning cleaning up pizza boxes and plates and empty beer bottles in his living room. Once he was done, he paced nervously, jumping every time his cell rang. He had brief conversations with Michael and Gil, both concerned about Jackson and his mom. He got them off the phone as quickly as he could without being rude, giving them a sketch of what happened and promising more later. It wasn't until after eleven that Jackson called, telling him the hospital was releasing his mom at noon. Relieved, David swept up his keys and hurried out of his house.

Jackson greeted him with a warm smile, alleviating the gut-clenching fear that kept David awake most of the night. Fear Jackson had been looking for comfort when he kissed him, that he hadn't really meant it and he couldn't possibly want someone as average as David. Jackson so clearly wasn't average. At all. David had almost managed to convince himself

Jackson's erection was the result of gratitude, even though he knew how damned near impossible that was. He was a nervous wreck when he pulled up in front of the house. Then Jackson smiled at him as he got in the car and David's fear bled away, leaving giddiness in its place.

It lasted until Jackson accompanied his mom's wheelchair out through the hospital's huge sliding doors, and David saw the anger and concern he was trying—unsuccessfully—to hide. David understood the source of it when Shirley was unable to stand by herself, needing her son to lift her from the chair.

David hustled to help, holding the door open, poised to step in if Jackson needed him. When she was settled in and her seat belt fastened, David got a good look at her face. The heavy bandage around her head covered her hair but her face was revealed, and she was almost as white as the gauze. Most alarming, though, was the far away, confused expression on her face.

When the door was closed behind her, David looked at Jackson. "Is she all right?"

"Does she look all right?" Jackson snapped. David took a step back, stung, but immediately Jackson reached for his arm. "I'm sorry, David."

"It's okay."

"No, it isn't." Jackson sighed. "None of this is your fault, I'm...." He broke off, running his hand roughly through his thick hair, something David noticed he did when he was frustrated. "No, she isn't all right, but they're releasing her anyway. Insurance." He spat the word, and David caught his hand for a moment in a hard squeeze.

"I understand." He lowered his voice. "My dad." That had been one of the worst parts of the ordeal around losing his dad. Hearing some insurance lackey describe a kidney transplant as "elective surgery" had been infuriating. Oh yes, he understood.

Jackson returned the pressure of his hand, his eyes full as they held David's.

There hadn't been much conversation as they drove Shirley home. She dozed and Jackson sat in the backseat, perched on the edge, his hand on her shoulder. If David hadn't already had feelings for him, that would have clinched it. As it was his heart felt so full and sore on Jackson's behalf, it was hard for him to take a deep breath.

The hospital had provided a walker for Shirley but she became agitated if it was even mentioned. As a result, they each took an arm and walked her carefully up the front walk and helped to lift her into her living room. When she collapsed into a small rose-colored swivel rocker, exhausted, David found himself wondering how Jackson was ever going to get her into bed by himself that night.

"Mom has made some meals for the two of you," David said when Jackson walked him back out to his car. "But if you'd rather not have company today…."

"No, it's fine." Jackson glanced back toward the house, his arms crossed over his chest, his hands gripping his biceps so tight his knuckles were white. The defensive posture was hard for David to see. "I know she'd like to see your mom, and frankly whatever she's made would have to be better than anything I could manage."

David looked at the house. "I feel like I'm abandoning you for some reason."

Jackson's tight posture relaxed slightly. "You aren't. Go on. I'll see you later."

David wanted to kiss him, but the next-door neighbor came out at that moment to mow his lawn, so he touched Jackson's arm briefly in passing before he climbed into his car.

WHEN DAVID and his mother arrived at Shirley's small house, a sporty black Audi with a white racing stripe sat parked at the curb. David studied it for a moment as he pulled into the driveway and hoped the expensive little car didn't belong to Travis.

His mother got out of the car and walked onto the porch. Even though it was cool outside, the door to the house was open to the screen. David stood at her shoulder and glanced into the dim living room. Shirley Henry hadn't moved from her chair. There was a knitted afghan over her legs, and the television was on but her eyes were closed. Jackson was nowhere to be seen.

David was reaching in his pocket for his phone to call him when Beverley reached out and tapped firmly on the screen door.

Shirley lifted her head and looked around. "Hello?"

"Hello, hon," David's mother called. "It's Beverley Snyder. May I come in?"

"Oh, Beverley." Shirley looked as if she was going to try to stand and Beverley was through the screen door so fast David was stunned. She went to her friend and put her hand on her shoulder.

"Don't you dare get out of that chair," she scolded gently, but there was underlying steel in the tone. "Your son would have my head if you fell again because you were trying to open the door." Beverley bent, taking one of Shirley's hands. "How are you, hon?"

Shirley looked up at her, and her lost expression was heartbreaking. "I hit my head."

"So I heard. Does it hurt?"

Shirley's trembling hand went to the bandage above her eyes. "I have a bit of a headache."

"I imagine you do. Honey, where is Jackson?"

Shirley blinked. "I think he's talking to... someone." She closed her eyes. "I'm not sure who...."

There were voices coming from another part of the house as David let the screen shut behind him. They weren't loud; he doubted they'd disturbed Shirley while she napped. But they were loud enough he could hear them clearly.

"You can't be here for even a few hours a day?" Jackson sounded exasperated.

"I have the girls, Jackson. Besides, this is why you came home, isn't it?" Her voice was waspish and David didn't like it.

"I have to work, Mickey," Jackson shot back. So this was the sister.

"Why? Live off the money Daddy left. You don't have to work. And if you think you do, you could always hire someone to be here with Mom during the day. It's inconvenient for me right now."

"The money is Mom's, Mickey, not mine. I won't touch it." Jackson sounded tired when David wanted him to be angry. David was angry for him.

"Well, that's stupid. He left it for her care. If you want to be a martyr, that's on you. I'll come by if I can, but I can't make any promises."

The voices were getting closer, and moments later a slender woman with longish dark hair came out of the hall. If she was surprised to find people in her mother's living room, she didn't show it. All but muscling his mother aside, she went to Shirley and grasped one of her hands, bending forward to speak to her.

"I'll see you sometime this week, Mama." She spoke so loudly that Shirley flinched at the noise.

David studied the woman dispassionately, comparing her to her brothers. He supposed she was pretty in a manufactured way. Expensive haircut, french manicure, pricey jeans, and a short, fitted leather jacket. She actually reminded him a bit of Juanita but her face held none of the other woman's humor or warmth. "I have a busy schedule with the girls, but I'll try to get by."

"I'd love to see the girls." Shirley sighed wistfully.

"Oh, Mom, I can't bring them here while you have that big bandage on your head. It would scare them."

Shirley's hand drifted to her head and David saw the way it was shaking. He wanted to go to her and hold it, just so she wouldn't look so very frail.

"Of course." Shirley dropped her hand to her lap.

"Michelle," Beverley said. David recognized the tone of voice and glanced at Jackson. He had his arms crossed defensively as he stood not far from David, his gaze on the floor. David wondered if he ought to give him some sort of warning about what was coming but couldn't catch his eye without being obvious about it. He stifled a sigh as his mother went on. "Dear, how old are your girls now?"

Michelle straightened, turning to look at David's mother. "They're eight and ten. Have we met?"

"I'm Beverley Snyder. This is my son, David." She gestured and Michelle glanced at him without interest. "Your mom and I became friends at the garden club. I met you at your father's memorial."

"Oh." Michelle dismissed Beverley too, and David saw her bristle. Beth might be more outspoken than his mother, but Beverley was no slouch when she was irritated. This should prove interesting.

"You know, Michelle," Beverley went on, lifting her chin, "there really isn't any need to shield children when they're the age of your girls."

Michelle blinked. David wondered if anyone besides Jackson ever told *Mickey* what they actually thought.

"I beg your pardon?" If voices could cause frostbite, hers would have.

Beverley wasn't dissuaded. "You simply tell them Grandma fell and hit her head. It might do your mother a world of good to see her grandchildren, don't you think? You could manage that, couldn't you? Unless something has changed recently and you've gone back to work?"

Beverley eyed her expectantly. For her part, Michelle looked as if Beverley had slapped her.

"I'll... see what I can do. But I need to go now. Good-bye, Mom." She squeezed her hand and backed away, and David realized it wasn't the little girls who would have a problem with the heavy bandage. Jackson told him about how his sister handled illness; David could see it happening right then in the tidy living room.

Michelle left quickly and Jackson followed her. David and his mother exchanged a long look.

"I'll start bringing in the food."

"That would be good." Beverley leaned over her friend, asking softly when she'd had her last pain pill.

David walked out, determined to go to the car and mind his own business. But the moment he was out of the door, he knew it would be impossible.

Jackson stood in the street, speaking stridently to his sister through the open window of her sporty car. David couldn't hear exactly what was being said, but he didn't need to. He popped the hatch and began to unload, one eye on the little drama taking place in the street. He was nearly to the door with a casserole when the little car jerked from the curb with a short screech of tires and sped away. Jackson stood watching her leave, and the exhaustion and disappointment on his face made David want to take him in his arms and whisper soothing words of comfort.

Was that what Jackson had been doing all his life? Taking the hits from his family, forcing himself to accept their failings? Jackson saw David waiting just steps from the porch and came to him, taking one of the dishes without a word. David didn't offer any either.

The kitchen in the little house was small and quaint, and fortunately there wasn't much in the refrigerator. David placed the dishes inside.

"Is there more that needs to be brought in?" Jackson asked.

David huffed out a wry chuckle. "Yes, there's more. You won't need to go to the store for a week."

"Are you serious?"

"So very serious."

"Good God." Jackson stared when they arrived back at the full car. "What was she cooking for?"

"The invasion of Normandy." David lifted the Crock-Pot and held it out. When Jackson would have taken it, David held on and waited for him to look up. He was haggard. He also looked sad. "What can I do?" David's voice dropped to a whisper.

Jackson swallowed and another of those long, pregnant pauses dragged out. "You're doing it," he finally answered. "You're here."

"JACKSON, DEAR," Beverley said two hours later. "Would you like for me to help your mother get ready for bed?"

"Oh, you don't need to do that," he said quickly. "I can do it."

Beverley gave him a level look. It wasn't unkind, but it was purposeful. "Have you had to help your mother in the bathroom or to change her clothes before?"

He hesitated. "No, ma'am."

"Then I doubt it would make her any more comfortable than it would make you. Allow me to do this, all right?"

Jackson looked at Shirley, who was dozing in her chair. "Okay. Thank you."

Beverley pushed herself to her feet. "Now, where is that walker?"

The walker was fetched and placed before the chair, and Beverley woke Shirley gently. "We need to get you into bed, hon. Up you go." Shirley began to grumble about the "damned walker," but Beverley wouldn't hear it. "So, you want Jackson to have to carry you around, is that it? Because that's the alternative, Shirley. With the walker you can at least do this part on your own."

That line of reasoning did the trick. Beverley put her hand under her arm, and with the walker moved close, Shirley was able to leverage herself to her feet. Jackson hovered nearby, but she did it on her own. They started slowly for the hall and Beverley shot Jackson a stern look.

"Go eat."

Jackson didn't move until the bathroom door opened and closed. David pushed to his feet.

"Have you eaten anything at all today?"

Jackson paused. "No."

David sighed. "Come on, then. You either do it on your own, or she'll sit here and watch every bite."

"Dude, your mom is pushy."

David's laugh was wry. "I noticed."

They went into the kitchen and Jackson's steps were dragging. Hoping the soup would help, David got down a bowl and filled it with soup.

"Aren't you having any?"

He was so close behind David that he startled a little. He turned his head and found Jackson's face inches from his.

"Mom made it for you."

"And there's enough for the neighborhood." He leaned over David's shoulder, looking into the pot. "It smells phenomenal. What is it?"

"Italian wedding soup. It tastes as good as it smells."

Jackson pressed his hard body against David from his shoulder blades to his knees. "Eat with me, okay?" he whispered against David's ear. "So I don't have to eat alone?"

With him standing so close, David thought he'd agree to anything. "Okay."

They sat across from each other at the tiny kitchen table, eating the rich, flavorful soup and taking rolls from an open Tupperware bowl between them. The soft golden light from the fixture created the illusion of privacy, an oasis of warmth cut off from the cold, dark night outside the windows. They didn't talk much, but the homey feel made David long for more of this in his life.

He and Trevor had never really made dinner at home; they ate out a lot because their schedules conflicted and it was easier. The closest they got to meals at home was ordering in and eating in front of the massive television. He couldn't think a single time they'd shared a meal at the ridiculously expensive chrome and glass dining set in the condo's kitchen. David had always wanted this: dinner at a kitchen table, the way it had been for him growing up. He stared down into his soup. His whole body ached to have this with Jackson, every day, all the time.

He startled when a large, warm hand covered his on the top of the ugly Formica. He looked up into weary blue eyes.

"What's the matter?" Jackson's voice was worn but gentle. The sound slid down David's spine like a caress and his cock twitched. This was so not the time, not with his mom down the hall.

"Nothing," he answered quickly.

One of Jackson's dark eyebrows shot up. "Try again." His calloused thumb moved over David's knuckles.

"I'm… concerned about your mom," David improvised.

"So am I. But you looked… sad."

"No, really, I'm fine." Jackson didn't look convinced, but Beverley bustled into the room at that moment. She got a glass of ice water and ignored the hands held on the table, pulling out a chair and settling in.

"She's already asleep," she said before Jackson could ask. "Poor thing is worn out. A hospital is no place to rest. I think that's why her hands were trembling so. That and the terrible blow to the head."

"That's what the ER doc said." Jackson pushed his empty bowl aside. "We should expect the trauma to her head to increase the MS symptoms for a few days."

"I thought that must be the case." Beverley pursed her lips, her hands wrapped around the glass. "Forgive me, Jackson, but I couldn't help but overhear some of your conversation with your sister earlier."

Jackson didn't react other than a tightening at the corners of his mouth. David linked their fingers, and Jackson's were warm and solid between his.

"I took care of David's father," Beverley said. "I speak from experience when I say I know how difficult being a full-time caregiver is. I have a thought, if you don't mind me speaking my mind."

Jackson's face relaxed into a tired, resigned smile. "No offense, Beverley, but I doubt I could stop you."

"You've got that right," David murmured, squeezing his hand. The small smile Jackson sent him was all the reward he needed.

"Hush, you," Beverley said to David. When she returned her attention to Jackson, her voice was soft but insistent. "When you told your sister you have to work, you're right. You can't give up your livelihood in order to take care of your mother. I know you're worried about her, but I'm hoping you'll allow me to help you."

"You've already helped so much. I mean all the food...."

Beverley made a dismissive gesture with her hand. "The food is easy, honey. It's the other stuff that's hard. Getting her up and dressed, keeping track of the meds, making sure she's steady on her feet. And making sure she uses that damned walker whether she wants to or not. This level of care is very consuming."

Jackson released David's hand with a squeeze, then flattened his palms on the old tabletop, his fingers tense. The tips were white where he pressed them into the surface. "I can do all of that." He sounded faintly defensive, but David knew his mother wasn't deterred.

"Of course you can," she said. "But while you're doing it, you can't do anything else. Believe me, I know. I'm not doing anything else right now other than futzing about in my garden. I'm not trying to build a business, and I don't have clients. I can take care of your mom during the daytime, and that way you can keep working."

Jackson's fingers pushed harder into the tabletop, and David wondered if he even knew it.

"I can't let you do that," Jackson finally murmured. "Not without paying you."

A steely light entered his mother's eyes. "Jackson, I've grown quite fond of you and clearly David has too"—David knew his face and ears were probably bright red—"but you're about to offend me."

"Beverley, the offer is lovely and I know my mom is comfortable with you, but...."

"But what?"

He didn't say anything for another of his long, thoughtful pauses.

"I'm supposed to take care of her," he said at last. "It's why I'm here. It's why I came back."

Beverley reached across the table and gently laid her hand on his arm. "Jackson, honey, is it what your mom would want?"

Jackson's Adam's apple bobbed when he swallowed.

"I happen to know she wasn't happy about you moving home. Don't misunderstand," she said quickly when he stiffened. "She loves having you here, but she hates that you felt pressured into doing it."

"She told you that?"

Beverley nodded. "Shirley's a proud person. And for the next few weeks, she won't be able to bathe without help. Right now she can't even go to the toilet by herself. You're her baby, honey. Having you take care of her at this level is going to prove embarrassing to you both. Would you want her helping you into the tub?"

Jackson stared at the tabletop for long seconds. "No."

An awkward silence settled over the kitchen. "How about this," Beverley said finally. "I have things that need to be done around my house. We could do an exchange of services. I'll take care of Shirley for you for the next few weeks, and you can do my repairs for me."

"What repairs, Mom?" David asked, frowning. "You haven't said anything to me…." She gave him a cross look and kicked his shin under the table. "Ouch. That hurt."

Jackson actually managed a small smile.

She huffed. "Honestly, David. I don't tell you everything. And not to offend you, sweetheart, but you're not the handiest person I've ever met."

It was true, but hearing it said like that was kind of embarrassing. Especially in front of Jackson. But when he glanced at him, Jackson was looking back at him with a fond, soft expression on his face.

"So, do we have a deal?" Beverley held her hand out to Jackson and waited. After what seemed a long time, and David wondered if he'd ever get used to the lengthy pauses, Jackson took her hand and shook it.

"Excellent!" Beverley smiled at him, clearly pleased. "What time do you start work in the morning so I know when to be here?" They settled on seven forty-five.

"David." His mother stood and pushed her chair in. She scooped up the canvas bags the food had come in and held them out. "Take these out to the car, will you please? I'm going to put the bowls in the dishwasher, and I'll be right behind you."

"Beverley, seriously, I can load the dishwasher," Jackson protested.

"I'm sure you can, and no doubt you'll get the opportunity to quite a bit in the next few weeks." She gave him a pointed look. "For right now I thought you'd rather walk my son to his car."

David felt a surge of embarrassment at his mother's forwardness. He loved her, but honestly. "Maybe he doesn't want to."

"No, actually." A smile curled Jackson's lips. "He really wants to. Thank you, Beverley."

She smiled at him sweetly. "You're more than welcome, Jackson."

Jackson caught David's free hand, pulling him up from the table, then through the doorway into the living room. "My jacket," David said as they walked by, and Jackson didn't even pause, just grabbed it from the back of a chair, tossed it over his broad shoulder, and pulled David out through the front door.

When they got to the red car in the driveway, he opened the door to the backseat and tossed in the padded carrying bags.

"Are you cold?" Jackson pushed the door closed.

"A little," David admitted. Actually he was a lot cold. The temperature had plummeted with the sun and now their breath made soft clouds of condensation around their heads. Jackson held up David's jacket, waiting. Charmed by the courtly gesture, David slipped his arms into the sleeves. He hadn't even settled the heavy fabric on his shoulders when Jackson gripped his arms and turned him.

David's eyes widened when Jackson grabbed the open front of his jacket, pulling him in until they were pressed together.

"I don't know what I'd have done today without you." Jackson's voice was rough.

David searched the handsome face so close to his. "I can't imagine not being here. You needed someone."

Jackson slowly shook his head. "Not just someone. You. I needed you."

Jackson bracketed David's face with his hands and his palms felt warm against David's cheeks. He leaned forward and kissed David, a sweet, smooth brush of lips. Then he leaned back, staring into David's eyes, and he must have found what he was looking for because the next kiss was anything but sweet. Jackson pulled him in, angling his mouth over David's in a kiss both firm and unmistakably carnal, and David let his eyes drift shut. He leaned into the firm body and opened his mouth when Jackson's tongue pressed insistently against his lips. He let him in on a welcoming sigh.

Jackson's tongue tasted of italian wedding soup, but the homey flavor mingled with something else, something that was Jackson's alone. David responded to it, chasing the flavors through the warm heat of Jackson's mouth, and when he caught David's tongue and sucked on it, David's knees went weak. Jackson encircled him with his arms and pressed David's back against the car. Jackson's coiled strength and heat pressed into his body and his heart began to pound hard. One of Jackson's knees slid between his legs and he whimpered when Jackson lifted his muscled thigh and pressed it against his balls.

The screen door slammed loudly and Jackson jerked back, ending the kiss abruptly. David looked up into his eyes, his breath short and his cock aching as Jackson gathered himself and stepped back reluctantly. David managed, with difficulty, to straighten where he stood, glaring at his mother as she calmly walked down the curved brick walkway.

"I'll see you tomorrow," Jackson murmured, then turned to Beverley. "I'll see you in the morning, Beverley."

"Oh yes, you will." She reached out and patted his arm as she passed, then she was standing before David where he still leaned against the car trying to gather himself. She looked up at him, her head cocked to one side. "You plan on driving, dear? Because the steering wheel is in the front seat."

Beverley walked around the car to get in on the passenger side, and Jackson gave him a wry smile as he held David's gaze. David couldn't help but return his smile, and he didn't notice the passing of time or the cold or anything at all. Until his mother beeped the car's horn.

David jumped at the sound and Jackson chuckled.

"She's not that funny," David muttered.

"Oh, I don't know." Jackson dropped his hands into his pockets. "She's pretty funny."

"Don't ever let her hear you say that. I have to live with it."

Jackson's teeth flashed white in the light from his porch, and regretfully David opened the door to the car and got in, when what he wanted to do was climb inside of Jackson's shirt and stay there.

"I wondered if you planned to go. Or if you were going to let me sit here all night."

David gritted his teeth, started the car, and backed out of the driveway. Beverley waved brightly to the tall, slender man who lifted one hand in farewell.

"I'd have stood in the living room a little longer, David, but it looked like things were about to get out of hand in the driveway, which wouldn't have done Jackson any good in this neighborhood."

"You were watching us?" He ignored the fact his voice had gone up at least an octave. "Jesus, Mom!"

"Well, honey, there were only two bowls. It didn't take that long to load the dishwasher." She sent him a grin. "It does look like the boy knows his way around a kiss."

David thought he must be glowing in the dark, his face was so hot. "I am not discussing this with you."

She smirked as he drove her home.

CHAPTER TWELVE

DAVID HAD just dropped into his desk chair when a soft knock sounded on his office door. It had been another hellish, pointless day, and he wanted to hide and ignore it. He was relieved when he saw it was Michael, who closed the door as he came in. Collapsing in one of the chairs facing David's desk, Michael hooked one long leg over the arm. He was wearing designer jeans and a V-neck sweater, the sleeves pushed up on his slender arms, and he looked casually elegant. But then, Michael always did.

"Please tell me we're going to stop using Conderson's," he said, referring to a very tardy furniture manufacturer. "This is the third time, David."

"I know." David leaned back in his chair. "But I didn't pick them. The client did."

"Can we gently suggest someone else next time? Or pull their photos out of the sales book? Something? Because we're the one left holding the bag when they can't deliver."

"I know we have to do something. I can't keep making excuses for them." David pressed his fingers into his temples where a headache brewed. "I've got to tell you, Michael. We keep having more and more days like this. I'm getting to the point where I'd rather be doing almost anything else." David had never said it out loud, but it was true, truer by the day.

Michael linked his hands around his knee, his expression pensive. "All I have to say is if you ever decide you're leaving, you need to take me with you."

"But if I left, you're next in line for department head."

Michael grimaced. "And do it without you? No, thank you." He gave David a searching look. "You're serious, aren't you?"

David stared at his blotter. So many things in his life were changing. Financially it was probably the very worst time to be considering a career change. But for his peace of mind, and his life?

"I won't lie to you. It's tempting."

"Yeah," Michael replied, his eyes beginning to shine. "But you do have to eat."

David smirked. "Well, there is that." David's cell phone buzzed, and when he picked it up, he felt a surge of pleasure when he recognized the number. He scooped the phone up with a bright smile.

"Oh my God, look at that smile." Michael gave him a crooked grin.

"You hush," David scolded, and his ears were hot. He pressed an icon on the screen. "Hello?"

"Hey."

Just the one word in Jackson's deep voice had chills dancing over David's shoulders. He smothered a happy sigh. "Hi."

"Sorry to call you at work...."

"No, it's fine. I'd so much rather talk to you than the other people I've had to deal with today."

"I think I'm offended," Michael said in a stage whisper. David flipped him off.

"I have a couple of things I wanted to touch base on."

"Okay." David knew he sounded breathless. The more Jackson talked, the more David wanted to drive home, climb in his back pocket, and live there.

"I have some guys who can get to that roof patch this weekend, if it's okay with you."

"That's fine. I'm delighted I don't have to replace the whole thing."

"I knew you'd like that part." Jackson was smiling, and David could hear it in his voice. "Manny's also available on Saturday to put a camera through the pipe to the street to see if there's a break in that line. We don't want to wait on that. If they have to dig it up, it needs to be done before the ground freezes. That way you can start showering at home."

"That would be nice," David answered. He had to get up forty minutes early in order to run over and shower at his mom's. She didn't mind, but heading out at six thirty when the temperatures were in the low thirties was no fun.

"Oh, and if you wanted to hire Gil to paint, now would be a good time." Jackson paused, another of those weighted pauses David had come to expect. "He'd been hired to paint a house out in the valley." His voice went soft, but there was something faintly off in it. "The owners pulled out of the job at the last minute. It was a big contract too. He's lost a couple of grand. It's not so hard on Gil, but it really hurts Vern when they lose the labor."

"Why did the owners pull out?" David frowned. There was something Jackson wasn't saying; David could hear it.

"Gil's not positive," Jackson answered, "but he thinks it might have something to do with the rainbow-flag decal on his truck's bumper."

"Seriously?"

"You know how it is, David." Jackson didn't need to elaborate for David to interpret what he was hearing in his voice. He'd lost jobs for the same reason, and David clenched his teeth.

"Yeah, well, it's crap."

"What's crap?" Michael whispered, a frown between his brows. David held up his hand and Michael subsided but remained watchful.

"The people paid for the paint," Jackson went on. "But Gil lost all of the profit on the labor."

"Well, their loss is my gain." David forced a bright note into his voice. "I'd love for him to get started at my place."

"He can bring paint chips by this evening, if you like."

"That would be perfect."

"I'll let him know." Another silence stretched out and David forced himself to wait. It wasn't easy. His first instinct was to fill the silences with mindless chatter; it's what he'd always done when he felt nervous. Jackson had taught him to wait. "Are you sure you can do that right now?"

"What, have Gil paint? Yeah, it's fine."

"As long as it's not going to cause you a budgeting problem."

"No, it's fine. Do you need any more…?"

"No, so far we're good." There was a weight to this hesitation. "Am I going to get to see you today?" His voice dropped even further into an intimate timbre that instantly made David's cock twitch and his balls feel heavy. He caught his breath, his pulse beginning to race at the base of his throat. "I told your mom I'd be home by six, and I know that's kind of early for you…."

"It isn't. I can leave here at five."

Michael's brows shot up and his smirk deepened.

"That's good." Jackson all but purred, and David swallowed heavily. If he said much more in that deep, rough voice, David wasn't going to be able to stand up without embarrassment. "See you then."

"See you."

David hung up, taking a deep breath and trying to get his erratic heartbeat into a normal rhythm.

"God, you've got it bad."

He looked up at Michael, a quick denial springing to his lips. But he couldn't say it, because it was true: he did have it bad. It had gone too quickly, and he should know better, but there it was.

"I'm so screwed," he said instead, laying his forehead heavily on his desk. "What am I doing?" A moment later he felt a soft touch on the back of his head.

He lifted it and found himself looking into Michael's face as he leaned forward over David's desk.

"Following your heart." Michael let his hand drop away, a small smile on his face. "Maybe this time, it'll be worth it."

David sighed. "God, I hope so."

Michael gave him a hopeful look. "Me too."

DAVID DROVE to his house, breathless excitement thrumming through his veins.

There had been a few raised eyebrows when he walked out at five, but Michael told everyone else they were getting out on time for a change. David hadn't even looked back, just headed out of the building and to his car with a spring in his step that hadn't been there in a very long time.

Rush hour traffic was heavy and even though he only lived ten miles from downtown, it took him close to twenty-five minutes until he was turning onto his street. He braked for some kids playing basketball and waved to Jordyn, who was walking down the sidewalk pushing a stroller, Bootsy trotting along at her side. He gave one happy bark when he saw David waving, and David liked to think the little dog recognized him. Then there was Jackson's truck parked in front of his house, and he pulled into his driveway, his heart drumming rapidly at the base of his throat.

The makeshift workstation wasn't in the driveway when David parked in front of the garage. He stepped out of the warmth of his car and a cold wind lifted his hair and chilled his cheeks. Fall had arrived in earnest and the temperatures were in the high forties. He hurried up his front steps and tried the knob, grateful to find the door unlocked. Warmth brushed his face and he closed the door behind him, leaning against it.

Gil's dad's elegant furniture gave David a rush of pleasure, and he noticed immediately the discordant note in the room was gone; the ugly recliner was missing from its place near the wall.

"Hi."

David looked up to find Jackson leaning casually against the wall between his living room and dining room, arms crossed over his chest and one ankle crossed over the other. He was wearing jeans and a snug T-shirt, his dark hair windblown, and he looked like sex on legs. His tool belt was missing, and David wondered if he had finished up early and was waiting for him.

He hoped so.

"The chair?"

"I gave it to some Jehovah's witnesses who knocked on the door." Jackson's lip curled in his slow smile. David arched a brow skeptically. "Okay, fine. I took it out behind the garage. I didn't think you'd mind."

"You're right. I don't mind." David walked to him slowly. "How's your mom doing?"

"Surprisingly well. More alert after a night's sleep than she was yesterday."

"That's good." David smiled.

"Yeah. She was glad to see your mom. They were having coffee and eating homemade cinnamon rolls when I left."

"She brought you cinnamon rolls and didn't save any for me?" David huffed. "I may have to disown her."

Jackson grinned. "Good luck with that."

David stopped a couple of feet in front of him. "I'm glad your mom is better, and I'm glad my mom is there with her. It gives you a chance to work without worrying, and my mom something to do. It's a win-win."

Jackson reached out and caught the front of David's coat, tugging him closer. "You getting off work earlier than usual is a win-win." The long-fingered hand curled in the fabric and David caught his breath as he pulled them together. "Are we done catching up?" One dark brow arched as Jackson's full lips curled in a smile. "Because it's almost five thirty, and this is cutting into our make-out time."

David's mouth went dry. "Oh. We're going to make out?"

Jackson nodded, slipping his strong arm around David's waist and bringing him taut against his chest. David's hands came up to cup Jackson's biceps. God, they were hard. "We are so going to make out." Jackson lifted one calloused hand to cup David's jaw, his thumb stroking across David's lips. "Now—" The arm around David's waist tightened. "—can we stop talking, please?"

David nodded, and Jackson's smile ripened as he leaned forward and captured David's lips.

Where the kisses they'd shared before began tentatively enough, this one didn't. Jackson almost immediately pressed his tongue forward and David opened to him. Jackson's kiss was searching and anything but uncertain, and in a daze, David lifted his arms and wrapped them around Jackson's neck, letting Jackson take him wherever he wanted to go.

There was nothing sloppy about Jackson's tongue in David's mouth. He curled it around David's, stroking slowly then sucking, and David moaned as the sensation sent a thrill of need straight to his groin. He'd been half-hard in anticipation when he walked in the door, but he was so hard he ached now.

With a nudge from Jackson's hand, David's coat slid from his shoulders and fell to the floor. Jackson kicked it aside and took a few steps, and David held on and let himself be walked backward. He was maneuvered until the backs of his knees hit a soft surface, and Jackson turned them, falling, pulling David down. They were horizontal on the long leather couch, David sprawled on top before he knew what was happening.

He pulled back, looking down into Jackson's bright blue eyes. "Very smooth." David speared his fingers into Jackson's dark hair.

"Thanks. But you're talking when I can think of much better things for you to do with that mouth."

David pressed down with his hips. "Me too, but I can't imagine there's time."

Jackson shifted slightly, spreading his muscular thighs, and David slipped perfectly between them as if it was his place. "Tease," Jackson growled.

"Not teasing." David dove back in for another openmouthed kiss.

Their cocks pressed together, and even the layers of cloth couldn't diminish the thrill of arousal. Jackson slid a hand down to cup David's asscheek and he pulled him in, lifting one thigh over David's hip, arching his pelvis up to meet his groin. David groaned at the rush of heat, even as Jackson curled his other hand around David's neck.

Jackson's grip tightened on his ass, strong fingers digging in. David spread his hands on Jackson's ribcage and rotated his hips, providing needed friction, and Jackson made a delicious sound in the back of his throat.

Jackson lifted enough to suck on the skin below David's chin, and the feeling was so exquisite, the ache in his groin so pronounced, that David was afraid he was about to do something he hadn't done since he was fifteen. He fumbled and pressed his hand between them, his palm at the base of Jackson's throat. He could feel Jackson's Adam's apple moving beneath his fingers. "Wait," he gasped. "Jackson, wait."

Jackson drew back, releasing David's neck with a soft pop. "Why?"

"Because I'm about to come in my pants and it will humiliate me so completely I'll never be able to look you in the face again."

Jackson huffed out a ragged chuckle and let his head fall back against the sofa cushion. "Damn. I really want to watch you come undone."

Another wave of desire rolled over David, and he took a deep breath before running his hand down Jackson's chest, gratified to find Jackson's heart pounding as hard as his. "You have to get home."

Jackson closed his eyes on a groan. "Yeah. This whole making-out thing was a very bad idea." He pressed his forehead against David's throat. "It's been a long damned time since I had to cut off something this good to get home to my mother's house."

David laughed weakly. "Yeah, and this time you have to face *my* mother when you get there too."

Jackson settled his hands on David's waist, not stroking, just holding. "I like your mom."

"I like her too. But I wouldn't want to have to talk to her right now." He glanced down meaningfully and Jackson chuckled.

David pushed up onto his hands and knees and Jackson reluctantly let him go. He settled in the corner of the sofa, and Jackson lifted his hips to reach into the front of his jeans to adjust himself. When he was done, he sighed, and David eyed the long bulge that filled the front of Jackson's pants with a longing he tried very hard not to show. His palm itched to reach over and cup him, and restraining himself was difficult.

"Well, hopefully it's cold enough outside that it will take care of this hard-on before I get home." He gave David a slight smile. "You're driving me crazy, you know that, right?"

David found it hard to believe and thrilling, all at once. "That goes both ways, Jackson."

"Good." Jackson leaned in and kissed him quickly. "I'll see you tomorrow."

David followed him to the door, giving Jackson one last brief kiss before he stepped out onto the porch. David glanced around the darkened street, but he didn't feel the crawling sensation of someone watching him he did some nights. Still, he watched Jackson go to his truck, giving one last wave as he pulled from the curb. Then he closed the door and leaned against it. He was still so hard it hurt, and he pressed his palm against his aching cock.

"I'm driving you crazy?" he muttered. "This is going to kill me." He pushed away from the door and bent very cautiously to pick his coat up off the floor, then decided it wasn't worth doing himself permanent injury and left it where it was.

DAVID WAS still floating on a wave of euphoria the next morning. His phone sounded off with a text message at seven thirty as he stood in his kitchen, finishing up a hasty cup of coffee. Jackson's number flashed on the screen.

How did your meeting with Gil go?

David smiled, setting his cup aside to answer.

Excellent. I picked out colors for the outside of the house and the living room, dining room, and bathrooms.

What, not the kitchen?

David laughed. He glanced at the discolored paint above the stove and around the handles on the cabinet doors.

And the kitchen. I may be eating ramen noodles for a while, but at least the kitchen will be presentable.

I have a big picture of you eating ramen.

David could almost imagine his slow smile.

I'll have you know I make a mean ramen. And peanut butter and jelly. And Kraft's mac and cheese.

Yeah, but Kraft's mac and cheese is gourmet fare compared to ketchup and saltine sandwiches.

David laughed again.

Clearly, we need to exchange recipes.

Yeah, if I never eat another saltine with ketchup it'll be too soon. There was a pause. *The delayed gratification may kill me, but I still want to kiss you senseless the next time I see you. Will it be this afternoon?*

David smiled so wide his cheeks hurt.

At the risk of seeming desperate, he texted back, *I'll be here by five thirty.*

Desperate would be four thirty.

No, desperate would be calling out sick and waiting for you in nothing more than a blanket and a smile.

Let me picture that. There was another short pause. *Okay, I have to stop picturing that, you damned tease, or I'll never get your new back door installed.*

David laughed again.

Okay, I'll stop. And I'm leaving you a check on the coffee table. See you at five thirty.

He'd written out a check for another thousand dollars, reminding himself to adjust his savings balance, and left for work.

He hadn't noticed the purple mark on his neck until he shaved that morning, and even the sight of it sent a shiver of remembered pleasure through him. Because he really did need to present a professional image, he'd pulled a high-necked russet sweater on before donning a black sports coat, and that pretty much covered the spot. Unless of course you were Michael Crane, who apparently had hickey radar. He spotted the mark instantly and spent most of the day giving David a good-natured ration of crap, but he was too happy to care. Even another tense phone call with Conderson's Manufacturing couldn't put a dent in his mood. When his assistant's distinctive, rhythmic rap sounded at about four while David was going over a spreadsheet for the disputed job, David fought a grin.

"Aren't you getting tired of ragging on me yet?"

His door opened and Michael stuck his head through the gap, but the cheeky smile David expected was nowhere in sight. Instead, he was frowning.

"There's a man here to see you," he said, his voice low. "He won't tell me what he wants, but insists he has to see you, personally."

David mulled that for a moment. "Well, show him in, I guess."

Michael didn't look like he thought it was a great idea, but he opened the door wider, admitting a middle-aged man wearing a suit with a long, dark wool coat over it and holding a briefcase in one hand.

David stood. "I'm David Snyder." He offered his hand. "How can I help you?"

Instead of shaking his hand, the man slapped an envelope into his palm. "You've been served," he said tautly, then pushed past Michael, who had lingered, and out through the office door.

David's throat was dry. He knew what "you've been served" indicated. He opened the envelope, pulling out the thick sheaf of papers and unfolding them. A large, hard lump settled in the middle of his chest.

Across the top it read *"The Superior Court of Washington, In re the domestic partnership of petitioner Trevor Connor Blankenship and respondent David Wayne Snyder. Motion and Declaration for Temporary order of support."*

Hands trembling, he read further.

"...Requires the respondent, Mr. Snyder, to pay existing mortgage, monthly support, temporary attorney fees, other professional fees, and costs in the amount of $12,000 per month to Mr. Blankenship, until such time as indicated by the court."

David felt like he might throw up. Twelve grand? Twelve grand a month? Trevor knew he didn't have that kind of money. The payment on the condo was twelve hundred. If he had to pay this, it would wipe him out in a couple of months.

"My God, David, you're white as a ghost. What is it?"

David lowered himself to sit on the edge of his desk and handed the documents to Michael.

Michael took them, scanning down the page. "Oh, for fuck's sakes," he exploded.

David stirred from his shock enough to see his office door was still open. He pushed up and closed it, leaning heavily against the wood.

"He can't do this." Michael asked David, "Can he?"

"I have no idea," David said, still stunned. "I mean, clearly he can...." He gestured weakly toward the documents Michael still held.

"But twelve thousand dollars a month?" Michael lowered his voice, but it still sounded as loud as a shout in David's head. "He can't be serious."

"I think he's completely serious."

"You have a lawyer, right?" Michael tossed the papers on David's desk. "Call him."

"Her," David corrected absently, staring at the documents. "My lawyer's a her."

"Fine, call her. You have to fight this, David. You can't let him get away with it."

David nodded, crossing to sit in his chair.

WHEN HE walked in the front door of his house at nearly six, he still felt shell-shocked and sick to his stomach. He'd called his attorney's office only to be told she was in court, so he made an appointment for the next morning. He then called his broker, and he confirmed what David already knew: if he had to liquidate enough of his assets to meet Trevor's financial demands, ten years of hard work would be wiped out in three months. He didn't think Trevor could touch the 401(k), but he wasn't sure about that either. By the time David got off the phone with him, his most pressing desire was to vomit, then curl up in a fetal position around a bottle of scotch.

"I was beginning to think you stood me up."

David looked up. It was dim in his living room, the only light coming from the kitchen doorway on the other side of the dining room.

It took him a moment to find the outline of Jackson sitting in the rocking chair near the fireplace.

"I was getting ready to leave."

"I'm sorry, I... something came up and... I...." He paused, cleared his throat. "I'm sorry." His voice sounded raw even to his own ears.

"David?" The light on the end table nearest Jackson flared to life, and David winced. Jackson stared at him for a long moment before pushing slowly to his feet. "What's wrong?"

It probably should have occurred to David not to tell him, but it never did. He reached into the deep inside breast pocket of his coat, fished out the papers, and held them out, hating that his hand was still trembling. Jackson took the documents, turning so that the light from the lamp fell across the top page.

Jackson didn't say anything as he read through the pages. He was so still and silent that David's shakes began to worsen. Finally, Jackson reached into his pocket and pulled out his cell phone. He looked down and thumbed in a number, and waited.

"Beverley?" he said finally. "Hi. Do you mind staying with my mom for a few more minutes? I'll be there by seven.... Thank you." He hung up, putting the phone back into his jacket pocket. He searched David's face. Instead of speaking, he took the two steps that separated them and pulled David into his arms.

"It'll be okay," he murmured next to David's ear. "Take a deep breath. It'll be okay."

David leaned into the strength of Jackson's body, wrapped his arms around his waist, and pressed his face against Jackson's throat. He didn't know if it would be okay or not, but it felt a lot less scary while held in Jackson's embrace.

They talked quietly, Jackson holding David, reassuring him again and again that everything would be okay until he had to leave. After Jackson was gone, David made himself a light dinner of tomato soup and a grilled cheese sandwich, unsure before he ate if he'd even be able to keep it down, but the food helped to settle his stomach. He opened a bottle of red wine and drank a glass far more quickly than the fine vintage deserved, then poured a second and took it into the bedroom. He'd been going to browse the Internet for some accessories for the house, but the idea of spending enough for even some throw pillows and a bedspread caused so much anxiety, he dismissed the idea. Instead he turned on the television and changed into sweats, then stretched out against the headboard, sipping his wine. He tried, really hard, not to worry. But he'd never been very good at that. And Michael knew him as well as anyone. David got a text at just after nine.

Stop worrying and have another glass of wine. It will all work out okay.

David smiled faintly. *Do you have a hidden camera in my bedroom or something?*

No, but if you plan to start fucking the lovely Jackson anytime soon, I might invest in one.

Fuck off very much, thank you.

He could almost hear Michael laughing.

Love you, too. I'll see you tomorrow.

David put the phone next to him on the comforter and tried to concentrate on some show he didn't know the title of.

When his phone buzzed near his hip at nearly ten o'clock, and he had no more idea what he'd been watching than he had the hour before, he frowned and scooped it up. His frown faded when he saw the displayed number. A wave of relief slipped through him as he muted the television.

"Hi."

"Hey." Jackson's deep voice slid into his ear, and David closed his eyes. The sound of his voice moved over David like a caress.

"How's your mom?" David's voice dropped into the same, intimate timbre.

"Sleeping. She's doing a lot better."

"I'm glad. I keep meaning to call my mom and ask."

"I didn't say anything to her, by the way." He could hear Jackson shifting, and he wondered if he was in bed too. "To your mom, I mean."

"Oh, thank you. I'll tell her, but I want to wait until I talk to my lawyer first."

"Yeah." There was a pause. "Are you okay?"

Was he? "Yeah. More pissed off than anything now."

"Good. I'd rather you were pissed off than blaming yourself."

David frowned. "I wasn't...."

"Weren't you?"

David thought about it. How many times since the server left his office had he thought "if only I hadn't walked out the way I did," or "if only I hadn't trusted Trevor to begin with."

"Okay, maybe a little."

Jackson grunted softly. "You do get that your ex is an asshole, right?"

"Oh, yeah. But...." David stopped, moving his thumb around the top edge of his wine glass.

"But what?"

David hesitated, knowing even before he said it that it was probably going to sound stupid.

"Come on, David. Talk to me."

The quiet acceptance in Jackson's tone made it possible for him to say what he'd only allowed himself to think before. "I chose him, didn't I? I mean, he didn't suddenly become an asshole. He's always been one. And I think I knew it. And still, I stayed. What does that say about me?"

There was another of Jackson's patented silences. When he spoke his voice was even softer.

"All it says about you is that you wanted someone to love you. And that isn't a crime, David. Don't we all want that, ultimately?"

"You wouldn't have done it. You wouldn't have let someone treat you like that."

Jackson exhaled heavily. "Do you remember the night in the car, when we were talking about why I moved home?"

Of course he remembered. David had thought more than once that Jackson's ex must be some sort of idiot to let him go. "Yeah."

"His name is Stephen. Stephen Addison Hall the third."

"Wow, that's pretentious."

Jackson chuckled. "That should have been my first clue actually. That he lived up to the name. He comes from money—a lot of it. His dad is a lawyer. It was something we had in common, although his dad is in the DA's office and mine was always in corporate law. I met him at a friend's housewarming. I thought he was the most beautiful thing I'd ever seen."

David didn't want to be jealous of an ex, but he was.

"I should have looked closer. Listened more carefully when he was dismissive of people. He has a wicked sense of humor, but what I thought was him being funny was actually him being a jerk. It wasn't so bad, until he turned it on me."

"Was he stupid?"

Jackson chuckled darkly. "No, but I was. The first time I let him make me the butt of a joke, I should have walked away. But I didn't. I stayed, and every time he made a little joke and was 'just kidding,' I let him take a little bit more of my self-worth." He paused, then cleared his throat roughly. "The point is, you aren't the only one who's put his faith in the wrong person, okay?"

It was David's turn to pause. He couldn't imagine anyone being dumb enough to let Jackson go. He supposed he should be grateful, though. For both Trevor and Stephen. Without them, he and Jackson wouldn't be where they were. "Yeah, okay."

"And I want you to listen to me." David could imagine the look on Jackson's face that went with the resolute tone: eyes level, his chin dropped down so that he was looking at David from beneath the arched brows. "No judge is going to order you to pay more than you make every month. So try to relax, try to let it go for tonight, and try to get a good night's sleep. Have a glass of wine or four, all right? Not so much you end up with a headache, but enough you can relax."

David laughed. "I have glass number two in my hand as we speak."

"Excellent." David took a sip when Jackson paused. "And listen, I don't want you to worry about the work at the house getting done. I won't let it go unfinished. Neither will Gil. So stop worrying about that."

"Jackson, I can't let you and Gil do the work if I can't afford to pay you for it."

"David?"

David rolled his eyes. Even for as short a time as they'd known each other, David recognized that stubborn, unyielding tone of voice. "Yes?"

"Shut up, okay? Just… let us do this. The house is worth a couple hundred grand more than you paid for it. I figure I'll get paid. If I'm not worried about it, and Gil isn't worried about it, maybe you shouldn't be either."

David had to blink against a sudden and wholly shocking sting of tears. He hadn't allowed himself to cry during the whole of the Trevor mess, and now he was afraid if he started, he'd never stop. He swallowed around the lump in his throat. "Yeah, okay," David managed, sounding breathless but not weepy. That was a relief. "Thanks."

"You're welcome." There was another pause, and even though they'd said everything that needed saying, it was like neither of them wanted to hang up.

"So, what time is your appointment with your lawyer?"

"Nine."

"Okay."

David could count his heartbeats during the following silence. One, two, three....

"Are you... okay, going alone?"

David's heart warmed. "Yeah, I'm okay. But thanks for offering."

"Sure."

One, two, three....

"I should hang up now. Six comes early."

"It does."

David could feel his heart beat. Thud-thud, thud-thud, thud-thud....

"I wish I was there, holding you." Jackson's voice was so deep, so soft, and David let it wrap around him like a blanket.

He took in a deep, shuddering breath. "I wish you were too."

"See you tomorrow."

"Absolutely."

"Good night, David."

"Good night."

David thumbed his phone off, and despite the way his afternoon had gone, and despite the uncertainty of the situation with Trevor, he went to sleep warmed clear through, a smile on his face.

CHAPTER THIRTEEN

HE WORE a suit the next morning. He didn't ordinarily wear suits; in fact, the one he took out of the closet he'd only worn once, to a cousin's wedding the year before. He'd picked it out alone, loving the cut and the dark blue color. Of course Trevor hated it, saying the lapels were too wide and the trousers cut wrong, which is probably why he never wore it again. But on this sunny fall morning, when the temperature was in the midtwenties, he donned a white oxford button-down and a blue striped tie with the dark blue suit. He added a pair of black leather loafers that had cost more than his car payment, and he even tucked a pocket square in the pocket of his jacket. He'd never actually met his lawyer face-to-face, but he figured when you were paying someone two hundred and fifty dollars an hour, looking like you could afford her might be a good thing. Plus the suit made him feel empowered, and after the day before, he figured any little bit of empowerment couldn't hurt. When he studied himself in the mirror, he thought he still looked like an effeminate nerd, but at least a prosperous one.

He laid his long black overcoat and gloves on the back of the sofa, then walked through the dining room, intent on starting a pot of coffee. He had paused to admire the way the sun filtered through the two stained glass windows above the built-ins in his dining room when the front doorbell rang.

David checked his watch. It was only seven thirty. Dark hair and the strong lines of Jackson's face were visible through the small windows in the front door, and he was smiling when he opened it.

"Good morning," he said.

Jackson was wearing his bulky denim jacket and knit gloves, and the cold had brought color to his strong cheekbones and the tip of his nose. He held a tray with two Dunkin' Donuts cups and a small brown paper bag, and he looked at David, his brows shooting up.

"Wow. Look at you."

He came in through the open door, his gaze moving up and down David with slow thoroughness, and David closed the door, feeling his cheeks fill with color.

"Damn." Jackson smiled slowly. "You look amazing."

"Better than my usual, preteen girl attire?"

Jackson grinned. "I like that too. But this is... impressive."

David looked down. "Thanks."

Jackson held out the small bag a bit awkwardly and David took it from him.

"Breakfast." Jackson indicated the tray, and David grinned.

"That was nice of you."

They crossed into the kitchen, and once he'd set the cups on the counter, Jackson reached out and curled his hands gently around his arms.

"You really do look... pretty amazing." Jackson smoothed his palms down to David's hands. "And I want to kiss you, but I don't want to muss your suit."

David smiled. "You won't. Much to the ex's chagrin, it's a polyester blend."

"The more I hear about this guy, the more convinced I am he wasn't good enough for you."

David's grin mellowed as his slipped his arms around Jackson's waist, inside his jacket.

"I don't think he was either."

He was still smiling when Jackson pulled him close and kissed him.

AFTER BREAKFAST sandwiches and a lovely hazelnut-blend coffee, David left his house at eight thirty. Gil was just arriving, and he parked on the street and grinned as he dropped the tailgate of his pickup.

"Looking good there, handsome," he called, and David waved with a grin. There was nothing as heartening as having two good-looking men admire the way you looked. It was a balm for an ego that had taken several hits in the last few weeks. Of course, having your lips still swollen from the kisses of one of those two men was even better. Vernon climbed out of the passenger side of Gil's truck and whistled as David started for the garage. David shot a grin over his shoulder.

The smile lasted all the way until he was pulling out into rush hour traffic and the packet of papers rustled in his breast pocket as he turned the corner. Anxiety made his skin feel too tight, but he took a deep breath, forcing the fear down. He wasn't going to jump to conclusions until he talked to his lawyer. It was why he'd hired her, after all.

Her offices were in a very nice high-rise building in the downtown corridor. He took the elevator to the sixth floor, and when he stepped off, he saw the entire floor was taken up with the law firm. Ridgeway, Ridgeway, and Cohen was emblazoned on the dark wood wall in eighteen-inch-tall golden letters, and a very attractive woman with short dark hair and a ready smile sat behind the reception desk.

He gave her his name and she picked up her phone, gesturing toward a coffee station in the corner. David had already reached his coffee limit for the morning, so he took a seat in a very comfortable chair in the corner to wait. He didn't sit there long.

Karen Ridgeway wore a sharp tweed skirt and a bronze silk blouse. Her blonde hair was cut in a blunt bob, and she wore gold hoops in her ears and a simple gold ring on her finger. Expert and subtly applied makeup highlighted her attractive features, and she approached and offered her hand with a friendly smile.

"David?"

He stood, taking the offered hand.

"It's nice to finally meet you face-to-face. Come on back."

She led the way down a long, wide hall. They passed several beautifully appointed offices and one large conference room, and finally ended up in a corner office with an impressive view of downtown and the river.

"Can I take your coat?"

"No, I'm fine, thank you."

She gestured toward a burgundy leather wingback chair facing a large mahogany desk, and settled into a matching swivel chair behind it. David's hands were clenched and he forced them to relax.

"All right," she began, "my message says you were served with court documents yesterday?"

"Yes." He reached into the pocket of his coat and pulled out the envelope. Once he'd placed it in her outstretched hand, he watched nervously as she pulled out the documents. It was a challenge to keep his knee from bouncing as she read the three pages carefully, a slight frown forming. After several minutes she touched a button on her desk phone.

"Brian, can you come in here, please?"

A young man answered the summons quickly. He was an attractive guy with reddish-blond hair, smartly dressed in dark slacks and a shirt and tie. She held the sheaf of papers out to him. "Could you call the courthouse for me and see if this case has been filed?"

He took the papers and glanced at the first page, frowning slightly. "But, this doesn't...."

"I know," she cut him off. "Just double-check, please."

"Yes, ma'am."

The man left as David's lawyer picked up her phone and quickly punched in a number, then leaned back in her chair.

"Tony Sugarton, please," she said to whomever answered the phone. She gave David a reassuring smile while she waited. It wasn't long. "Tony, Karen Ridgeway here. Listen, did you have documents served on David Snyder on behalf of your client Trevor Blankenship?" She listened for several minutes, her smile scarcely wavering. "Is that right? Okay, well, thanks so much. Give Mimi my love." She listened again for a moment. "Sure. Ron and I would love that. I'll give you a ring before the weekend."

She hung up as Brian walked back into the office. "It hasn't been filed." He handed the papers to her and, after giving David a fleeting smile, left the room.

Karen leaned forward, bracing her elbows on the top of her desk and linking her hands. She pursed her lips briefly, her thumbs bumping together a few times. "Well," she said finally. "It appears that your ex is trying to pull a fast one."

David stiffened. "Pardon?"

"His lawyer didn't draw up these documents. Mr. Blankenship probably downloaded them from the Internet. And it's not to say he couldn't file a lawsuit himself. He could. But—" She held his gaze. "—not with these papers."

"I'm sorry," David said. "I don't understand."

"You told me that you and Mr. Blankenship didn't register as domestic partners, correct?"

David nodded.

"Then it's impossible for him to apply for dissolution of something that doesn't exist. And what he apparently doesn't know because he didn't do his homework is that all domestic partnerships entered into in Washington State before 2014 were automatically registered as marriages once the law legalizing same-sex marital recognition passed. I was almost positive these papers weren't the work of his lawyer. In addition, I knew they probably weren't filed with the court."

"But, I was served," David said. "In my office."

Karen looked faintly apologetic. "He probably had someone he knows do it, someone you hadn't met." David thought of the man who had come to his office, and he could say without question he'd never seen him before. "Whoever he was, he wasn't an actual process server. I'm sorry, David, but I think your ex was simply trying to rattle your cage."

"Rattle my cage," David repeated through tight lips.

"He probably wanted to point out it would be a whole lot less expensive to make the condo payment than it would be if he got a settlement from a court, including support. Perhaps he thought this would instigate negotiations with you for what he wants. Apparently he doesn't know that because you weren't married, he isn't entitled to support."

A slow-burning anger filled David's chest. He reached across the desk and picked up the papers that had turned the last twenty-four hours of his life into a living hell. "So, let me understand: he did this so I would negotiate with him about the condo payment?"

"I think so, yes."

David's fingers tightened around the papers, and she studied him, a calm, perceptive expression settling over her features.

"Because his name is on the mortgage for the condo," she said, "he's entitled to half of the proceeds when it's sold, but certainly nothing in addition to that. And—" She steepled her hands beneath her chin. "—if you're no longer interested in keeping that property, you are within your legal rights to tell him he has the option of buying you out immediately or selling it." She studied him, her gaze unwavering. "So, are you ready to stop letting him walk all over you?"

David clenched his teeth, anger choking him. He forced a deep swallow. "You know, I believe I am." He was proud his voice sounded so calm. It was the exact opposite of what he was feeling.

A slow, predatory smile spread across her lips. "Good."

STILL SIMMERING with anger at the end of his appointment, David simply couldn't face the idea of putting up with his daily routine at work. He called Michael.

"How did it go?" Michael asked as he came on the line.

"Infuriating. The good news is I won't be paying anyone twelve grand a month. The bad news is my ex is an even bigger bastard than I thought."

"Oh God, did he do something else?"

"No, sending me fake court documents was the extent of this week's effort to drive me insane."

"Wait, he did what?"

"Listen, can we talk about this later? I'm not in the mood right now."

"Of course," Michael said quickly. "You're not coming in, are you?"

"That's why I'm calling. I'd really rather not."

"Don't worry about it. The only thing on today's schedule is that conference call with Conderson's, and I can handle that."

"I love you, Michael." David let his head fall back against the headrest. "If I had to take that call today, I'd probably tell them to just fuck off with their demands."

"You have no guarantee I won't do precisely the same thing." David gave a short laugh. "Listen," Michael went on, "I'll call you when I leave the office, okay? I need to hear what's going on."

"That'll be fine." David closed his eyes as relief washed over him. "And Michael? I owe you."

"So much more than you can ever pay," Michael agreed. "I'll call you later."

David drove home through the quiet neighborhood streets, passing school buses and young soccer moms in their minivans. When he pulled into the driveway, the sight of Jackson's silver truck parked in front of his house made his heart lift. Vern's truck was there too, the tailgate lowered and five-gallon buckets of paint sitting in the truck bed. David parked in front of the garage door, sitting in the car for a few minutes as weariness washed over him. He was so tired of the mess with Trevor, so tired of the nerves that struck him when darkness fell, so tired of the nastiness. Even with Karen's help in countermanding what Trevor had done, the whole thing made him feel ill.

His car door was pulled open, and he stiffened instinctively as cold air rushed over him. Jackson bent, looking at him with concern in his eyes, and David reached out.

Jackson took his hand, crouching beside him. "Babe, are you okay?"

David paused before he nodded. He'd never been much for endearments, but hearing Jackson call him babe sent a shaft of pleasure through him. "Yes, I'm fine."

"Did everything go okay?"

Jackson looked so worried, a crease between his brows, that David reached out and smoothed it with his thumb. "Yes. But let's go inside to talk, okay?"

Jackson glanced behind him. "Vern and Gil are prepping the bathroom. Do you want the conversation to stay private?" David appreciated his discretion, and he nodded. "Come with me?"

They walked shoulder to shoulder over to Jackson's truck, Jackson gripping his hand, and when they pulled away from the curb, David didn't even care where they were going. He closed his eyes, grateful for the heated seat, the way it fit to his spine. Tension seeped from his shoulders. Jackson's supportive, thoughtful silence did more to calm him than any assurances Karen Ridgeway had uttered.

When they'd been in the truck for several minutes, Jackson parked and David opened his eyes. "Where are we?"

He looked around with interest and saw towering pine trees and rocks, interspersed with bright red bushes. Down the hill was a fast-moving stream, the water frothy and sea green. On the other side were some small cabins tucked in between the trees.

"I came to Leadership camp here." Jackson put the truck in park and turned off the engine. "It's only fifteen minutes from downtown, but it might as well be a world away. I come up here when I need to just get out of town. There aren't any fish in the stream, but it hasn't stopped me from trying." He unfastened his seat belt, then leaned across the console between them and undid David's as well.

When he would have moved back to his own seat, David gripped the lapels of his denim jacket, stopping him. He kissed Jackson softly, his hands opening to smooth over the chest beneath the dark fabric.

Jackson leaned his elbow on the console. "You ready to talk?" David nodded. "Good." He gestured toward the backseat. "Care to step into my office?"

David grinned. "Did you just invite me to your backseat, sir?"

Jackson pretended to think about it. "I believe I did."

"Excellent."

David opened his door, stepping down. By the time he reached for the grab handle to climb into the backseat, Jackson was already inside, his hand extended. He helped David up onto the seat, closing the door behind him.

"Very smooth," David said, smiling. "One would think you've had practice."

"Hey, I was a teenager with an extended cab pickup. I won't lie."

David relaxed into the corner of the seat, one leg bent, the other out straight along the floor. "I'll bet this truck has seen its share of action."

Jackson leaned back across from him. "This one, not so much. The Toyota 4Runner I had in high school?" He shrugged. "Let's just say I had a very good time doing stuff my father never would have approved of."

"And you probably would have gotten arrested for it if you'd been caught."

David admired Jackson's long, lanky frame as he gave him an unrepentant smile. "Undoubtedly. Come here."

He opened his arms, and David gladly slid across the seat into them, slipping his arms around Jackson's waist. Jackson leaned back into the corner and accepted his weight, easing David's head down onto his shoulder. His large, calloused hands moved slowly up and down over the wool covering David's back and shoulders.

David closed his eyes, relaxing into his embrace. They didn't talk for quite a while. He'd nearly dozed off when Jackson finally spoke.

"You want to tell me what your lawyer had to say?"

Just that easily, Jackson asked and David answered. Jackson sat quietly, holding him. David laid out Karen's suggestions. She wanted him to get a restraining order against Trevor, telling him in black and white that the stalking behavior had to stop. Also, Trevor had to either pay for the condo or agree to its sale. When he was done, he lay against Jackson's shoulder, waiting.

"I think," Jackson said slowly, "that you hired a very smart lady and that you ought to listen to her."

"Yes, I know." David sighed. "You don't think getting a restraining order will just aggravate the situation? I was trying not to provoke him."

Jackson's hand slid to David's nape, his fingers gently kneading the tense muscles. "I don't think you've done anything to provoke him, and he's still figuring out ways to harass you. Isn't he?"

David's cell phone vibrated in his pocket as if on cue. He sat up and pulled it out, then shook his head at the irony after reading the screen. Trevor had texted.

Are you ready to settle this like an adult yet?

Without his asking, David handed Jackson the phone.

Jackson made an incredulous sound. "Wow, he may be the single most clueless individual I've ever seen."

David's phone buzzed again, then again, and Jackson studied the screen. "What would you like me to do with this?"

"I need to keep the texts for Karen, but just shut it off. Here."

Jackson handed it back, and David pushed the button, shutting the phone down. Then he dropped it to the floor and went back into Jackson's arms. He laid his head against Jackson's chest and closed his eyes. For some reason he suddenly felt like he could cry.

"Is it really stupid that I have this opportunity to jump you," he asked, his throat thick, "and all I want is for you to hold me?"

"No," Jackson said softly, tightening his hold. "No, it isn't stupid."

SATURDAY MORNING, two days after visiting his lawyer, David woke to the insistent ringing of his cell phone. Still groggy he answered it. "Hello?"

"We need to talk, David."

It took a moment for David to realize who it was. "Trevor?" David fumbled for his glasses, finally managing to place them on his face. The digital clock on his nightstand read six thirty. "What the hell, Trevor. It's six thirty. On a Saturday."

"I know what time and day it is," Trevor snapped back. "I said we need to talk, and you're ignoring my texts."

He had been. Trevor had sent at least a dozen texts the day before, all of them beginning with "we need to talk." David ignored them all. He wanted to delete them, but Karen told him to keep them in case they needed them.

"Trevor." David wearily rubbed his eyes beneath the lenses of his glasses. "I don't have anything to say to you."

"I have plenty to say to you," Trevor retorted. "A restraining order, David? Really?"

He'd gotten Karen's letter then. She warned Trevor that having the fraudulent papers delivered, entering David's office when he wasn't there, and following him to his residence, not to mention the dozens of texts and phone calls, was stalking behavior and constituted grounds for a restraining order. The letter was pretty clear: knock it off or the order would be filed immediately.

"You were caught going through my desk. At work."

"That little bitch assistant of yours has a big mouth."

"You broke the window out of my car!"

There was a startled pause. "What the hell are you talking about?"

"Don't play stupid with me, Trevor."

"Is that why the police were around here a couple of weeks ago, asking me a bunch of questions? Your car was vandalized?" He sounded genuinely surprised, but then David knew Trevor was a skilled liar. "I didn't do it, David."

David rolled onto his back, his hand going to his hair, not believing him for a moment. "Trevor, seriously. Stop calling me. Stop texting me. If you have an issue, call my lawyer. I believe you have her name and number."

"I don't want to sell the condo, David."

"Then refinance it."

"I can't!"

That made David pause. He closed his eyes. "What do you mean, you can't? You have a good job."

There was a long pause, but it didn't remind David of Jackson's. This one almost vibrated with tension.

Finally Trevor exhaled loudly. "I'm a bit… overextended, and as a result my credit rating is not high enough for me to be able to finance a loan on my own."

David stared at the ceiling, marshaling his resolve. He'd wondered, with all the clothes and expensive wine bought on a credit card. "That's not my fault, Trevor. It's not my fault you cheated on me, it's not my fault I had to move out, and it's not my fault you can't finance a loan."

"You didn't have to move out."

David's eyes narrowed. "Oh yes, I did."

There was another pause. "So what you're saying is you don't care if I lose my home over a blow job?" His voice vibrated with poorly suppressed fury, and David found that, where in the past it might have frightened him, now all it did was make him tired.

"I didn't say that. Of course I don't want you to lose your home. But I won't pay for you to live in it either."

"If you hadn't bought that fucking house, if you'd been reasonable to begin with, none of this would be happening."

David shook his head even though Trevor couldn't see it. He was beginning to think that in addition to having a cruel streak, the man was deluded. How had he never noticed that?

But he had, a small voice in his head replied. David had known Trevor could be unreasonable when he didn't get his way. How many shirts had he buried in his closet because Trevor didn't like them? How many times had he been afraid he was buying the wrong brand of crackers, the wrong type of cheese, the wrong bottle of wine? How many times over the course of five years had Trevor told him he was wrong? And how many times when Trevor went off into one of his tirades had David secretly been afraid his verbal anger would manifest itself into something physical? Trevor had managed to make David believe he had to go along and keep him happy, not only so that Trevor wouldn't harm him somehow, but because Trevor had him convinced no one else would ever want him. He was too thin, too white, too openly queer. And suddenly David had had enough. He sat up, every muscle in his body clenched tight.

"This conversation is over." He started to hang up the phone and Trevor spoke again.

"I've seen the new guy you're with, David." David stilled. "You made a real stink over a blow job, but it didn't take you long to hook up with someone else, did it?" Trevor's voice had dropped into a low, almost soothing timbre, but David knew better. "I know all about him. How he's taking care of his mom, where he lives, what he drives. But you shouldn't get used to him. No guy who looks like that one is going to hang around for long, not with you. And then you're going to be alone again, David. Alone and vulnerable."

A chill spread over David's skin. "What's that supposed to mean?"

"Just what I said. It means you'll be alone. I hope you have an alarm system installed. I'd hate to think what could happen to you, alone in that house."

David swallowed, determined to keep his voice steady. "Are you threatening me?"

"I'm just saying you can't be too safe, you know? There are a lot of bad people in the world, David. I'd hate to think one of them might find you, all alone in your cute little house. You might want to consider some sort of protection. I bought a gun last week because I wanted to be certain I could protect myself."

David curled his fingers in the sheets, making a tight fist, trying to think what to say, what to do. Finally it came to him.

"Trevor, you should know this call is being recorded, as will any future calls you make. And I've saved all the texts too."

The next pause sizzled with tension. David heard a soft click when the call disconnected.

His phone fell from nerveless fingers and he covered his face with his hands. Shaking, he didn't know what to do or who to call. It was only six forty-five, too early to call any of his friends. Too early to call Jackson, which was what he wanted to do. Was Trevor right? *No guy who looks like that one is going to hang around, not for long.* The words echoed in his head, and it felt like a fist closed around his heart, squeezing all the blood out of it. Suddenly unable to sit still, David threw back the sheets and blankets and got out of bed.

Trevor's words tried to insinuate themselves into his mind, but David wouldn't allow it. He wasn't the same man who had tolerated years of verbal and emotional toll on his ego. He'd never considered himself abused, but looking back on it, he could see he might have been wrong. Karen had said it and Michael had been saying it for years. Well, despite Trevor's veiled threats, David wasn't going to let him win, not this time.

He dressed carefully, wearing black jeans and a paisley print shirt in pink and green. It was almost like having a new wardrobe, getting reacquainted with the clothes Trevor hated. David looked in the mirror and he remembered what he'd loved about the shirt. The pale pink flattered his skin and his hair, and the hint of green in the paisley print brought out the sea-foam color of his eyes. Of course, right then he was pale as death and his eyes were so wide, a slender ring of white showed all around the iris. He pinched his cheeks hard to bring color up into them, then went into his room and methodically made the bed. He put on a pot of coffee and set a box of donuts he'd bought the night before on the counter. Several of the guys would be working in his house that day, and he wanted them to feel welcome. He used a dust mop on the hardwood floors until they gleamed and dusted the furniture and the built-ins, moving quickly, efficiently. But still his mind echoed with the words. *I hope you have an alarm system installed. I'd hate to think what could happen to you, alone in that house.*

At eight o'clock, when everything was done and David still felt like the frayed end of a live electrical cord, he called Karen Ridgeway's private number. She answered on the second ring, sounding as if she'd been up for hours.

"Karen, this is David Snyder."

"Well, good morning, David. What's up?"

He told her. He tried to remember the conversation verbatim, even though he was sure he missed things. But it was important, he knew that. When he got to the part about Trevor having bought a gun, she cut him off.

"This is what I want you to do. Sit down right now, while the conversation is fresh in your mind, and write it down. Either e-mail it to me or bring it to me first thing Monday, and I'll get it expedited so that the restraining order goes into effect as quickly as humanly possible. And call a security company and have an alarm installed today. This guy is going off the rails, and you don't want to be in the line of fire when he does."

"You think he means it?"

"I'm aware of too many murder victims who never thought their partner would actually go through with their threats. I think you have to treat this like he will." She paused. "It would be good if you weren't there alone right now. Maybe ask a friend to stay with you. This is a serious situation, David. Please treat it like one."

David felt sick to his stomach. "Okay, I will."

"And I'll look for that e-mail."

"I'll get it to you."

When she hung up, David sat for a minute, staring at the phone in his hand. Then he got up, retrieved his laptop from the office, and went to the living room. He sat on the couch, opened the computer, and pulled up a Word document. And stared at the blank screen, his mind whirling.

I'm aware of too many murder victims who never thought their partner would actually go through with their threats. I think you have to treat this like he will.

David didn't want to believe Trevor would hurt him, but what did he know about it? Unbidden, a memory of the pictures of Manny in the paper came back to him, his face a patchwork of scars and his eyes haunted. Manny probably hadn't believed George Wilkerson would beat him half to death either.

David stared at the blank page. Could he bring it back well enough to write it all down? He began to type, covering the basics, and was so engrossed in what he was doing that when the doorbell rang, he jerked back, his hand lifting to the place now throbbing in his throat. Broad shoulders and dark hair showed through the small windows in the door, and for a moment he stiffened. But he should have known better; when he jumped up and yanked the door open, Jackson stood there, his hands in his back pockets as he waited. He started to smile but must have seen something in David's face. He reached out, catching David's arm.

"What's wrong?"

David searched the street as he pulled Jackson inside, closing the door behind him. He stared into the pale eyes, trying to stay against the door, trying to firm his spine. But the obvious concern on Jackson's face pulled him in, and the next thing he knew, he'd wrapped his arms around Jackson's neck and stood there, trembling in his embrace.

"David, talk to me." One of Jackson's big hands lifted to the back of his head. "What's happened?"

David took a deep breath. "My phone rang at six thirty."

"And?"

David didn't know if he could repeat it all without babbling. He took a step back and gestured. "I called Karen. She told me to write it all down."

Jackson's searching gaze was still on his face. "Can I read it?"

"Please. I'd rather you did than have to repeat it all again out loud."

Jackson's brow furrowed, but he walked over to the couch, giving David one last concerned look before sitting and leaning over the keyboard.

"Do you want some coffee?"

Jackson nodded, his gaze moving over the screen.

David went into the kitchen and poured cups of coffee, doctoring his heavily with cream and sugar, leaving Jackson's black the way he said he liked it. He returned just as Jackson sat back on the couch, jaw set, eyes distant but hard. When David handed him his coffee, he took it but set it down immediately on the coffee table, standing.

"Jackson?"

"I'll be right back. I'm just going out to the truck."

David followed him, then stood in the open doorway as Jackson strode purposefully down the steps. He bent over the toolbox in the bed of his pickup, then came back with what looked like a small black lunch pail in his hands. David had no idea what it could be.

Jackson sat on the couch and patted the cushion beside him, then placed the box between them. He pulled his keys out of his pocket and fitted one in the small lock on the box's handle.

When he opened the lid, David recoiled. Inside, resting in a black foam space tooled specifically for that purpose, was a gun.

"Jackson!" he gasped. "What...."

"I bought it to keep in the truck when it was vandalized. The police suggested it actually. They told me if someone was willing to take a baseball bat to my truck, I should be prepared for them to take one to my head. Have you ever fired a gun?"

David put his coffee, which had begun to slosh alarmingly against the sides of the mug due to his trembling, on the coffee table and wrapped his arms tight across his chest, tucking his hands under his arms. "No, I've never even held one. And I don't want to start now."

"I understand," Jackson said, and if his expression was anything to go by, he did. "I didn't either. But you've been threatened, David. Pretty blatantly. I think you have to take steps to defend yourself."

"I'm calling an alarm company this morning."

"That's good, but I still think you need the gun too."

"Jackson, I don't even know how to fire it. Plus I don't think I could point it at anyone, knowing I couldn't pull the trigger."

"Okay." Jackson studied him calmly. "I want you to remember how you felt this morning when Trevor told you he'd purchased a gun, and the inference he was making."

David doubted he'd ever forget it. Just recalling it made his stomach cramp. He looked at the gun in the box. It wasn't big, but even lying there it looked lethal.

"If he somehow got in here without being invited, wouldn't it make you feel better to know you had backup?"

David hated how readily his mind went to *yes*. Still, he hesitated.

"Please, David," Jackson said softly, reaching over and taking David's hand. He looked deeply into his eyes. "I can't be here all of the time, not with what's going on with my mom. But every time I leave you, I'm going to worry. Let me leave the gun here, please."

David stared down at it, the gun a deadly blue-black against the dark gray egg crate foam. "What about you?" he asked faintly. Much as he hated to admit it, he would feel safer with the gun in the house, could even imagine picking it up in his hand. Something he never would have imagined before that day.

"My dad had a small arsenal and I kept some of it." Jackson's lips twisted wryly. "I'm covered at home, and I can put one of his pistols in the truck."

David took and released a deep breath. "You'll show me how to hold it?"

"I'll take you to the range and teach you how to shoot it."

149

Just the idea made David's palms sweat and he wiped them on his jeans, but he finally nodded. "Okay." He looked into Jackson's eyes again. "I really hate this."

"I know, baby."

The endearment warmed David even as Jackson slipped his big hand around his nape and pulled him in for a quick kiss. Out front the sound of car doors slamming echoed on the clear morning air. Jackson stood and went to the front window.

"It's Vern and Gil." He crossed back to David and scooped up the box. "I'll take this to the bedroom."

He moved quickly through the dining room, disappearing into the hall beyond. David felt odd, like people would know just by looking at him he had a weapon in the house. Which was patently absurd. He saved his document and shut the laptop as the doorbell rang.

"Good morning!" he said, forcing a bright smile as he opened the door. "Coffee and donuts in the kitchen."

Gil smiled at him as he passed. "Thanks, David."

"Morning, sweet cheeks." Vernon winked at him as he followed Gil, and David's smile felt less forced.

When Jackson joined them in the kitchen a few minutes later, his mug of coffee in his hand, Vern arched a steel-gray brow.

"Where've you been? The bedroom?" He wiggled both brows comically and David laughed. It was almost not forced at all.

"The john," Jackson answered, scowling at him.

"With your coffee?"

"I detoured back through the living room to get it." Jackson looked at the older man in exasperation. "What do you care, Vernon?"

"Oh, I don't know." Vern leaned over, studying the donuts in the box before selecting a maple bar. "Just trying to keep tabs on you love birds, that's all, Jackson." He took a huge bite of donut and grinned around it, and Jackson gave David a warm look.

By the time half the donuts were gone and Manny arrived, David no longer felt ragged around the edges at all.

CHAPTER FOURTEEN

DAVID SPENT time getting his home files squared away and his desk cleaned off in his office so nothing would be in Gil and Vern's way when they were ready to start in there. They were finishing up trim in the main bathroom and would be moving on to the walls in the office next. He took his laptop and sat at his desk long enough to send the document to Karen, then locked the computer away in his desk and vowed not to think about Trevor's phone call again.

Between the guys working in the bathroom and the others on the roof, it was pretty noisy inside of the house. By one o'clock, David decided he had to get out for a while, and making a run to keep the men fed was the least he could do. He decided to take lunch orders and grabbed his iPad.

He asked Gil and Vernon, who were finishing up the off-white trim in the bathroom, what they wanted from Subway, then headed out his front door. Jackson and Manny were standing in the front yard near the sidewalk. Jackson heard him coming, and the smile he gave David took the chill off the day.

"Hey, I was just going to come find you."

David gave him what he hoped was a flirtatious smile in return "And here I am."

Jackson slipped his arm around David's waist, his hand spreading on his lower back, and even the innocent touch made David feel heady.

"Manny finished scoping the pipe. Good news: nothing's broken."

"Oh, thank God. Manny, I'll name my firstborn after you."

Manny sent him a shy smile from beneath the brim of his baseball cap.

Jackson gave him a wry smirk. "Planning on having a firstborn, are you?"

"Well, not vaginally."

Both men laughed. After a moment, Manny spoke. It was the first time David had heard his voice. "You do have a slight blockage in your pipe out here," he offered softly, gesturing toward the curb. "I can use the snake and get rid of it for you, if you'd like."

David tamped down the giggle that was threatening. After the morning he'd had, his emotions were all over the place. "There are so many things my inner twelve-year-old would like to say in response to that," he finally managed, "but I think I'll leave it at 'I will appreciate being able to shower in my own home very much. Thank you.'"

Jackson gave him an amused look and Manny's cheeks turned pink. "Stop using sexual innuendo to harass my friends," Jackson muttered, but David could see he wanted to laugh.

"Killjoy," Manny tossed to Jackson, then walked away with an exaggerated swish to his hips. Jackson and David looked at each other before bursting into laughter. Jackson leaned forward, near David's ear, while David was still giggling.

"I haven't seen him joke around like that in months."

"I'm glad he's doing better." He put his hand on Jackson's chest. "I came out here to get your lunch order."

"Can I have whatever I want?" Jackson's voice was low. "I like this, by the way." He ran his finger down the front of David's pink paisley button-down. "I'd like it better off you, but I like it."

The expression on his face made David's breath catch and sent a surge of heat south of his belt buckle. "You're a vicious tease, you know that, right?"

Jackson hooked his finger between two of the buttons on David's shirt and pulled him closer. "Baby, I'm not teasing. The minute I can figure out a way to be gone all evening, you and I are going on a proper date. With a proper date conclusion."

David licked his lips when the tip of Jackson's finger brushed his stomach and it quivered in response. "Oh, planning to kiss me good night on the front porch?"

Jackson's full lips pulled into a very sexy smirk. "Among other things."

"You two do realize you're standing in the middle of the front yard in broad daylight, right?"

David looked around, surprised to find Michael standing about four yards away. When had he gotten there?

"Yeah, I pulled up, got out of the car, and have been standing here, and you didn't even notice."

Jackson looked at him over David's shoulder. "Hello, Michael."

"Jackson." He approached over the dry grass, looking past them. "David, were you aware there are men on your roof?"

"Yes, I'd noticed." He took a regretful step back from Jackson's body heat. "They're fixing the leak over the service porch."

"Ah." Michael glanced toward the curb, his expression brightening. "Is that Gil's truck?"

"He and Vernon are finishing up the bathroom. Would you like to go in and say hello?" David teased. Michael flipped him off, and Jackson patted David just above his ass before walking away. David caught one of his belt loops, stopping him. "Jackson, wait. I did come out here for something, before I... well...."

"Lost your mind and decided to grope your boyfriend in the front yard?" Michael supplied dryly. David caught the impish gleam in Michael's eyes.

"Oh, shut up," David muttered at him.

"He wasn't groping me." Jackson grinned even as David's face heated. "I'd have noticed."

David rolled his eyes. "I came out here to find out what you and Manny wanted for lunch. I'm making a Subway run."

Manny shook his head. "You don't have to feed me, David. You did donuts."

"And you didn't have to snake out my plumbing on a Saturday afternoon either." Michael opened his mouth and David gave him a dark look. "Do not even go there."

Michael snapped his mouth shut, but his gray eyes were sparkling.

"Manny, I'm buying. You've got to eat. What do you want?"

Jackson nudged Manny. "Just let him buy. Then I won't have to hear about it later."

David raised a brow at him, but Jackson didn't look remotely intimidated. "A meatball sub with provolone on italian bread," Manny said finally. "And thank you."

"My pleasure." David typed it in. "And to drink?"

"Coke would be great."

"Okay. Jackson?"

"Actually I'll go with the same."

Michael shook his head. "How do you all keep those bodies if you eat like that?"

"Manual labor." David gave him a look as he walked around the side of the house. "You should try it sometime."

"And you should try not being a bitch," Michael shot after him, and David heard Jackson laugh.

"I will so fire you—"

"Stop saying it," Michael interrupted. "No one believes you anymore."

Michael was grinning as he followed David down the driveway. When David had everyone's order, he started for his car.

"Want to come with?" he asked Michael.

"Sure."

David tossed the tablet to Michael as he started the engine.

"How the hell do you get anything done around there?" Michael asked, fastening his seat belt.

"What do you mean?" David adjusted his mirrors as he put the Yaris into gear.

"The new ones? The roof guys? They're hot as hell. Where did they come from?"

"They're friends of Jackson's." David gave the man in question a small wave as they backed out of the driveway, and Jackson smiled in response. One of his slow smiles, the ones that dimpled his cheeks and went all the way to his eyes.

"Oh, dear God," Michael groaned. "That smile is lethal."

"Ain't it just?" David drove off down the street. "In answer to your question, Jackson is acting as general contractor for everything because I have no idea who to hire."

"Are they gay?"

"The roof guys?"

Michael nodded.

David shrugged. "No clue. I get the feeling they're batting for our team, though. It sounds like the guys toss each other jobs whenever they can. The construction industry here isn't exactly gay friendly."

"Hmm." Michael's lips twisted. "Big surprise there." He studied the tablet. "You know, it would be cheaper and easier to buy all of this soda pop at the grocery store than it would be to try to carry trays of drinks back."

"You're right. We'll make a stop."

"By the way, have you heard from the demon spawn yet?"

All of the lightness that had worked its way into the day faded. "As a matter of fact…."

David told Michael about the phone call. By the time he was done, Michael's fingers were white knuckled around the tablet.

"Jesus, David, the man is nuts. At least you aren't letting him get away with it."

"You know, I might have," David admitted softly. "If it hadn't been for Jackson, I very well might have."

"What do you mean?" Michael frowned. "Why is it different because you met Jackson?" David could feel Michael's inquisitive stare.

David hesitated before he answered, another habit he'd picked up from Jackson. He thought before he spoke now, which was very much a departure from how he'd been before. "I don't want him to think I'm weak," he finally admitted. "And if I'd let Trevor walk all over me, it would be weak."

He glanced at Michael and saw his satisfied expression. "Well, bravo Jackson, then. You deserve better, and Jackson certainly is better. And if you need someone to stay at the house with you until this mess with the dickwad is sorted out, I'd be happy to."

David reached across and squeezed Michael's hand. "Thank you."

Michael returned the pressure. "Of course."

They decided to go to the grocery store first, and when they pushed the cart loaded with soda and beer to the front end, the checker was wearing whiteface, a big red rubber nose, and a rainbow-hued fuzzy wig.

"What the hell?" David muttered. Michael laughed.

"It's Halloween, David. Didn't you see the little kids dressed up as superheroes in the parking lot?"

"I see kids dressed up every once in a while," David responded. "I didn't make the connection."

"So, the pumpkins and the cobwebs and ghosts all over the houses on your block didn't make an impression?"

155

"We never paid any attention to Halloween at the condo." A little girl skipped by in a princess outfit complete with tiara, and David smiled. "We'd better pick up some candy while we're here."

Michael ran back and got three giant bags of assorted candy bars.

"You live in the burbs now, buddy," Michael replied to David's horrified expression. "You'd better have enough candy so they don't smash a pumpkin on your porch. And you need good candy, not that hard syrup crap."

"I'll take your word for it." David added the candy to the drinks on the conveyor belt.

They went to Subway next, and the scent of the meatballs and marinara almost made David resent his turkey on whole grain. Almost. He'd never work it off doing his job, and a potbelly would not be cute. Since he hoped someone would be seeing him naked soon, the turkey was sounding better and better.

Michael was quiet after they left the grocery store, but David could see he was preoccupied. At one point he glanced over to see his friend chewing his lower lip, staring into the distance.

"Okay, spill it."

Michael blinked "What?"

"You've got something on your mind. What is it?"

Michael pursed his lips. "The other day, when Gil lost that job in the valley, it was because he's gay, wasn't it?"

"Of course no one would say so, but they think that was the reason, yes."

"So, if all of those guys are gay, and the opportunity for gays in other construction companies isn't so great here, why don't they band together and start their own company?"

David frowned. "I don't know, Michael. Some of the problem is with the major contractors not wanting to hire them. But Gil lost that job from a private client. I doubt they'd want to band together and make themselves an even bigger target."

Michael shrugged. "It was just a thought."

One that would return to David several times over the afternoon.

THE WORK Gil and Vernon had done in his bathroom was beautiful. The woodwork and the wainscoting gleamed a glossy off-white, and the

David, Renewed

wall from the shining chair rail to the ceiling was now a soft, dusky blue that matched the tile on the floor. David had been convinced he'd need to replace the ugly flooring, which would have necessitated tearing out the pedestal sink and the claw-foot tub. Now that the paint was finished, the blue hexagon tiles on the floor looked perfect. There wasn't a drip or a mark of paint anywhere, and David studied the finished product carefully. The crews he hired to do the painting for the firm were good, but not this good. He wandered to the office doorway and watched as Gil and Vernon carefully covered the hardwood floors, taping down a tarp around the edges, protecting the floorboards and furniture with more plastic. Gil looked up and noticed him.

"Hey, David. Is everything okay?"

"Oh, yes, it's fine." David smiled. "The bathroom looks beautiful."

Gil grinned, and David spotted a speck of paint on his chin. "We aim to please." He winked, then opened the can of paint on the floor. David had picked a soft, mossy green for the walls, but Gil talked him into a darker, richer color. Now the paint was sitting there against the floorboards, David could see Gil was right; it did work better with the woodwork and the old frosted-glass ceiling fixture.

"That's going to be perfect." David gestured to the paint Vernon was pouring. "You were right."

"I knew you'd like it better when we got right down to it."

"Yeah, and he's so fucking modest about it." Vern cleaned the side of the can with an angled brush, then pressed the lid back in place.

"Hey, there's nothing wrong with knowing you're good at something," Gil said mildly.

"Yeah, yeah, Mary. Get over here and pick up a roller before I prove how little work you actually do." Vernon picked up a smaller container of the dark green paint and began to cut in expertly around the doorframe.

"Isn't he sweet?" Gil took a new roller out of a sleeve of plastic. "I keep him around because I figure you've got to be nice to old people, you know?"

Without missing a beat, Vernon flipped him off along the back of the paintbrush, and David grinned. As he wandered toward the front of the house, he was thinking about what Michael had suggested, and the quality of

157

the work Gil and Vern did. The crews he hired for the firm did mass projects with spray guns and hundreds of gallons of paint. Gil was an artist, expertly finishing each wall, not a drop of paint ending up where it shouldn't. Except for on his chin. They really should be working with an interior decorator, getting paid what they deserved.

Dusk was streaking the sky in shades of pale orange and cotton candy pink, and it was downright cold by the time most of the guys left. Manny and the roofers were finished and gone, and Vern and Gil bid David good-bye, grabbing candy bars out of the giant ceramic bowl he'd set next to the door. Michael had settled in on the couch, announcing he was going to help hand out candy and stay the night, when Jackson opened the front door. He acknowledged Michael, and then held out his hand to David.

"Can I show you something?"

"Oh, I'm sure…," Michael started.

"Do remember who you work for," David interrupted, and Michael rolled his eyes.

"Bitch, please."

David shot him a stern look as Jackson pulled him out through the front door.

He linked their fingers as he led David down the steps, and then paused near the side of the house where the shadows were deep and cool. He stopped so quickly David almost collided with his back. He turned around and took David's biceps in his hands.

"I liked that, earlier."

David studied his face in the dying light. "What?"

"When Michael said I was your boyfriend. So, we're there, right?"

He seemed almost wary, as if he was afraid David felt something different, wanted something different than he did. David cupped Jackson's hard jaw. His chin felt rough against the skin of his palm. "Yeah, we're there."

Jackson's full lips curved in that devastating smile, the one that went all the way to his eyes, and he curved his arm around David's waist. "God, I feel like I'm in high school."

"I didn't know anyone who looked like you in high school. And even if I had, they wouldn't have noticed me. I was a terrible band geek. I'll bet you weren't."

"No, I wasn't in band." Jackson's thumb moved against his back and sent a shiver up David's spine.

"So, what did you do?"

Jackson looked sheepish. "I was a shop geek. Between wood shop and metal shop, I rarely left the vocational building."

"They didn't have an interiors class when I was in high school. Hence, band."

"What did you play?"

David sighed, dropping his forehead onto Jackson's shoulder.

"Come on, David. What did you play?"

"The flute," David finally answered, his voice muffled. "Go ahead. Laugh."

"Does it sound like I'm laughing?"

It didn't. David raised his head and angled it, studying Jackson's expression. He was smiling but there wasn't any ridicule in it.

"I think it's cool."

"You are seriously the first gay man I've ever met who didn't have something snarky or filthy to say about the fact I played the flute."

Jackson appeared to think about it for a moment, then shook his head. "Nah, too easy."

David laughed softly and Jackson pulled him closer. Wrapping his arms around the strong neck, David leaned into Jackson's body.

"So Michael is staying with you tonight?"

"He said he'd stay as much as I needed him to."

"He's a good friend."

"He is."

"I wish it was me." Jackson pulled him even tighter. "I wish I could stay with you."

David sighed. "Me too."

Jackson slid his hand down David's back, letting it come to rest on his ass. He gripped David's asscheek and pressed his groin forward. David felt the hardness pressed into him and his cock began to fill.

"This is really unfair, you know, when you're going to get in your truck and leave."

"If I wasn't pretty sure some little kid dressed as Iron Man and his nice soccer mom was about to walk along the sidewalk, I'd drop to my knees and blow you right here."

David's breath stalled, and he was about to lose his composure all together and beg Jackson to do just that when, as if he'd conjured it with his words, a child's laughter carried to them on the chill breeze. David groaned and Jackson squeezed him before letting go. He brought their lips together in a sweet and disappointingly brief kiss.

"I'll call you after I get Mom squared away for the night, okay?"

"Okay." David hesitated. "Is it really stupid to say I'll miss you?"

Jackson favored him with another sweet smile. "Not when I'm going to be missing you too."

Their shoulders bumped and fingers linked as Jackson walked him up the porch steps to the door. David opened it and Jackson leaned in far enough to bid Michael good night, kissed David quickly, then made his way down the steps. David enjoyed the view of the square shoulders and narrow hips.

"You're watching his ass, aren't you?"

David sent Michael an exasperated look before closing the door, and his friend looked pointedly at David's groin, one of his brows arching above the dark frames of his glasses.

"Oh, you're vile," David huffed, adjusting himself. Michael gave him a cheeky grin.

It was less than ten minutes later when the doorbell rang and the first of a parade of trick-or-treaters made the pilgrimage to his front door. There were grade school kids dressed as zombies and even high school kids dressed in camo and wearing white sheets with holes cut out for the eyes. There was one teenage girl wearing a T-shirt that read, "This is my costume. Now give me the damned candy." Michael laughed at it when he answered the door, and the flirtatious grins she shot him made David smirk.

"I thought she was going to give you her number," he teased when Michael closed the door.

Michael shuddered. "God save me from teenage girls. I didn't know what to do with them when I was a teenager. You're up."

The doorbell pealed again, and David pushed up from the couch. This time it was his turn to laugh.

His neighbor Jordyn held her baby, who was dressed as a football player in Seattle Seahawk blue and chartreuse green, a large three on the jersey. Boots stood on a leash beside her, his little butt wiggling. He was wearing a taupe-colored fuzzy sheath from his neck to just above his tail, with wide white lacings in the center of his back. Clearly he was the football. He looked up at David, doggy grin in place.

"Okay, you win best costume."

The baby held out a pumpkin bucket in his tiny fist, and David smiled at him as he dropped in three candy bars. "One for Mom, one for Dad, and one for you." He looked down at the little dog. "Sorry, boy. I'm going to have to stock up on biscuits for your next visit."

Michael had come up next to him and dropped to one knee with a giggle, scratching Boots behind one bat-shaped ear. "Oh God, I think I'm in love."

"Bootsy, meet Michael. Michael, this is Bootsy and his owner, Jordyn." He gestured to the baby. "And this is clearly Russell Wilson."

"Actually his name is Colin. And I'm surprised you know football players."

"I'm gay, I don't live in a cave."

Jordyn chuckled but it faded quickly, and David noticed she looked harried.

"Are you okay?"

"Yeah, I'm fine." She spoke quickly, then sighed and shook her head. "Just rushed. We got news that Paul's grandmother died this afternoon."

"Oh, I'm sorry."

She dropped the leash as Michael continued to pet the dog, and pushed some wayward dark hair behind her ear. For his part, Boots had apparently decided Michael was his new best friend and nudged his hand every time he looked like he was going to stop petting him. "She's been sick for a while, but they didn't expect it this soon. His family is all in Michigan, so we have to fly. Paul is making reservations and I should be packing. It's just, this is his first Halloween and I didn't want him to miss it…."

"I understand." David smiled at the baby who was studying him with disarming seriousness again, and this time his little bow-shaped mouth pulled up at one corner. He gave David a gummy smile.

"We can't get out before nine, but we have to get ready and drop Bootsy at the kennel on our way to the airport." She made a face. "It's in his vet's office, and I hate to take him there, but we can't leave him at home."

David shook his head. "Jordyn, don't take him there. I'll watch him for you."

"Oh, David, thank you, but…." She looked down at the dog, who had rolled to his back and was leaning into Michael's hand as he rubbed his head. "Really?"

"Absolutely."

"We'll only be gone until Tuesday, but I don't want to put you out."

"Jordyn, it won't be putting me out. Boots and I are buddies. It'll be fine."

Her eyes lit up for the first time since David had opened the door. "Really? I mean, he's really good. I leave him in the house for hours sometimes, and he doesn't bother a thing. And he likes to take walks, but it isn't really necessary. He eats in the morning and the evening, but I can bring you his bowls and food and everything. Oh, David, are you sure?"

"I'm positive. I grew up with dogs. Besides, I've been thinking about getting one, so this is perfect timing. It can remind me what goes into it before I lose my mind and go buy a corgi puppy."

She smiled. "He isn't going to help with that."

"Yeah, I sort of figured. Go do what you need to do. We'll be here."

Jordyn looked at Michael as he stood, her cheeks turning a pretty pink. "I'm sorry. You're Michael?"

She offered her hand and Michael shook it, sending David a bemused look.

"Are you and David dating, or…?"

Michael shuddered. "Good God, no. We're just friends. The one he's dating is the hunk with the silver pickup truck."

"Michael," David scolded.

"What? It's the truth." Michael grabbed a Snickers from the bowl in David's hand and went back to the couch.

Jordyn's sloped brows arched. "The one with the dark hair and the chiseled chin?" David nodded, feeling his cheeks turn pink. She gave him a sassy grin. "Nice job, David." She leaned around the doorframe and looked at Michael. "Oh, and you're very handsome too. In fact there's been nothing but good-looking guys around here all day today. The scenery was lovely while I pulled weeds. Okay, I need to get going, but we'll drop this guy off in an hour or so."

She gave David a relieved smile and made her way down the steps.

"I like her." Michael bit into his candy bar.

"Of course you do." David closed the door. "She told you you're handsome."

"Well, I am," Michael replied without a trace of arrogance. "It's still nice to hear it every once in a while." He crossed his long legs and licked chocolate off his fingers, and David answered the door when the bell chimed again.

CHAPTER FIFTEEN

THE STREAM of costumed children waned by eight thirty. Jordyn and a haggard-looking Paul brought Bootsy by, along with a reusable shopping bag full of his food, bowls, biscuits, a medium-sized plush bed, and even a stuffed toy shaped like a hedgehog. Jordyn said it was his "baby," and Boots certainly seemed attached to it. When Michael offered it to him, he took it in his mouth, lay down by the couch, and propped his chin on it, bright eyes surveying the room.

"Oh God." Michael scratched his ruff. "This animal is going to make me want a dog, and it's not allowed in my lease."

David sat next to Boots on the floor and started to pet his head. He looked up at David in adoration, and David smiled. "So move."

"I plan to when the lease is up."

"Oh, yeah?" David leaned back on his hands. "Where do you want to go?"

"Up here, actually. I'd love to find a little house to rent."

"I'll keep my eyes open."

David's cell phone buzzed in his back pocket, and he lifted onto one hip to retrieve it. He saw the number and answered with a smile. "Hey. Is your mom already in bed?"

"Actually she's sitting right here and Evelyn is giving candy to a bunch of miniature zombies."

David chuckled. "Yeah, zombies are big this year."

"I have a feeling zombies are big most years. Hang on a second." Jackson murmured something, a door closed, and then there was a short pause before he spoke again. "Okay, now I can hear you. What do you have planned for tonight?"

David glanced at his houseguests, who were clearly enjoying one another's company. Michael was petting Boots and the little dog was luxuriating in the attention. "Michael and I were going to order Chinese, I think. Why?"

"Do you think Michael would mind if I stole you?"

Even as delight filled him, David was confused. "Jackson, what's going on?"

"Well, I kept thinking about our discussion this afternoon, about a real date. Mom's been doing so much better, and Evelyn offered to stay with her whenever I needed her. So... I asked, she's staying, and I'm taking you on a date."

David's heart rate sped up. "Seriously?"

"Very seriously. Evelyn is going to stay until tomorrow morning."

"You're going to spend the night, then?"

"I realize that I'm inviting myself, but I sure hope so."

David was so excited he felt a little light-headed, but he hesitated. "Can you hold on for a second?"

"Sure."

David covered the speaker and looked at Michael. "Do you mind if I—?"

"Oh, for God's sakes, don't be stupid." Michael grinned at him. "Boots and I will hang out, eat the rest of the candy bars, and then I'll go home."

"I'll buy your dinner."

"The fuck." Michael shook his head. "I can buy my own. That way I don't have to eat any shitty kung pao chicken."

"You're sure?"

Michael looked at him in exasperation. "David, tell the man yes already. If you don't go, I'll just have to watch you pout all evening."

David wanted to protest, except he knew it was more than likely the truth. He removed his hand. "Mr. Henry, I'd love to go."

"Excellent." He could hear the smile in Jackson's voice. "I'll pick you up in about half an hour. Is that enough time?"

"That should be fine."

"And David?"

"Yeah?"

"Wear something sexy."

David was still giggling when he hung up, then slapped his hand over his mouth. "Tell me I wasn't giggling."

"You weren't giggling." Michael smirked at him.

"Oh my God, you liar."

"Hey, you told me to tell you that you weren't giggling. Never let it be said I'm not a supportive friend."

"I've got to shower." David pushed up from the floor.

"Yeah." Michael leaned back, his hands behind his head and a wry grin on his face. "You'll want to get really, thoroughly clean. Everywhere. If you get my drift."

David felt his face flame. "Oh, be quiet, you perv!"

Michael's laugh followed him into the bathroom.

WHEN DAVID emerged from his bedroom, Jackson was crouched near the door rubbing Boots's stomach, and the little dog was wiggling with joy. He and Michael looked up when David came into the room and Jackson's hand stilled in the white fur, his gaze slowly moving over David from his feet to his head.

David was so nervous his skin felt electrified, but he managed to stand still under Jackson's intense gaze. When Jackson said "wear something sexy," David threw caution to the wind and dove into his old wardrobe. He had on tight black skinny jeans, an untucked bright green button-down with a gray pinstripe, and a gray V-neck sweater over that. Over all of it was looped a large mint-green-and-white scarf, and on his feet he wore zip-up half boots with a slight heel. His hair had taken longer than picking out the clothes, and he'd gone for messy, but not too messy. He knew he looked very thin and hoped he'd achieved more hip than overdressed nerd.

Jackson stood up, and the appreciation on his face was unmistakable. "Wow. You look great."

Michael leaned back against the sofa cushions with his hands behind his head. He gave David a slow, approving smile.

"Thanks. So do you."

And Jackson did. He had on well-worn jeans, but they were spotless. His button-down shirt was black, and the black suede jacket over it looked like it would be soft to the touch. It accented his broad shoulders and clung to his musculature in all the right places. But what David noticed the most was that his stubble was gone. His square chin and upper lip were without their usual shadow, and his thick, dark brown hair was neat but slightly rumpled, as if he'd run his fingers through it. David wanted to run his fingers through it too.

Boots wasn't fond of being ignored, and he butted Jackson's calf with his head. Jackson looked down with a grin. "Michael told me you have a houseguest."

"A pretty pushy one too, apparently. Or I have a rival for your affections."

Jackson looked at David with a sly little grin. "He's cute, but not really my type. You ready to go?"

David got a black wool peacoat out of the closet and let Jackson slip it over his shoulders. He looked over at Michael. "I'll see you later."

"Yep. And while you're gone, I'm going to eat all your food and order porn on pay-per-view." David sent him a withering look and preceded Jackson out the door. "You kids have fun," Michael called after them. "Make good choices." His cackle followed them out into the night.

Jackson chuckled as he closed the door behind them. "He's in a good mood."

"Too much chocolate," David replied. "And he's a lunatic."

Jackson's teeth flashed in the porch light. When he reached for David's hand and linked their fingers, David leaned into his shoulder.

"So, where are we going?"

"Well, I thought we'd take in a movie first and then go to a late dinner. How does that sound?"

"Perfect." Actually David didn't care where they went. He was just glad to be in Jackson's company. He stepped closer to Jackson, and Jackson released David's hand and slipped his arm around his shoulders. The solid heat of him felt good.

A soft sound echoed from behind them on the dark driveway, like the step of a foot on concrete, and David stiffened. The hair on the back of his neck twitched, and Jackson stopped at his side.

"What's the matter?" Jackson frowned. David peered into the dark shadows near the back of his house. Had something moved there? He couldn't be sure, and he stepped closer to Jackson. "David?"

"I'm probably jumping at shadows," David murmured. "But ever since the night Trevor followed me, then sat out in his car watching me, I keep thinking I'm hearing and seeing things."

"Do you want me to check?"

"No." It came out more emphatically than he meant for it to, but he really didn't want Jackson walking off into the shadows by himself. "Let's go have a good time. I'm sure I'm imagining it."

Jackson didn't look convinced, but when David curled his hand around his arm and headed for the car in the driveway, he allowed himself to be pulled along.

CHAPTER SIXTEEN

DAVID FORGOT the noise in the shadows when he saw a sleek black Mercedes parked in the driveway. "Wow. Is that yours?"

"Mom's." Jackson pressed the fob on the keys and the lights flashed briefly. "Actually it was Dad's. It's about the only thing she still has that was his."

David admired the car as he walked around to the passenger door and got in. Spotless black leather upholstery covered the seats and exotic wood trim broke up the sleek leather lines. The dash surrounding the driver's seat had so many dials and buttons, it looked like something out of a fighter jet.

"This is really beautiful." David fastened his seat belt, then ran his hand appreciatively over the soft leather inserts on his door.

"I thought it would be nicer for a date than the pickup."

"I like the pickup." David looked over at Jackson in time to catch the smile sent in his direction.

"I do too. But this is easier to park."

When Jackson started the car, the lights illuminated the driveway, chasing away the shadows, and David sat back with a silent sigh of relief when he saw nothing out of the ordinary.

He glanced at Jackson. "Did your dad like expensive cars?"

Jackson's lips twisted. "My dad liked expensive everything. He made a lot of money, and he liked to spend it. When I was growing up, my folks lived down on Mill Wood just off of Northwest."

David's brows shot up. The area Jackson described was an exclusive neighborhood closer to downtown known as Knoll Ridge. It was the fairly exclusive domain of cardiologists and neurosurgeons. And lawyers.

"In a six-bedroom house full of expensive stuff my mother didn't give a damn about, but he was big on 'keeping up appearances' with the other partners at his firm and their wives. When Dad died we found out the house was mortgaged to the rafters and he was in debt up to his ass. Memberships to exclusive country clubs and a string of mistresses ate up a lot of his income." He sounded bitter, and David couldn't blame him.

"Did your mom know?"

"I think she knew something wasn't right, but it was the only thing Travis and I have ever agreed on. We didn't say anything to her. We paid off his credit cards, including the hotel bills and several thousand dollars' worth of jewelry that didn't go to Mom, then advised her to sell the house because he'd made some lousy investments. She didn't ask a lot of questions; he'd always insisted on managing their money and she trusted him." Jackson's lip curled. "Like he deserved it. We managed to pay this off"—he patted the steering wheel with his thumb—"and I was able to convince her that Travis didn't need another Mercedes and she should keep it, no matter how he bitched about it. By the time we made sure she wasn't stuck with Dad's debts, there wasn't much of monetary value left." He pulled out onto the main boulevard heading toward downtown, looking as at home driving the Mercedes as he did in his truck. "My siblings took what they wanted from the house, and Mom donated the rest to charity. He left her a moderate life insurance policy, so if she's careful she'll be okay. And she never was attached to the old place and all of the stuff the way he was. The house she's living in now belonged to my grandparents, and it looks pretty much the same as it did when they were alive. Except we took out part of the lawn and put in a rose garden out back."

"My mom said it's beautiful."

"She loves it, which is all I care about."

"How is she doing today?"

Jackson's lips relaxed in a smile. "A lot better. I don't know if it's her own determination, or if it's your mom's presence, but she's doing well. I think she could be alone during the day now, except I also think they're having a good time. I came home last night and they were playing poker for blueberries."

David laughed. That sounded like his mom. "Has Shirley been back to see her doctor?"

"Yeah. He pretty much told her to behave herself and not do anything stupid before the stitches come out on Tuesday. I believe the minute they're out, she and Beverley plan to go to the beauty parlor and then out to lunch." David vowed to call his mom the next day. He owed her big time for Jackson being able to finish the work on his house. David smiled when Jackson reached over the console and caught his hand, holding it as he drove. A few minutes later, he pulled the sleek car into an underground parking structure at the downtown mall, home to their local Regal Cinemas.

Later, David wouldn't be able to tell anyone what movie they saw. It was a comedy, but beyond that he wouldn't be able to relate anything about the plot. He laughed, but he was more aware of the Junior Mints Jackson teasingly popped in his mouth, the large Diet Coke they shared, and the feeling of Jackson holding his hand in the darkness of the theater, his thumb moving over David's knuckles in slow, steadily arousing caresses. David was so wrapped up in Jackson, he didn't even notice if anyone around them had a problem with two men holding hands. In the past he'd never been able to ignore the reactions of others, but tonight he didn't even notice there were people around them.

After the movie, Jackson drove a few blocks to a popular Italian restaurant named Luigi's situated in the heart of downtown. It was in one of the original buildings, built just before the turn of the nineteenth century. The old brick facade hid a charming interior with heavy, darkly upholstered banquettes and a gorgeous old bar along the back wall. A huge mirror hung above it, reflecting the dozens of bottles of high-end liquor. David had been there once or twice with his parents, but Trevor didn't like Italian food, so....

They split an antipasto platter heaped with mozzarella, capers, and salami, with a side of crostini and a bottle of Sangiovese. David knew next to nothing about Italian wine; Trevor was the wine expert and wasted no opportunity to tell him he had no palate. He might not, he thought, taking another sip of the excellent red wine, but he knew he liked this. And he vowed to be done thinking about Trevor.

He and Jackson chatted easily over the appetizer, David quietly thrilled when Jackson's booted toes ended up resting against the outside of David's ankle, moving gently against the soft leather of his boot. It was such a small thing, but it was reassuring and a sweet reminder that the handsome man across from him was so much more than just his handyman.

For dinner, David ordered the chicken piccata and Jackson the lasagna, but they ended up having most of it packaged to take home. They walked slowly back to the parked Mercedes, shoulders brushing, laughing softly. David's heart felt lighter than it had in a long time, and any remaining stress from the morning phone call seemed very far away.

The porch light was still on when Jackson pulled into the driveway and parked the car, and they silently climbed out and walked across the lawn hand in hand. There wasn't any reason to talk; they both knew where they were headed. David's heart was racing and he was nervous, but he also wanted Jackson as desperately as he'd ever wanted anything in his life. He unlocked the front door, pushed it open, and jerked back when they were met with a sharp bark. Boots stuck his head around the frame and David laughed, pressing his hand over his heart.

"He scared you?" Jackson pressed his chest to David's back.

"I forgot he was here." David bent to push Boots gently back, keenly aware of Jackson close behind him as he ruffled the fur behind the dog's ears. "Good boy," he praised the little dog. "Go lie down now. Go on."

Boots licked his hand, then trotted over to the fleece-lined bed Jordyn and Paul had dropped off, climbing in and curling around his toy hedgehog. David closed and locked the door, and large hands closed over his shoulders. He was gently turned, his back pressed against the door, and all he could see was Jackson: Jackson's eyes, Jackson's mouth.

"Hi," David managed, breathless.

"Hi." Jackson smiled, a devilish curl of his lips, and placed his hands on the door on either side of David's head. He leaned in, and when Jackson's weight settled against him, David let out a shaky sigh.

David knew Jackson had to be able to feel his heart pounding, and the way his desperate body strained hard against him. He'd been half-erect all evening; the press of Jackson against him finished the job. Jackson rolled his pelvis forward, and David felt hardness corresponding to his against his hip. He slid his hand up Jackson's side under his jacket.

"Is Michael still here?"

David hummed as his fingers spread over Jackson's ribs. He could feel bands of hard muscle over his rib cage.

He shook his head. "No, he said he was leaving about ten."

"Good." Jackson leaned in and nuzzled under David's chin, and the rasp of his barely there stubble sent a shaft of shivering want down David's spine. "Then all we have to worry about is the neighbors."

David chuckled. "Old houses are built solid."

Jackson leaned back, his mouth curved in a slightly lopsided grin. "Are they soundproof?"

David's body hummed at the implication. "I'm not noisy," he said, almost apologetically. "I never have been."

Jackson's smile deepened. "Maybe not before."

Heat flooded his face and he knew that, once again, it was flaming bright red. He touched his hot cheek. "God, I wish I could stop blushing."

Jackson pressed his lips where David's fingers had been. "I love that you blush. I look forward to seeing if it's confined to your face, or if you blush all over."

David shivered. Maybe the restraint of a lifetime would be changed in Jackson's arms. David wanted him so badly he could taste it, and that was certainly new.

Jackson took a step back, taking David's hand and leading the way toward the darkened hallway, and David let himself be led.

"Oh, wait one second," he said when they arrived at the door. David detoured back to the living room to scoop up the nearly forgotten bag holding their meals, then hurried into the kitchen to put them in the refrigerator. He grabbed a couple of dog biscuits from the box on the counter and crouched at the little dog's side to give him the treat. "You're a good boy," he murmured.

Boots began to chew on a hard biscuit, crunching happily.

Jackson eyed David indulgently when he straightened. "You're going to spoil him."

"I don't care. He's only here until Tuesday. I doubt I can do much damage." He grabbed Jackson's hand, and it was his turn to lead the way to his bedroom, pausing when he saw the door ajar. He peered in to find the room empty but the light on the nightstand glowing softly. The dark bedding was neatly folded at the foot of the bed, revealing the pristine burgundy sheets and carefully fluffed pillows. A bottle of lube and several condoms were on the nightstand and a snack-sized Snickers on each pillow. David closed his eyes, sighing in embarrassed exasperation.

"What?" Jackson pressed against his back, his breath on David's neck.

David shivered. "My best friend truly does have many good qualities, but subtlety isn't one of them. Apparently he felt the need to provide deluxe turn-down service."

David pushed the door open farther, and Jackson sputtered out a startled laugh. He walked to the bed and picked up one of the candy bars.

"Funny guy." Jackson smirked and set the candy next to the bottle of lube. "Well, between my neighbor and your best friend, everyone seems to be trying to tell us we're moving too slowly."

David closed the door and leaned against it. "I think we're right where we should be, when we should be."

Jackson slipped the jacket from his broad shoulders, then hung it over a chair in the corner before returning to David. "I think you're right." He pulled David away from the door and slipped the heavy wool jacket down his arms. "And I think we've talked enough. For now."

CHAPTER SEVENTEEN

JACKSON TOSSED the jacket on the chair too, and David slipped the scarf over his head, throwing it in the same general direction, not actually caring where it landed. Jackson stepped closer, sliding his hand around David's nape, pulling him in for a slow, toe-curling kiss.

David didn't know what he expected, but the leisurely, sweet tempo of Jackson's seduction wasn't it. He kissed David long and thoroughly, then separated from him just long enough to slip his fingers under the hem of David's sweater, and pull it off over his head. He unbuttoned his own shirt, and David stared at what was revealed of Jackson's chest, framed by the black fabric of his shirt. His heart pounded a slow, heavy beat at the sight of Jackson's chest hair swirling from his sternum to curl around each copper-colored nipple. The dark hair delineated his six-pack before narrowing to disappear into the waistband of his jeans, and David groaned, reaching out to run his fingers through the slender trail on Jackson's lower belly. He loved a man with hair on his chest and stomach, and it was softer than it looked.

Jackson slid his hand down David's arm, pressing against his hand, holding his palm harder to his abs. "What was that sound for?"

"You're so perfect." David pushed Jackson's shirt back, then lifted both hands to cover the full slabs of pectoral muscle, thumbs caressing his nipples. Jackson's pupils dilated and his chest filled as he inhaled sharply, and David experienced a moment of heady delight at being able to cause the reaction. Then Jackson began to unbutton David's shirt from the bottom up, and David felt a quavering moment of fear. He caught Jackson's fingers, stilling them.

Jackson looked up into his eyes. "David?"

David licked his lips but his mouth was so dry it scarcely helped. "I don't look like this," he murmured, once again smoothing his palm over Jackson's chest, unable to stop touching him. "I don't compare to this."

Jackson lifted his hand and caught David's jaw, holding him in place and leaning in to kiss him, his teeth nipping David's lower lip. "Bullshit, David," he breathed against his mouth. "You're slender and you're fair, and you have the most beautiful eyes I've ever seen." He reached around, filling his hand with one of David's asscheeks, squeezing, "And this has kept me awake nights."

The capacity for anything like an intelligent response flew out the window when Jackson leaned forward and opened his lips on David's throat.

"Oh God." David felt Jackson's tongue touch his skin. His neck had always been sensitive, but that one spot, just at the point where his neck curved toward his shoulder, made his knees weak. He curled his fingers around Jackson's wrist and leaned into his touch when Jackson spread his fingers to cup David's jaw. Jackson slid his lips farther up David's throat, nudging aside his collar as his teeth teased the pale skin and his fingers moved back to the buttons of David's shirt, sliding them through the holes.

"Jackson," David gasped, lifting his hand to the back of Jackson's head, fingers spearing into the thick softness of his hair. He groaned when Jackson took another sharp nip on his neck.

"Yes, David?" he murmured against David's skin.

"I just… I want…." David's ramblings faded when Jackson slipped his shirt from his shoulders and pulled him in against his bare chest. The soft hair brushed against David's nipples and they stiffened into hardened peaks. He shuddered. "God, I want—" David tried to collect his thoughts, but they were as intangible as clouds torn apart by a breeze. "I want…," he tried again, and Jackson pulled him in closer, slipping his thigh between David's legs.

"You want what?" Jackson murmured.

It was taking every ounce of self-control David had not to hump his thigh, and now he wanted him to talk? It was almost alarming how aroused he was. He'd never felt anything like it before in his life.

"You," David finally managed, gasping when Jackson pressed his thigh against his aching balls. "I want you."

"That's a good thing," Jackson said, his voice rough. "Because I want you too."

David's shirt had pooled at his elbows, and Jackson ran his rough palms over the exposed skin of his back and shoulders. "Your skin is so soft, so beautiful." He opened his lips farther on David's throat, pulling on the skin. David clutched a handful of pectoral muscle and fisted his other hand in Jackson's hair.

"I—God." David groaned, and Jackson's swirling tongue soothed the spot when it began to ache. David gave in and rubbed his erection against Jackson's thigh.

"This has been the longest damned day of my life," Jackson muttered.

David let his shirt slip off his arms and pushed Jackson's to the floor as well. "It has?"

Jackson nodded. "I can't remember the last time I wanted someone this much."

David stared at the man in front of him, unable to come up with a single rational thing to say. Jackson was lean and golden brown, and his jeans rode low enough that David could see the caps of muscle atop each hip bone. Every move of his hands caused his biceps to bunch, his sturdy forearms to flex. He was stunning, and David wanted to lick every inch of him. Jackson was so fucking beautiful, and David stammered out something to that effect but doubted he made sense.

Jackson curled his hands around David's rib cage on each side. "So are you, David," he said. "You're perfect."

David made a scoffing noise before he could stop himself.

Jackson's gaze was level and earnest. "God, I really want to kick your ex's ass." He leaned closer, and his face blocked out everything else. His lips hovered just inches from David's. "I don't want anyone else in this room tonight but you and me. And I love everything about the way you look." Jackson slid his hands to bracket David's spine and pulled David in until their chests were once again pressed firmly together. David caught his breath. "I even love your glasses."

The feeling of Jackson's skin combined with his words made David light-headed.

Jackson took his mouth in a deep kiss, and his lips moved on David's, persuasive, urging them to part. When his tongue slipped between David's teeth, the feel of it, slick and mobile, pulled a moan from David's chest. He wrapped his arms around Jackson's neck, clinging.

Jackson turned as the kiss deepened, easing David onto his back on the bed, his knee sinking into the mattress next to David's hips as he lowered himself to cover him with his body.

They kissed until David's bones were liquid and the only thing anchoring him to the bed was his arms around Jackson's neck. Finally, Jackson lifted to his knees and his hands went to the waistband of David's tight jeans. David heard his belt being unbuckled and felt the back of Jackson's fingers brush against the skin just above the pale brown curls at his groin. His knuckles brushed David's cock as he was unzipped, and David was so hard he almost came from that contact alone. Jeans and briefs were peeled down his legs and his boots were yanked off, the whole bundle dropped to the floor with a dull thud. Then Jackson was back, his face hovering over David's erect cock, which was red and bobbing damply against his belly.

David clenched his eyes closed and felt his face heating. He wasn't embarrassed by his size; he'd gotten over that in tenth-grade gym when he realized he was pretty much average. But having Jackson stare at him while he was hard with want was both thrilling and terrifying. Jackson sifted his fingers through the pale brown hair at the base of David's cock, and David shivered. Then Jackson curled his hand around him, and he came back up, his lips near David's ear.

"This," he said with a squeeze, "is nothing to be embarrassed about. It's beautiful." He stroked David expertly and slid back down, his face so close his heated breath felt like feathers brushing the stretched skin.

The first touch of Jackson's tongue to the tip, licking precome from the slit, sucked all the air from David's lungs. He forced his eyes open and looked down, gasping, watching in amazement as Jackson opened his mouth, relaxed his throat, and took him in to the root. He pulled slowly back, his blue eyes looking up the length of David's body to meet his eyes.

"Oh my God," David murmured, one of his hands going into his own hair, fisting, trying to moor himself in place. The sensation of the warm, wet heat worked in concert with the intense look in Jackson's eyes.

Jackson took David in deep again, swallowing around the head, then pulled back and concentrated his tongue around the tip, sliding his hand up David's thigh. Jackson eased David's legs apart, curling long fingers around his balls before he pressed behind them. David fought the urge to thrust into Jackson's mouth, holding a fist in front of his lips, trying to muffle the series of ragged moans issuing from his throat. The blue eyes continued to watch him, gauging his response.

It didn't take long for David's skin to feel tingly and too tight and his legs to fall farther apart. He pulled his knees up closer to his chest, and he didn't have the neurons left to be embarrassed at how needy he sounded or must have looked. "Jackson," he warned, his voice strangled. "I'm so close."

Jackson pulled back, sliding his palm over the swollen head of David's cock with a slow twist. David shuddered. "Is that a problem?" Jackson asked.

David took a deep breath, fighting back the orgasm that threatened. "I don't want it to be over so soon."

"Ah, sweetheart." Jackson ghosted his fingers over the furled entrance David had exposed and offered up like a gift. "Just because you come doesn't mean we're done."

David finally understood the term "gagging for it," because that was the sound he made.

Jackson gave one slow lick on David's reddened prick from the base to the head, then rolled to his side. David felt his erection bob wetly against his lower belly as Jackson's hands went to his own jeans and he yanked them open, shoving them down along with his briefs. He kicked them away and straightened, and David took in the long, muscular thighs, the prominent hip bones, and the perfect, uncut cock rising dark red from the nest of dark curls between his legs.

David's mouth watered for a taste of him. "This." He curled his fingers around Jackson's thick erection. "Bring this up here."

"Yes, sir." Jackson gave him a slight smile, lifting until he was straddling David's chest. His cock was right there, and David could see the swollen head peeking out of its cuff of skin, could smell his arousal. He inhaled the musky scent and reached out, clutching Jackson's hips and pulling him closer. When he nuzzled the thickened flesh, rubbing his cheek against it, Jackson grunted deep in his throat.

David opened his mouth and took him in, and the salty, faintly bitter taste made him groan. He felt Jackson's hand curl around his nape, not pulling, just holding, his thumb caressing the base of David's skull. Relaxing his throat, David took him in as far as he could until his nose brushed springy black curls and his throat was full. When he pulled back, he slipped his tongue under Jackson's foreskin, curling it around the shiny head before sucking hard. Jackson caught his breath, then pulled away.

David looked up at him, frowning. "Did I do something wrong?"

"You did it too right. I was about to embarrass myself and pop off after one suck." Jackson scooted back to kiss him, running his tongue along David's lower lip before turning and reaching for the bottle of lube.

David got his first glimpse of the tattoo on Jackson's hip: it was an upside-down pink triangle outlined with a thick black line. He reached out and touched it, smoothing over the inked skin with his fingertips, feeling the slightly raised edge of the black outline. It was the only tattoo Jackson had, and David recognized the significance.

Jackson's heated gaze returned to his face. "Scoot up," he ordered softly.

David scrambled to make his limbs cooperate and hoped he didn't look like some kind of pale, long-legged insect flailing about. When his head was on one of the pillows, Jackson leaned over him, spreading his hand on David's chest as he looked down into his eyes.

"Just to clarify," Jackson said, "what do you want?"

David knew what he was asking and hoped he didn't go up in embarrassed flames as he fought to say the words aloud. "I want you inside of me."

Jackson closed his eyes and took a deep breath. "And I want to be there. I'm just not sure how long I'll last. It's been a while."

David lifted one of his hands to the back of Jackson's neck. "That doesn't matter." His fingers slipped up into his dark hair. "And it's been a while for me too. Longer than you'd think."

Jackson smiled, his hand sliding down David's stomach, raising gooseflesh on his chest and causing his nipples to turn into hard pebbles. "Is it juvenile of me that it pleases me to hear that?"

Jackson lowered his head and kissed him, his tongue sliding immediately between David's lips. David linked his arms around Jackson's neck and heard the cap of the lube bottle snick open.

Lube was always cold when first applied, and David mentally braced for it, lifting one leg and wrapping it over Jackson's hip. But Jackson kissed him again, and when David felt a feather-light touch behind his balls, then along the taut skin to his ass, the lube had been warmed in Jackson's hand. David sighed softly as Jackson rubbed a finger almost delicately around his rim. By the time he slipped the tip inside, David was angling his hips up, almost on the point of begging.

Trevor had always said David was a "natural-born bottom," but there had been a little sneer in his voice that insinuated there was something wrong with that, and something wrong with David because of it. It made him fight against that part of himself, to close off his pleasure in it, and ultimately killed his sex life with Trevor. The knowledge that while Trevor had enjoyed making use of David's body, he didn't respect him, made David unable to relax, and Trevor had been unable to understand why he couldn't.

But he had no trouble relaxing with Jackson. Jackson's finger slid inside with just the slightest bit of bearing down on David's part, and they both moaned when Jackson was inside of him to the second knuckle. When Jackson hooked his finger and found his prostate, David cried out, his back arching off the sheets.

"Good?" Jackson watched him carefully and stroked him again, and David gasped, trying to lift his other leg, arching his hips to take him even deeper.

"God, yes—I—please."

"Please what, David?"

David turned his face away from Jackson's penetrating gaze, feeling even more than naked. If Jackson mocked him or sneered at him, David wasn't sure he'd ever recover from the disappointment. "Don't make me beg, Jackson," he said, shocked by how close he was to tears.

"David." David pulled his upper lip between his teeth, squeezed his eyes closed, his erection beginning to fade. "David, please look at me."

David forced his eyes open and found Jackson's, but instead of the cool, mocking derision he'd seen in Trevor's eyes, in Jackson's he found quiet but desperate longing.

"I just wanted to know if you needed more preparation or if I could...."
His words trailed off into silence, but the hunger in his eyes didn't fade. "The

only way this will be good for me is if it's good for you too. But you need to tell me what to do."

David's smile was tremulous; he was feeling very much on the brink of tears again, but for an entirely different reason. "I'm ready."

"You're still so tight, though."

Jackson's finger moved inside of him, then nearly out, and David clamped his muscles down to keep it from leaving him empty and waiting. "I like… to start that way," David said, unable to simply admit he liked the burn of his body stretching around a thick cock. "Just, slowly. Okay?"

Jackson took a deep breath and nodded. David heard the tear of the condom wrapper, knew Jackson rolled it into place, but he didn't look down; he watched Jackson's face. He took in the concentration on his even, handsome features, watched him shiver as if just touching himself was almost too much.

Then Jackson was looming over him, and David lifted his legs to his chest with his hands behind his knees, waiting. Jackson held his weight on one stiffened arm and used his other hand to line himself up. He pressed forward and David bore down, gasping as Jackson slid slowly inside. It took all of David's concentration to stay relaxed through the stretch.

When Jackson's hip bones were pressed flush to his ass, David cried out, lifting one hand and digging his fingers into Jackson's arm. He'd almost forgotten how this felt, how stretched he was, how full.

"Too fast? I'm sorry, I just—"

"No, not—not too fast. Just—" David's mouth fell open and his eyes rolled back. He was unable to concentrate on anything other than the delicious burn spreading through his ass and up his spine. "One second, just…." He managed to regulate his breathing and pushed back against the welcome intrusion. The burn faded, and the wonderful, complete feeling he loved replaced it. He forced himself to look up at Jackson and saw the lines of strain around his mouth, the beads of sweat on his forehead.

David reached up and smoothed his hand over the side of Jackson's taut face. "Move," he whispered, and Jackson's grateful sigh sounded like it came from his soul. He pulled back and pushed in again slowly, and David's hips rose to meet him. "You can go faster," he murmured.

Jackson's next thrust was faster, the one after that faster still, and he reached beneath David with one hand, angling his hips higher.

David gave a strangled cry of pleasure when Jackson's cock nudged the swollen bundle of nerve endings inside of him. At that angle, Jackson hit his prostate with each thrust and David lost track of everything but the sweeping, overpowering rush of pleasure. His neck arched and his vision grayed and he babbled, his head moving on the pillow as every muscle in his body grew tighter and tighter. He begged for more, harder, faster, and felt the bedframe begin to shake. He could hear the sound of Jackson's skin slapping against his, feel the slick sweat on his sides when he tried to grip him.

Finally, Jackson's voice broke through to him. "Come on, babe," he urged. "Come on."

David couldn't find words to answer.

"David, please!"

Jackson gasped, and his desperation, along with the powerful pounding in David's ass, pushed him over the edge. He came so hard without ever touching his cock that stars burst to life behind his eyelids and the ocean roared in his ears. David cried out and clung to Jackson until he thrust in hard and stayed there, his strong body shuddering, his cock twitching hard enough that one of David's aftershocks felt like another smaller, but no less shattering orgasm.

David was aware that Jackson collapsed on top of him, but he didn't stay there long. He withdrew carefully and rolled to David's side, and David's legs flopped to the bed like overcooked spaghetti noodles. He didn't care. He was drained, and he didn't feel connected to his body at the moment. If he had to move, it would have been next to impossible.

The bed shifted and Jackson sat on the edge, then bent and pulled on his jeans before standing.

"Jackson?" David's voice sounded rough and felt even rougher.

Jackson gave him a soft smile and leaned over to kiss him. "I'll be right back."

He walked toward the bedroom door. David stared at his beautiful broad back and could just see the top of his tattoo over the jeans riding low on his hips. He closed his eyes, and the next thing he knew, the hardwood floor creaked and the bed dipped at his side. A warm, damp cloth began to move over his stomach.

David opened his eyes and looked up, and Jackson smiled down at him.

"You okay?"

David blinked sluggishly. "Mm-hmm. Although the old phrase 'getting your brains fucked out' might be a real thing. I feel like mine leaked out my ears."

Jackson chuckled softly. "I have to say that was pretty spectacular." He kissed David. "Thank you."

David let his hand come to rest on Jackson's chest. "You're welcome. Although I don't feel like I did a whole lot."

Jackson laughed. "You're mistaken." He stood up long enough to toss the washcloth in the hamper and divest himself of his jeans, then came back to the bed.

Even as sated as David had ever been in his life, Jackson took David's breath. "You're incredible."

Jackson slipped back into the bed, gloriously naked, and leaned in to give David a lingering kiss. "Thank you. So are you."

David wasn't going to argue with him. Instead he watched as Jackson bent to pull the covers up over them.

The upside-down pink-triangle tattoo on Jackson's hip came into view, and David reached out and touched it. Jackson stilled, looking at him over his shoulder.

"I like this."

"Thanks." Jackson waited until David's hand fell away, then pulled the comforter up, covering David before lying on his side, facing him. "We're German on my mom's side of the family." His expression and deep voice were pensive as he reached up to push some of David's damp hair from his forehead. "They lived outside of Düsseldorf before World War II. Her grandmother had a brother named Erich. He was away at college in Munich when the Nazis started rounding up the Jews. And the gays. He wasn't out or anything—his parents never would have forgiven him. But he lived with another man, and I guess in those days that was enough. They never found out exactly what happened to him, but after the war a neighbor told the family both Erich and his lover disappeared one night." Jackson closed his eyes for a moment. "I think people, even people in my family, like to forget that gay people went to the gas chambers too."

David felt his eyes begin to burn. He cupped Jackson's cheek, and Jackson pressed his lips into David's palm.

"I would have liked to know him," Jackson said. "My grandmother told me I look like him."

"Do you have any pictures?"

"My mom does."

"I'd like to see them."

Jackson brushed his knuckles down David's cheek. "I'll show them to you."

David scooted closer and curved his hand over Jackson's hip where the tattoo marked his skin, and he rubbed his palm over it. Jackson was warm, and the heat radiated between them. Jackson wrapped his arm loosely around David's waist as their legs tangled, and David felt the soft, comforting weight of Jackson's cock pressed against his thigh. Usually this was David's favorite time, the cuddling after, but tonight the sex had been so amazing he didn't know how pillow talk could compete. In fact, he wondered how soon they could go again, even though his penis wasn't particularly interested at the moment. He was so preoccupied, he didn't realize he was basically petting Jackson's ass until Jackson arched back into his hand.

"Oh, sorry." David snatched his hand away.

"I like it." Jackson grabbed David's hand and put it back over his tattoo.

"You do?" Jackson hummed in the affirmative. "How long ago did you have the tat done?"

Jackson ran his fingers down David's spine. "About eighteen months ago. I saw a movie called *Bent* with Clive Owen and Sir Ian McKellen. Mick Jagger was even in it." He stopped and took a deep breath. "I don't think most of us know what they went through. I know I didn't. Just watching the movie is a harrowing experience. I won't ever forget it. I went out and got the tattoo the next day." He stared somberly across the room. "Stephen thought it was stupid."

"Trevor would have too. I doubt they would have liked anything that wasn't in tribute to them."

Jackson's mouth curled to one side. "Truer words. I just think we need to remember, that's all."

"We do. Especially right now. The marriage decision made so many people angry. I knew it would upset some people, but I didn't expect the kind of backlash there's been."

"I did." Jackson's jaw was tight. "And I don't care if they like it or not. I pay my damned taxes. I should be able to get married if I want to."

David slipped his hand up Jackson's side. "I agree with you."

Jackson exhaled. "I know you do. But it was the weekend after the court's decision that some asshole went after my truck."

David continued to slide his hand over Jackson's smooth skin. He couldn't seem to get enough of touching him. The muscles under Jackson's skin were tight at the moment, and David wanted to relax them, soothe him. "Did the police ever find out who did it?"

Jackson shook his head. "And they won't. Not that the cops here in town don't care, because I think they do. There's just so much more important crime for them to worry about. I don't think a gay guy having his truck trashed rates very high on their list."

"Did they designate it a hate crime?"

"Yeah. But it was property damage and not a physical assault, so it's still pretty low on the priority list."

"Like my car window," David mused.

"Yeah, probably," Jackson admitted, his voice soft.

David bit his lip thoughtfully, cushioning his head with his free hand. "You know, Michael mentioned something to me earlier today and I haven't been able to stop thinking about it."

Jackson mirrored his pose and tucked his hand under his head as well. "What's that?"

"Were the guys working on the roof today gay?"

"One of them was. The other was his brother. Why?"

"I just wondered something. Do you know framing and drywall guys that're gay?"

Jackson looked intrigued. "I probably know people in all phases of construction and remodeling that are gay, or related to someone who is. There aren't that many of us, truthfully, and this isn't that big a town. We toss one another work when we can."

David reached out, his fingers finding their way into Jackson's chest hair seemingly of their own volition. The hair was silky, not wiry. It also gave David something to do with hands that were beginning to tremble with nervous anticipation. "Jackson, if you're all gay, and we know that local construction on a whole isn't good about hiring gay skilled labor, why not form your own company?"

When Jackson didn't immediately respond, David ventured a peek at his face.

Jackson was looking at him with an unreadable expression. He studied David for the space of several heartbeats. "Like, a company where we're all out?" he asked finally.

"Maybe not just out. Maybe… even advertise that you're out. Make the fact it's a gay-friendly company a selling point."

One of Jackson's brows arched. "You think that's a plus?"

"Maybe."

Jackson entered one of his long, thoughtful pauses, but he didn't seem to think it was a bad idea, and that emboldened David to elaborate.

"I know there's an active gay community here in town. A pretty good-sized one, considering. And I know some of them have serious cash. I also know straight people who would hire an openly gay renovation company."

"There are also some who would find out we're gay and fire us."

"But see, that's the beauty of this idea. They'd know going in. Gil would never get fired again because of a bumper sticker. Neither would you."

"You don't think we'd be painting a big target on our backs?"

"I don't know. I don't think so. I mean, yeah, there would be assholes. But there are always going to be assholes. And it might take a while for word of mouth to spread, but you're awesome at what you do. So is Gil. And there's Manny and the other guys doing the work on their own because major construction crews won't hire them. What if you and Gil and Vern and the others concentrated on doing renovation as a team? Like the work being done here. You could advertise as the company to hire if you own a turn-of-the-century home in need of everything from minor repairs to major restoration. You could even advertise as a company that specializes in the work of Andrej Janic. How many of those houses are there?"

"Thirty-six," Jackson answered without hesitation. "Four that have already been renovated and six more that are currently in some phase of restoration. Including yours."

"See? You know that right off the top of your head. I'll bet you've seen every one of them too, haven't you?"

Jackson shrugged one shoulder, then stopped and nodded.

"Which means there are twenty-six that remain untouched. And even if they aren't Janic's, there are hundreds of old houses up here, just on this side of town. And the owners of those houses are people who can afford to update and restore. And that's to say nothing of the parts of old town the city is trying to revitalize. I would think it would be something they'd be interested in, showing diversity with a company made up of LGBT people."

Jackson's lips quirked. "Well, not so much on the L, the B, or the T."

"But if word got out there was a company like that hiring, there might be."

Jackson continued to watch him, but now David could see speculation in his eyes. "You've really thought about this, haven't you?"

It was David's turn to shrug now.

"I think," Jackson said slowly, "what would be an even bigger draw would be having an interior designer attached to this too. That way renovation jobs could be taken from start to finish, including decor."

David gave him a small smile. "The thought had occurred to me."

"Seriously?" Jackson looked surprised.

"I'm not really happy where I am anymore. The business has changed. It's more about how fast and cheap we can get it done rather than how well. I'd have to stay at it until we knew if this would work. We all would have to keep working. But I don't know." He looked down at Jackson's clavicle, following the pattern of the dark chest hair over it with his finger. "I keep telling myself all of the reasons it's a bad idea, and my mind keeps providing reasons it isn't."

Jackson caught David's hand, brought it to his mouth, and pressed his lips against the bony knuckles. "It's not a bad idea. I don't see any reason why we shouldn't at least float the idea to the others."

The *we* made David's toes curl in pleasure. He looked up with a smile. "Yeah?"

"Why not? The worst they can do is say no."

David leaned his forehead against Jackson's chin. "I'm just glad you don't think it's stupid."

Jackson ducked his head, his lips against David's ear. "I don't think it's stupid. I'm not sure what the others will say, but I do not think it's stupid." Jackson caught his chin and lifted it, looking into his eyes. "Now I really don't want to talk anymore."

David studied his calm features. "Are you tired?"

Jackson chuckled, pressing forward with his hips. David had been so wrapped up in the conversation he hadn't noticed that Jackson's cock had thickened and lengthened and now pressed insistently against his thigh. "No, not really."

"Oh." David gave him a knowing smile. "You're not, huh?"

"No, not really."

"So, um—" David leaned forward and nipped Jackson's square jaw, and Jackson's eyes darkened. "—what did you have in mind?"

It was Jackson's turn to nip, and he pulled David's lower lip between his teeth before releasing it. "Well, if you're not too sore, I'd really love another shot at this." He reached around David, fingers sliding down the cleft of the object in question before skimming over his hole.

David shuddered. "I'm not too sore."

Jackson's slow smile was wicked, and that was all it took for blood to rush straight to David's cock.

"That's the best news I've had all day."

David laughed. "You're easily pleased."

Jackson's smile settled, mellowed. "Actually, I'm not." He wrapped his arm around David's waist, pulling him in until he was flush against his body. "I'm very particular about where I put my dick. And we're going to work on you being able to accept a compliment graciously."

"We are?" David had pretty much lost the thread of the conversation when he felt all the warm, bronzed skin against his. He looked up into Jackson's eyes, gleaming with suppressed amusement.

"We are. But not right now."

"Oh good." David angled his head and kissed him, then licked Jackson's lower lip. "Because I pretty much checked out when you said you wanted to fuck me again."

"Yeah, I know." Jackson leaned forward, his mouth opening on the same sensitive patch of throat he'd latched on to earlier. It was very vulnerable now, and his ramped-up arousal made David breathless as he rocked his pelvis forward. He gripped Jackson's bicep, fingers digging in.

"Can we stop talking now?" David whispered.

Jackson chuckled, and the sound went straight to David's spine, zinging down into his tailbone before leaving a sizzle behind in his ass.

"Absolutely." Jackson kissed David and rolled him to his back, pinning him beneath his weight.

David made a needy noise in the back of his throat, wrapped his long legs around Jackson's waist, and opened his mouth to the renewed sensual assault of Jackson's kisses.

CHAPTER EIGHTEEN

DAVID WAS deeply asleep when he was jerked abruptly awake. Panic roared through him when he realized a hand was pressed over his mouth. He gripped the hard arm attached to it, heart pounding as he tried to roll away.

"Baby, stop." Jackson's voice cut through the fear, and David stilled when he realized it was Jackson's hand. "There's someone in the house."

David blinked, sitting up as Jackson pushed off the bed. Moonlight shining through the window revealed a blurry image of Jackson yanking on his jeans, and David fumbled on the nightstand and found his glasses. He pushed them onto his face.

"What did you hear?" he asked as Jackson came into focus.

"Shh," Jackson urged, holding his hand up.

A muted thud came from the back of the house and then the sound of a dog growling. It sounded like Boots was right on the other side of the door. They froze and stared at each other, and then Jackson crossed on silent feet to carefully ease open the bottom drawer of the dresser.

"Call 911," he said.

David heard a couple of soft metallic clicks, and then Jackson was standing with the gun in his hand. David had all but forgotten about the pistol, and he stared at it in alarm.

"Jackson," he whispered, not wanting him to leave the room. He'd called a home security company that morning, but the first available appointment was Tuesday. Now there was an intruder in his house, but if there was a threat out there, he didn't want Jackson confronting it alone. Even with the gun.

There was another, louder sound from the kitchen, and fear washed over him. Boots growled again, the sound low. It sent a chill down David's spine.

"Jackson, please. I'll call the police, and we'll let them…."

The hardwood floor somewhere in the house creaked, and David's voice died in his throat. Boots's growl grew in volume, and fear for him made David feel cold.

"Boots, Jackson," he whispered.

"I know," Jackson said, his voice hushed and his hand on the doorknob. "Nine one one. Now. Please."

With trembling hands, David grabbed his cell phone from its charger and punched in the numbers. His eyes never left Jackson as he stood next to the door, hand on the knob, his head angled to one side as he listened. There was another sharp *pop* of the old floors from either the living room or dining room, he couldn't be sure.

Boots whined, and it sounded like he was scratching at the bedroom door.

"Nine one one, what is your emergency?"

The voice in his ear startled David and he jumped. "There's someone in my house," he said, pressing his hand over where his heart was galloping in his chest, keeping his voice pitched low.

"There's an intruder in your house?"

A loud thud made the floor in the bedroom vibrate. Boots finally began to bark and it sounded like he ran down the hall. Jackson turned the doorknob.

"Jackson, please wait. Please."

"Sir? Did you say there's an intruder in your house?"

"Yes."

"What's the address?"

David gave it to her, his eyes beseeching Jackson to stay where it was safe. Boots sounded ferocious and far bigger than he was, and David held the faint hope he'd scare whoever was out there into leaving the house.

Then Boots yelped and fell silent.

"Oh God," David gasped, so afraid for the little dog tears stung his eyes.

"Sir, are you all right? Sir?"

Jackson rushed out of the bedroom, and David struggled to his feet, yanking the top sheet off the bed.

"Yes, I'm okay. But I have to hang up. My neighbor's dog… my boyfriend…." He didn't even care that he wasn't making sense. He wrapped the sheet around his waist, unwilling to take time to try to untangle his jeans from his underwear with the phone in his hand.

Jackson was already out of sight, and fear shot through David when he heard him shout "Don't move!" and then heard a man's garbled cry and a thud.

"Oh my God!" David rushed out of the bedroom, trying not to trip on the trailing bottom of the sheet.

"Sir, sir? Don't hang up the phone. Stay with me until the police arrive."

"I can't. I have to go."

"Sir, don't hang up!"

David struggled down the hall, the sheet threatening to trip him at every step.

When he arrived at the doorway between the dining room and the hall, he saw shadowed figures struggling on the floor in the darkness of his living room and heard Boots snarling. Grabbing the sheet tighter around him, he tossed his phone onto the dining room table and felt across the top for something, anything he could use as a weapon. For a moment he panicked, feeling only the smooth surface of the wood, but then his fingers encountered something thick and cool and heavy—the bowl he'd used for the Halloween candy. He grabbed it up and lurched into the living room.

There was enough moonlight streaming through the front window that he could see two men struggling on the floor. He realized with a jolt of fear that Jackson was on his back as the other man straddled him, and they were both fighting for possession of the gun. A dark ski mask covered the intruder's head, but there was enough light for David to aim, and he reared back and swung the bowl as hard as he could, slamming it into the side of the intruder's head. It exploded with a crash as the bowl shattered, small pieces flying everywhere, and the man stiffened for a moment, then fell to his side on the floor. Jackson shoved out from under him, pushing to his feet and pointing the gun at what David hoped was the unconscious man.

"Did you get 911 on the phone?" Jackson asked, his voice surprisingly steady.

"Oh!" David lurched back into the dining room, pausing to turn on the lights, and rescued his phone from the tabletop.

"Sir? Sir, are you there?"

"Yes, I'm here," David said breathlessly.

"Is everyone all right?"

David looked back into the living room. Jackson was standing over the intruder, his gun pointed down at him, his bare broad shoulders gleaming slightly in the light. Pieces of white ceramic littered the room, chips of it clinging to the shoulders of the intruder's black sweater and scattered on the floor around his head. There were also slivers on the ski mask, and snack-size candy bars were everywhere. David hadn't even noticed there was still candy in the bowl when he picked it up.

Boots, he saw with relief, was clinging to the man's ankle by his teeth, snarling and shaking his head, apparently none the worse for whatever had made him yelp.

"We got him," he said breathlessly into the phone. "I hit him with a bowl and my boyfriend has a gun, and—"

"Who has a gun?" the operator asked in alarm.

"My boyfriend. The intruder is—" David took a step or two closer. "—I think he's unconscious. Oh, and my neighbor's dog bit him." They heard the sound of screeching brakes outside and blue and red rotating lights splashed across the living room blinds. "The police just got here."

"Be sure before opening your door."

He almost said he didn't know anyone else with a rotating light on their car but thought that was probably hysteria talking. A heavy knock sounded on the door and he started to cross into the living room.

"Stay there! Don't come back in here," Jackson said. "There are pieces of that bowl everywhere, and you're barefooted."

"So are you," David replied.

"I'm already closer to the door." Jackson backed up, slid something out of the grip of his gun, and put both pieces on the small table next to the front door. He looked through the small windows in the door before he unlocked it.

"Someone called about an intruder?"

Jackson backed up, gesturing to the man in the ski mask lying on the floor. The first officer slipped his gun from its holster and stepped into the room. Boots was still snarling and shaking his head, his mouth around the unconscious man's ankle. The cop looked at him, then at Jackson.

"Can you call off the dog, please?"

"Boots, come here, boy," David said, patting his leg.

Boots looked up at him, and then with every appearance of reluctance, released the man's ankle. The dog went over to David, and David was alarmed when the stocky little guy limped. Boots sat at David's feet with a huff.

The police officer approached the man on the floor cautiously, his gun trained on him. He looked from Jackson to David. "What did you hit him with?"

"A ten-pound ceramic bowl," David answered. "Full of candy."

"I see that," the cop said, sounding faintly amused. He bent and snagged the ski mask and pulled it off the motionless man's head.

David gaped and felt the blood drain from his face, but why he was surprised, he couldn't say.

Trevor's head lolled to one side.

The second cop stopped just inside the door. "He looks like you hit him pretty hard."

The first officer, whose tag read Hernandez, checked for a pulse just under Trevor's chin. They all waited silently. When the officer pulled his hand back and holstered his gun, David felt a moment of alarm.

"He isn't dead, is he?"

Hernandez looked up at him. "No, his pulse is strong." He pushed back the long hair that had spilled over Trevor's forehead. "But he's got a hell of a bump coming up."

Even from where he stood, David could see the bruising lump rising on his temple, and he grimaced.

The second officer, named Johnson, leaned forward, studying Trevor's forehead. "We'll call for transport?"

"Yeah. That's a pretty good goose egg." Officer Hernandez rolled Trevor's limp body over, pulled out his handcuffs, and secured his arms behind his back. He stood. "I'll go radio for an ambulance and alert the scene investigation unit."

Johnson agreed, and Hernandez walked out the front door.

Officer Johnson glanced over at David, then returned his attention to Trevor. "Do either of you know him?"

David stepped closer. "He and I used to live together. His name is Trevor Blankenship."

"Okay." Johnson slipped a small tablet from the breast pocket of his black uniform shirt. "Can you spell that for me, please?" He pulled a pen from his pocket as well. David spelled Trevor's name. "And who is the owner of the house?"

"Me. I mean, I am."

"And your name?" He gave it to him and spelled it. "Any idea why he'd be breaking into your house in a ski mask, Mr. Snyder?"

David tried to think of a brief answer and couldn't. "It's kind of a long story."

Johnson nodded. "Well, why don't you get dressed and then you can tell me."

David felt heat wash up his neck from his chest when he was reminded he was standing there in nothing more than a sheet. He nodded gratefully. "That would probably be good."

CHAPTER NINETEEN

W̲HEN M̲ICHAEL arrived not long after the paramedics, David had been perplexed by his presence. That was until Michael whispered that Jackson had called him, saying he thought David could use his best friend.

David had been hanging on to his composure by a thread at that point, and the thoughtfulness of the gesture sent his emotions spiraling. He'd begun to shake, and tears filled his eyes. Michael took him back to his bedroom while Jackson dealt with the police. Michael wrapped him in his arms and held him, letting the shakes and the tears play out until David felt composed enough to come back out and make his statement to the police. Now they sat side by side on the porch steps, watching as the paramedics loaded Trevor into the back of the ambulance.

He was handcuffed to the gurney but still managed to put on quite a show of being injured, moaning about his head and his leg. They hadn't noticed until after the paramedics arrived, but Boots managed to chew on more than his pant leg. Trevor's ankle had several neat round puncture holes ringing it. They'd also discovered that Trevor's blood alcohol was three times the legal limit, which might have explained why he stayed unconscious for as long as he did. It wouldn't help him dodge the breaking-and-entering charge.

"You okay?" Michael asked David, bumping his shoulder.

"Yeah." He smoothed his hand gently over the sleek sable fur on Boots's side and the dog laid his head on David's thigh. "I want them to leave so I can take Boots to the emergency vet."

"They should probably X-ray him to make sure nothing is broken." He leaned forward and reached across David, scratching the little dog's head. "You're such a good boy," he said when Boots licked his hand. "Biting the bad man's leg. Too bad you weren't a little bit taller and right at crotch level."

David gave Michael a wry look but couldn't hold on to it.

197

"Are they going to give Jackson back his gun?"

They looked to where Jackson stood next to a patrol car, talking to Detective Mitchell. He'd arrived not long after the uniformed officers.

When the first responders saw the gun and clip sitting on the small table next to the door, they had thought it belonged to Trevor and seized it as evidence. Even with Jackson providing them his registration and the gun's serial number, it could be a day or two before they returned the weapon. They'd bagged up the shards of ceramic and the crowbar Trevor used to break in through the back door, and the ski mask he'd had on his head.

Michael linked his hands around his skinny knees, leaning forward and watching Jackson.

"So."

David glanced over at him. "So?"

"So." Michael rocked slightly forward and back. "I gather Jackson is a spectacular fuck."

"Michael!" David smacked him on his arm.

"Hey, you can't blame me. I'm just observant."

"What could you possibly have observed that gives you that impression?"

"Well," Michael said slowly. "I mean, exhibit A: look at the man." He gestured, and David looked. Jackson was standing in the driveway talking to the detective. His hair was mussed and his shirt was half-unbuttoned, hanging over his hips and out from under his jacket. Actually he looked like he'd just climbed out of bed, which was nothing but the truth. "Any man who looks so pleasantly rumpled but so supremely self-satisfied must have had a lovely fuck." David huffed in exasperation. "Also you sat down on this step pretty gingerly, my friend."

"Oh God." David buried his face in the crook of his arm. "No one should know that much about their friend's sex life. I may spontaneously combust."

Michael poked him in the ribs and David batted at his hand. "So come on, spill. He's amazing, isn't he?"

David looked into his avid eyes, a grin pulling at his lips. "He was, in fact, spectacular. Twice."

Michael crowed, "You hussy."

David rolled his eyes, then leaned forward and buried his face in Boots's fur. "Oh, shut up."

"Why? I'm just teasing."

David rolled his head and peeked at Michael, who was grinning.

"Actually I'm incredibly jealous," his best friend went on. "I mean, how often is it that the performance lives up to the wrapping, particularly when the wrapping looks like that?"

It didn't seem to matter what Jackson did, or how rumpled he was; he was gorgeous. He glanced over at David and winked, and David sighed before he could stop himself.

Michael snorted. "You're ridiculous."

David thought about retorting, then decided he really didn't care if Michael thought he was absurd or not. "Yeah, I guess I am."

"Well, if it's any consolation, when compared to that—" He gestured toward Trevor, who was still moaning and groaning in the back of the ambulance. "—this time you hit the lotto."

Trevor's pale face was lit by the interior lights of the ambulance, and they could hear the petulant, almost cranky sound of his voice. "What could he possibly have been thinking," Michael went on, "breaking into the house like that?"

"I have no idea. He'll say he was drunk, like that's an excuse. I'm just glad Jackson had a gun."

"Why?" Michael gave him a half smile. "You didn't need a gun. You half brained him with a candy bowl."

David sat a bit taller. "I wasn't going to let him hurt the dog."

Michael laid his head on David's shoulder. "I love that you were protecting him."

"We're buddies." David smoothed his palm over the little dog again. "Aren't we, boy?" This time Boots climbed into David's lap, and David laughed softly as Michael ran his long, thin fingers over Boots's head.

One of the ambulance attendants slammed the back doors before going around to the driver's side, and moments later it pulled out of the driveway without the lights or siren. Trevor might be bitching a blue streak, but the attendants had assured David they didn't think he was badly hurt. Jackson laughed at something the detective muttered under his breath.

David's throat felt full and he forced down a swallow. When he spoke his voice sounded tight. "I'm in love with him."

Michael straightened, eyes wide. "Are you sure?"

He nodded. "Pretty sure, yeah."

Michael caught David's hand, linking their fingers, squeezing. "Does it feel… different?"

David knew what he was asking. "So different. Like… I'd say night and day, but it's bigger than that, more profound than that. What I felt for Trevor doesn't hold a candle to this." He released a shaky sigh. "It scares the crap out of me."

Risking his heart again, so soon after Trevor, was probably foolish. But he couldn't help it; it was already done.

Michael squeezed his hand. "It'll be okay."

David stared into Michael's eyes. "You can't promise that."

"Yes, I can." Michael gave him a small smile. "I believe it."

Jackson and Detective Mitchell started for the porch, and Michael slipped his hand from David's, returning it to Boots's head.

"Mr. Snyder, please make sure your attorney gets that restraining order," Mitchell said. "They're taking Blankenship to the ER to have his head checked, and then transporting him to the county lockup. He probably won't be arraigned until Monday at the earliest, and then he won't be released unless he can afford bail. But don't take any chances, particularly not with him already threatening you. I'm not sure how stable the guy is."

"I already talked to my lawyer," David said. He'd called Karen once Trevor was safely in custody, and she promised to file the restraining order first thing Monday morning.

"Good. All right, I'll be in touch."

He shook each of their hands, then made his way to the dark sedan parked out front.

Jackson stuck his hands in his jacket pockets, looking down at them. "Well, this has been an eventful evening."

"It's not over yet." David lifted Boots gently from his lap and stood up. "I want to take Boots into the emergency vet to make sure nothing's broken."

"Okay. I'll drive."

David gave him a wry look. "I love him, but we aren't taking the dog to the vet in your mother's Mercedes. We can take my car. I don't have leather upholstery."

"I'll get the leash and your keys," Michael said as he stood.

Jackson looked between them. "Are we all going?"

"Of course," Michael answered. "It's after 2:00 a.m. What else would we do?" He went into the house, and Boots followed him, limping slightly.

David started to follow when Jackson caught his hand, pulling him back. He was standing on the bottom step, which put him about six inches below David's head. He looked up at him.

"We haven't had a second to talk. Are you okay?"

"Yes. Why?"

"You had a few rough minutes."

David closed his eyes, exhaling softly. "Yeah, I did."

Jackson's eyes searched David's face. "I thought, it being your ex, this might be hard for you."

David gave him a grim smile. "What was hard for me was that I only got to swing that bowl at his damned head once."

Jackson squeezed his hand. "Really. Are you okay?"

David let the smile fall away. "Yes, really. I'm all right. I'm grateful if he has a gun he chose not to bring it with him." He shuddered, releasing Jackson's hand and wrapping his arms around himself, more than the cold making him shiver. "This could have been so much worse, Jackson. So much worse."

Jackson caught his wrist and David allowed himself to be pulled off the step and into his arms. Jackson held on tight, and gradually the cold David had felt slipped away. He encircled Jackson's waist with his arms, laying his head on his shoulder.

Jackson kissed the back of David's head. "I'm glad he can't hurt you."

"Me too."

"God, David…. Once he's out of jail, how am I supposed to sleep at night if you're here alone?"

"The alarm is being installed on Tuesday."

"Good. That's good." Jackson squeezed him again. "Maybe you need a dog too."

"I've been thinking the same thing."

Jackson was silent, his mouth still pressed to David's head. David felt the hot, moist breath through his hair, and he felt the shudder that moved through Jackson's arms.

David lifted his head, startled to see Jackson's eyes bright with tears. "Jackson?"

Jackson swallowed, his Adam's apple bobbing as he blinked quickly. He released David but cupped his face. "Nothing can happen to you, David," he said finally. "Nothing."

David curled his fingers around Jackson's wrists. "I'm okay, Jackson. And I'm not going to do anything stupid."

"Good. I'm going to hold you to that. Because if anything happened to you.... I don't even want to think about it." He looked haggard and frightened, and David believed him.

"Hush." David put his fingers over Jackson's lips. "I'm fine. And I'm going to stay fine. I promise."

Jackson gave him a weak smile, then pulled him in and kissed him.

"Oh my God." Michael came out of the house with Boots on his leash beside him. "Will you queers quit making out in the front yard so we can take this dog to the vet?"

David pulled back and shot Michael a baleful look over his shoulder, but Michael smiled brightly after he'd locked the front door.

"I'll pull the Mercedes out."

"Bring it back in once I've backed out," David said quickly. "Park it in the garage. I would hate for anything to happen to it."

"Okay."

Jackson gave David another fleeting kiss, then jogged toward the expensive coupe.

Michael picked Boots up with a soft grunt, carrying him as he fell into step with David. They walked to the garage, and Michael climbed in the back with Boots, then reached forward between the bucket seats and gripped David's shoulder.

"I told you."

"You told me what?" David deflected, but he knew what Michael was going to say and the thought of it made his pulse jump.

"I told you it would be okay." Michael squeezed his shoulder, leaning close. "He's as much in love with you as you are with him. So relax."

David took a deep breath as he backed his car out of the driveway. "Michael, someday, when you fall desperately head over heels in love, I'm going to tell you what you told me. And we'll see how good you are at 'relaxing.'"

Michael laughed as he settled into the backseat, Boots immediately climbing over his lap. "Never going to happen."

David waited for Jackson to jog back to the car, smiling slightly as he looked at his friend in the rearview mirror. "Famous last words."

"You can take them to the bank. I don't do love."

Jackson climbed in the passenger seat, and David headed off for the vet. Jackson caught his hand and linked their fingers.

"God, could you two knock it off?" Michael teased. "There's an impressionable dog present."

Jackson laughed, and David made a mental note to remember what Michael had said about love.

Because someday he would fall too. And payback was a bitch.

CHAPTER TWENTY

DAVID WAS nervous. Philosophically he knew he had no reason to be, but that didn't stop the butterflies in his stomach or the faint tremor in his hands as he meticulously layered cheese and deli meats on the large tray. Why he was so insistent on everything being perfect, he couldn't have explained if he had to. He just knew that for tonight, it was important that everything be as seamless as he could make it.

It had been a momentous six weeks since the night Trevor broke into his house. First there were the charges filed against him: first-degree burglary, because the crowbar he'd carried to break in was considered a weapon. In the state of Washington, the sentence could be lengthy prison time and a fine up to fifty thousand dollars. Trevor told his attorney all he'd wanted was to talk to David, but that didn't really explain his forcibly breaking through the back door. In addition, Karen wanted a menacing charge added for the office break-in, the phone calls, and the number of threatening texts. Had he been convicted of those charges, it could have added an additional twenty-four months to his sentence.

Initially Jackson, Michael, and even his mother had wanted David to press charges and shoot for the maximum sentence. And at first, David considered it. But then he went and sat down with Karen, and after that he wasn't so sure anymore.

"What happens to him if I press charges and he's convicted?" he had asked her.

She linked her fingers on her desk. "He'll go to prison. And I don't mean the county jail. I mean prison. He might get time off for good behavior, but he'll serve at least half of the sentence. When he gets out, he'll be on probation, probably for another year. As a convicted felon, he'll have a hell of a time getting a job. He won't be able to serve on a jury, which frankly is no great loss, but he won't have the right to own a firearm. Or to vote."

David looked at his hands in his lap. Is that what he wanted to do? Send Trevor to prison? Yes, he'd broken into his house, and yes, he made threatening statements on the phone. But it could also take up to two years to come to trial, which meant this thing would be hanging over his head, like a dark cloud over what could be the best time in his life. Did he want that?

"Are you having second thoughts?"

David bit his lip. At that point, Trevor had been out of jail for two weeks and David hadn't seen hide nor hair of him. That was a good sign, wasn't it?

"Do we have options besides a trial?"

"Sure," she answered. "We can always suggest a deal to the Assistant District Attorney in place of pressing charges."

"A deal?"

She nodded. "We can request supervised probation, with attached terms and conditions. There's no guarantee the ADA will accept the suggestions, but it doesn't hurt to try."

"What terms and suggestions do you think are appropriate?"

She leaned back in her chair, rocking slightly. "Well, I'd certainly keep the restraining order and make zero contact a term. At this point you might also stipulate the jointly owned property be sold. That way the two of you don't have to have anything to do with each other, but Trevor doesn't come out of it with nothing, which might mollify him a bit. I have to say, his attorney did tell me he didn't do very well during the two days he was at county. He said something to another prisoner and got punched in the mouth for his trouble. He ended up back in the ER before he'd been in custody four hours. I doubt we're going to have a hard time selling him on this, if it's the way you want to go." She gave him a level stare. "Actually it's entirely up to you and what you want."

"Can I get back to you?"

"Of course."

That night, David sat down with his mother, his sister, Jackson, and Michael. Predictably, Michael and Beth were out for blood and wanted Trevor to serve the maximum sentence on bread and water.

"I don't think we can stipulate the menu," David said, voice wry. "If it goes to trial, we can't really stipulate anything."

"Meaning he could get off." Jackson's eyes were narrowed as he spoke, and David nodded.

"He could. Karen says you never know what's going to happen with a jury. Besides that, I'm pissed at Trevor, but I don't know that I want to be responsible for him losing everything."

"David." Michael's voice was tinged with disbelief. "He broke into your house. With a crowbar."

"He was drunk!" David shot back. "How many of us have done dumbass things when we were drunk?"

"Well, I may have done dumb shit," Michael retorted, "but I've never committed a felony." He huffed and looked at the ceiling. "I can't believe you're even considering forgiving this guy."

"Oh, wait a minute." David leaned forward, his hand fisted on the table. "I'm not forgiving anything."

"Then what the hell are you talking about?" Beth's brow was furrowed in an irritated frown. "If he doesn't go to jail, and it's you making the concessions, then he gets away with it."

Beverley gave her a quelling look. "Beth, let your brother explain."

Jackson put his hand over David's on the table. "Tell us what you and Karen discussed, babe."

David drew calm from Jackson's unflappable, steady support. The warmth from his hand helped center him. "If he would agree to a deal, and his lawyer thinks he would, he'd be on probation."

"For how long?" Michael asked.

"For however long the judge decides. He's the final arbiter over whether this happens or not, but Karen says if I choose not to push for a trial, then he almost certainly will order probation for—well, she said at least eighteen months. He'd have to check in with a probation officer once a month. The restraining order would remain in effect, so he wouldn't be able to have any contact with me or come within five hundred feet of where I am at any time. He couldn't own a weapon, so if he actually did buy a gun, and it should be registered if he did, it would have to be sold or surrendered. He wouldn't be able to leave the state. He wouldn't be able to drink, and they'd do random blood tests to make sure he wasn't." He looked at the concerned faces around him. "And as a special term of his probation, anything he jointly owned with me would have to be sold."

"Meaning he'd have to sell the condo." Michael now looked thoughtful instead of angry.

"And he'd have to return his car. I signed the lease papers on the Mini Cooper, not him."

Michael smirked. "Well, there's a low down dirty shame."

Silence settled around the dining room table in his mother's house, and it remained for several seconds.

"And if he comes near you?" Jackson finally spoke into the quiet.

"If he so much as drives past the house, I can have him picked up and the deal is off the table." David looked from face to face. "My first impulse was to go for the trial too. I wanted him to suffer. But then I had to ask myself, what did I want him to suffer for? Breaking into the house, the harassing phone calls? Or cheating on me to begin with?" David shook his head. "I don't want to be that person," he finally said, his voice soft. "I want everything with Trevor to be over, done, but I don't have to destroy him to accomplish that."

Silence settled again.

Jackson cleared his throat. "You do what feels right to you, David. I'll back up any decision you make."

Michael huffed. "Nice, Jackson. Make the rest of us look like assholes if we disagree." He scowled. "Fine, but I don't have to like it."

David looked at his family. "Mom? Beth?"

Beth rolled her eyes. "You're a better person than I am. You know how I feel about the bastard, but ultimately it's up to you."

Beverley leaned across the table and put her hand on top of Jackson's and David's where they were linked. "I'll do whatever you want me to do, honey. But understand if I see him—" She gave him a matronly smile. "—I reserve the right to kick his ass."

David felt a bone-deep wave of relief. "Duly noted."

Jackson squeezed his fingers. "And I still think you should get a dog."

David leaned against Jackson's shoulder. "Agreed."

As expected, Trevor took the deal. The last and only time David saw him was at the hearing where the judge rubber-stamped what the ADA presented. They didn't speak. Trevor gave him one lingering look from where he sat beside his lawyer, but David wouldn't return his gaze, and he finally looked away. The condo sold within the first thirty days, for what David considered to be a reasonable profit. He let Trevor keep the furniture; he didn't want any of it anymore.

Boots had a couple of bruised ribs from where Trevor had kicked him, but was declared fine in less than a month. Jordyn and Paul were more than understanding about the whole thing, and the little dog continued to pay David visits on a regular basis when he escaped through their front door. David wanted to find a dog like him, but after searching the local humane society and rescue groups, he found out that corgis were extremely popular and didn't remain unclaimed very long. He'd about given up when Jackson called bright and early one brisk Saturday morning.

"What're you doin'?"

"Just waiting for you to get back," David answered. "I thought we were going to breakfast after the appetite you worked up." Jackson had spent several athletic hours the night before in David's bed and had only been gone about five hours. Shirley had recovered from her fall and was doing well, but Jackson still wasn't comfortable leaving her alone overnight. David looked forward to a time when they could go to sleep and wake up in each other's arms, but he understood his lover's caution.

"Change of plans, but I'll be over in about ten. Put on something warm."

David didn't even have a chance to say good-bye before he was gone. "Put on something warm?" David looked at his phone in confusion before slipping it into his pocket.

He assumed Jackson meant layers and went to his closet to change into a lavender polo with his purple Dolly Parton sweatshirt over the top. Michael had joked about the returned *queering* of his wardrobe, but Jackson liked all the color, which was good. David was done changing himself for anyone, even Jackson.

Exactly ten minutes after the phone call, his front door opened. Jackson still had his key and David hoped he never felt the need to give it back.

"David?"

"I'm here." David came out of the hallway and found Jackson all but bouncing on his toes. "What's going on?"

Jackson grabbed his hand, pulling him toward the door. "I found you something."

"Okay." David laughed as he allowed himself to be pulled outside.

It was overcast and cold, and the trees were bare and the lawns beginning to turn yellow. David had two giant urns of fall mums on his steps and bronze cushions with burgundy pillows on his swing, but that was about the only color in his yard. If you didn't take into account the bright red bandana around the neck of the black-and-tan corgi at the feet of a woman standing near the sidewalk. She bent with a smile and unhooked the leash from the dog's collar, and Jackson whistled.

"Come here, Scooter," he called, and the bat-like ears shot up, shoe-button black eyes bright. It ran to Jackson as fast as its short little white legs would allow, and Jackson crouched down, petting the dog when it arrived at his feet.

David stared at the beautiful little dog, his heart beating hard at the base of his throat. Jackson looked up at him where he stood on the porch.

"Well? Aren't you going to come and say hello?"

David came slowly down the steps, looking from Jackson to the dog. "Is it—?"

"Yours?" Jackson scratched behind the dog's ears. "Yes. If you want her."

David crouched on the dry lawn. "Her name is Scooter?"

Jackson nodded. "She belonged to an older lady who passed away recently. She just popped up on the corgi message boards yesterday morning. I called and the rescue lady Kate drove her over from Idaho this morning. She's a great little dog, David. She's three years old, completely housebroken and crate trained. And she's got a great personality."

David couldn't seem to think of a single thing to say. He couldn't recall a time in his life when anyone had gone out of their way for him since his parents. He reached out and touched the dog's fur, and it was every bit as soft as Boots's. She was a little smaller, and when she looked up at David, head cocked to one side and expression charming and alert, David lost his heart right there in his front yard.

"David?"

It finally registered that Jackson sounded worried, and David looked up at him quickly to find his dark brow furrowed with concern and perhaps a little hurt in his light eyes.

"Don't you like her?"

David pushed down the lump in his throat and threw his arms around Jackson's neck, knocking him to his ass right there on the lawn. He ended up sitting on Jackson's lap.

"I'd say that's a yes," the woman, who had walked closer, said from above them. David looked up at her, blinking back tears. She was beaming at him, and he managed a watery smile.

"That is most definitely a yes."

Scooter and Boots became fast friends. Jackson installed a doggie door leading out to the backyard and a fence to enclose it, and every few days Jordyn would bring Boots down for a "playdate." They'd race in and out of the door, and they were so damned cute David couldn't even be annoyed by the almost constant flapping. Michael adored her, although he laughed uproariously when David told him her name.

"Scooter? And Bootsy? Scoots and Boots for short? God, they're a country song."

David laughed along with him, but he didn't call her "Scoots." Having her greet him at the door when he came home was second only to having Jackson greet him with a kiss.

David shook off the memories, picked up the tray of meat and cheese he'd been arranging, and took it into the dining room, putting it on one of several large red serving dishes that were already arranged on his table. It wasn't really a full buffet meal, just snacks, but it looked festive and appetizing. There was a red runner down the center of the table, a clear bowl holding golden Christmas ornaments with spilling gold filigree ribbon at the center. Candles were already lit in large candleholders on the table and on the built-ins, and a fire burned brightly in the fireplace in the living room, not far from the Christmas tree. The tree was in the center of the front window and was decked out in white lights, gold bows, and mirrored glass ornaments. Jackson teased him that the place looked like a Pier 1 showroom floor, but David was proud of his home and wanted to show it off. The repairs and renovations were finally done, the floors gleamed, and the furniture was perfect on the jewel-toned area rugs, pillows and throws complimenting the furnishings. David would be the first to admit the house looked professionally decorated, but it was homey and elegant, and if it didn't look like an interior decorator had been involved, clearly he was doing something wrong.

There was a sound on the front porch and David turned in anticipation of Jackson's arrival. When Scooter went to the door, instead of her usual happy bark, she growled, and David stiffened.

"What's the matter?" he asked her. He looked out through the small glass windows in the door, but all he saw was refracted reflections of the lights from the tree in the beveled glass. He opened the door cautiously and peered out, but the porch was empty, as was the yard beyond. Scooter pushed past him, the hair down her spine standing at attention, her growls a low rumble as she peered around the dark yard.

It wasn't the first time it had happened since the night Trevor broke into the house. David tried to relax, told himself he had the alarm and the dog, and Trevor wasn't coming back, but he couldn't shake the feeling that someone was out there, watching him, waiting. He'd even spoken with Karen about it, but the fear remained. She told him to be easy on himself, that it would take time. He didn't like that answer at all.

David stepped out onto the porch, trying to peer into the shadows by his driveway. A blur of white dashed beneath the bushes near the street and Scooter barked again. Moments later a small gray-and-white cat darted out into the street. David felt the knots in his shoulders begin to unwind, and he laughed unsteadily.

"That's Precious, you goober," he said to the little dog. Precious belonged to his neighbor on the left, Mrs. Pearson. The cat was forever coming into the yard, and David wished the woman would keep her in the house. Vern said he wished it was legal to make her into a throw pillow. "Come on, Scooter. It's freezing out here."

They went back into the house, and he bent and ruffled the fur on her neck above her festive tartan collar.

"You're a good girl." She went back to her bed and David returned to the dining room, rearranging the platters. Again. It took a while for the trembling to go away, and by then he was heartily tired of it. Why couldn't he convince himself that everything was fine? Karen suggested he see a counselor to talk out his fears, and he was beginning to think it wasn't a bad idea.

Fifteen minutes later the front door opened and Jackson blew in on a gust of cold air. He was wearing a heavy dark blue jacket and a knitted skullcap, and held a bakery box in his hands. Scooter darted out of her plush bed and bounced around his feet like a windup toy.

"Hey, baby girl," Jackson greeted, rubbing her head. David crossed to him and took the white box from his hands, and Jackson kissed him quickly. His lips were cold. "Hey, babe." He kissed David again before pulling off his gloves and reaching up to snatch the hat from his head. He ran his fingers through his mussed dark hair. "Sorry I'm late. The traffic downtown was a bitch. Feels like snow out there tonight."

"It's in the forecast." David headed for the kitchen as Jackson shoved his gloves and hat into his jacket pocket, then hung everything on the wall-mounted coatrack David found in one of the antique stores downtown.

David took a deep breath as he walked into the kitchen. Now that Jackson was there, his nerves began to settle. And he didn't want Jackson to know how jittery he still was sometimes, jumping at shadows.

"What is that great smell?" Jackson followed David into the kitchen.

"Well, it's either the sandalwood candles or the Swedish meatballs in the Crock-Pot."

"Definitely something edible." Jackson lifted the lid on the Crock-Pot and inhaled deeply in appreciation. "Your mom make these?"

"She did," David said, arranging the elegantly decorated Christmas cookies on a platter that was waiting for them, a white snowflake doily covering the bottom. "And I won't even pretend to be insulted that you didn't think I was capable of making meatballs."

"I'm quite sure you're capable." Jackson reached over David's shoulder and grabbed a few cashews from a filled dish on the counter. "But why would you want to when she's so good at it?"

David kissed Jackson on the cheek. "And this is just one of the many reasons I love you. You get me."

"I love you too." Jackson's hands came to rest on David's hips. "New sweater?"

The deep red cable-knit had all but sung to him when he'd been in Nordstrom the afternoon before, and thank goodness it had been on sale at 50 percent off.

"Yes."

"The color looks great on you," Jackson said, appreciation in his eyes. "How soon can I take it off?"

David shot him a tolerant look over his shoulder. "After the party." Jackson grunted softly and grabbed another fistful of cashews. David picked up the crystal dish and handed it to him. "How about you take these out and put them on the table?"

"Sure."

David returned to putting the rest of the cookies on another platter and carried both of them into the dining room, setting one at each end of the table, then moving the cashews from next to the meat and cheese to next to a tray of chocolates. Jackson watched him with amusement.

"What?"

Jackson's teeth flashed. "Anyone ever tell you you're the teeniest bit anal?"

David straightened the napkins and plates for the fiftieth time. "Well, we all know you're anal," he quipped. Jackson laughed and grabbed David around the waist, pulling him in close.

"I certainly am," he growled playfully against David's ear, one of his hands sliding down over the soft gabardine covering David's ass as he nibbled the lobe of his ear.

The back door opened and closed loudly and a cool breeze slid through the dining room. A moment later, Michael appeared carrying a large portfolio. He made a show of covering his eyes.

"Mommy, make Daddy stop touching you in a naughty place."

David huffed in exasperation.

"I'm waiting on the paternity test results before you're in the will." Jackson patted David's ass and let his hand fall away.

Michael crossed to the living room and leaned the portfolio against the wall. "Did you hear that? My own father doesn't want me. Is it any wonder I need therapy? Hello, princess." He squatted down next to Scooter's bed and leaned forward, accepting her delicate lick on his chin. "This is the only one of you I'm claiming."

"Fine, you're both adopted." David turned to Jackson. "Sweetheart, will you get the wine glasses down from the cupboard for me?"

"Sure, babe. Where do you want them?"

David gestured to the top of the built-ins, where two bottles of red wine already sat. "Next to those."

Jackson took more of the nuts in his hand and sauntered out of the room, and David watched him go, loving the way his black jeans and dark blue sweater hugged his body.

"Oh my God, you two are nauseating." Michael stood up and walked over to David. "*Babe, sweetheart*." He bent and studied the cookies. "It's enough to make me erp. These are pretty. Where did you get them?"

"What makes you think I didn't make them?" Michael shot him a sardonic look and David laughed. "The bakery on Eighth." He took a step closer to Michael, his voice lowered. "Did you get it?"

Michael nodded. "It looks great."

"I wish there was time—" The doorbell rang and David sighed. "I guess it'll have to wait."

He answered the door, and for the next two hours, hosting took his mind off everything else.

His house was full of laughter and good friends, and it quelled a lot of David's nervous energy. His mother was there, taking much deserved praise for her meatballs and spinach dip. Gil and Vern arrived together, pink cheeked from the cold and presenting David with a bottle of champagne.

"Hostess gift," Vern quipped, winking.

Manny came in alone, looking faintly uncomfortable until Jackson managed to get him to drink a glass of wine. Slowly the tension in his shoulders eased, and he ended up sitting on the sofa with Beverley, eating her meatballs and having an animated conversation about gardening.

Tommy and his brother arrived with the news that the snow had finally begun to fall, and everyone took a few minutes to adjourn to the porch to watch the tiny white flakes drifting down. They weren't sticking yet, but David hoped there would be enough to cover the lights he'd strung in the bushes out front. He loved the way Christmas lights looked through snow. It was one of the things he'd missed when living in the condo; there'd been nowhere to hang Christmas lights. They all stood transfixed by the drifting flakes until Vern growled.

"It's just fucking snow, people. I'm going back inside before I freeze my nuts off." He stalked through the door.

"Charming, Vernon," Gil called after him. "Really. It's that sparkling personality that garners you the best invitations."

"Blow me, Gilbert."

Gil rolled his eyes to the sound of laughter. Gradually they all returned inside, and people settled into conversation groups around the room. Michael and Gil snarked at each other, and Vern officiated. Manny and Beverley were joined by Tommy and his brother, balancing plates on their knees and setting wine glasses carefully on coasters on the coffee table.

Everyone seemed to be settling into a pleasantly full lull, and with a fresh jolt to his nerves, David realized it was time. He caught Michael's eye, nodding toward the office. Michael excused himself and gracefully navigated the legs of the other people sitting on the couch before he left the room. Jackson came to David in front of the fireplace and slipped his solid arm around his waist. "Take a couple of deep breaths."

David pressed his forehead to Jackson's shoulder. "Do I look as if I need them?"

"You're looking a little green around the gills. These are our friends, babe. You don't have anything to worry about. And if they don't like the idea, they can always work as contractors for me, the way they do now."

"True. I just thought they might want a part of it, you know?"

"Don't rule that out before you've even begun."

Michael passed them with a black easel and stood it up in front of the fireplace, reaching for the portfolio and lifting it into place.

David rubbed his hands together to try to get some circulation back into his fingers; they were freezing. "I wonder if I might have everyone's attention for a moment?" David had to repeat it, but finally all eyes were on him, and he felt a bit like a rabbit caught in a trap. "If it's okay with all of you, Michael and I had an idea we'd like to run past you."

"If it's a time-share in Florida, I'm out of here," Vern grumbled, and everyone laughed.

"It's not a time-share, I promise."

"Okay, Michael." Gil leaned back on the couch, his hands behind his head. "You've got my attention." He smirked and winked at Michael, and David noticed that Michael ignored him. But he blushed too.

"Okay." David rubbed his palms on his thighs to dry them. "The idea actually came from something Michael said to me on a day you were all here working together. He asked me if everyone on the crew here that day was gay, and we talked about the fact it's been universally hard to find work because of the mind-set of the major contractors here in town. Michael asked me, why didn't you all consider starting your own renovations business? We all know how much work is available to be done on this side of town, particularly with the Janic houses gaining in value. The work you do is beautiful, Gil. Truly, better than anything I can get done on my large-scale jobs."

Gil bowed his head slightly. "Thank you."

"And, Manny," David went on, turning to the other man, "how much work could be done on the plumbing of these places if you were attached to an actual contractor?"

"Quite a bit, I imagine." He looked as if he didn't want to be put on the spot, his face staining pink across his high cheekbones.

"But more than you're doing now?" David asked. Manny spent a moment thinking about it. The drawn-out silence reminded David of Jackson.

"Anytime a contractor pulls you in on a job, it can lead to more work."

"Same thing for you, Tommy. Do you make more money doing your own advertising and stuff, or do you make more contracted to someone else?"

Tommy looked at his brother. He shrugged. "We've only ever done it on our own. I gotta tell you, though, if there was somebody acting as contractor, pulling us in to work, that would be golden."

Gil's brows pulled down in the middle. "So, what exactly are you suggesting, David?"

David paused to center his whirling thoughts. "I'm suggesting that we pool our resources and start our own company, made up of gay employees and their allies." He nodded at Tommy's brother, who gave him a brief smile. "And I say we market it as precisely what it is: a renovation and design firm completely run by gays."

David could see Gil and Vern recoiling a bit, but he was prepared for that. "Gil, you lost a profitable job and you said you thought the reason was your bumper sticker, right?"

"Well, yeah. But I don't have any proof."

"I know it wasn't your skill, and they'd have known it too if a bumper sticker hadn't changed their mind. See, here's the beauty of this. If they hire us, they'll know we're gay going in because we won't be pretending to be anything else. What did you say to me, Jackson? We don't have to throw a parade and fart rainbow glitter, but anyone who hired us would know."

"How would they know?" Vern asked. "Pink shirts? Short shorts with suspenders? Dolly Parton sweatshirts?" There were scattered chuckles and David felt his face heat.

"They'd know," he said, turning to the easel, "because of our logo."

This was the part he'd been the most nervous about. He didn't know how Jackson was going to react and that made him feel off-center. When he pulled the piece of poster board from in front of the sturdy foam core sign, his hands were shaking. He set the board aside and waited.

On the foam core was a large, pale pink triangle, upside down, outlined with a thin black line. Superimposed over the top in elegant script was Delta, then below the point of the triangle in even block letters were the words Renovation, Restoration, and Design. The room settled into silence as the men studied it, but David was looking for only one reaction.

Jackson stared at the logo for a long time, then looked at David. David wasn't sure what he'd been expecting, but it certainly wasn't the raw, aching jumble of emotions that swirled in Jackson's expressive eyes.

Jackson leaned in, his forehead against David's. "It's perfect."

David released a shuddering breath.

There was a spirited debate about David's idea going on, and he wasn't sure any of the others were actually going to go for it. There were lots of details to be ironed out. But it was a start, at least a talking point. He hadn't given his notice yet. But if even Gil and Vern and Jackson were the only ones onboard, and he knew Michael was, well… that was a start. They could take work with that group and pull others in as the jobs demanded. David felt a kernel of excitement down where his passion for his degree had first smoldered, deep in his gut. This might actually work.

He closed his eyes and leaned against Jackson's side, surprised in all the touching he'd done since he arrived that Jackson hadn't felt the plastic wrap taped protectively just above David's right buttcheek. That was the other surprise for Jackson, the one he'd had done that morning after Jackson went home.

There was so much good happening in his life, and as he cued back in to listen to the conversation, he realized he and Jackson weren't the only ones who thought this was a good idea, after all.

Jackson dropped his arm around David's shoulders as they listened to the other men argue the salient points. He might actually be able to go back to doing what he loved, and all the guys might have regular work if they could get people comfortable with the idea. That was the question, wasn't it? Would anyone hire them?

The debate went on for another hour and a half, and nothing was really settled when their friends began to leave, but David felt most of them were at least willing to have further discussions about it. It was more than he'd expected, and a small ember of excitement glowed in his chest.

Michael and Beverley were the last to leave, and as she headed for the door, Beverley caught hold of Jackson's arm.

"I'm going to go and spend the night with your mother," she told him. "You stay here and help David straighten up, then you boys can sleep in tomorrow."

Jackson leaned in and pressed a kiss to Beverley's cheek. "Thank you, Beverley," he murmured. Beverley was trying to get him to call her Mom, but he said it was weird when she felt more like a friend than a parent.

She patted his chest fondly. "Such a nice boy." She wrapped David in a hug. "Everything was lovely." She lowered her voice when Jackson turned to Michael. "I'll text you."

David nodded, then helped her with her coat and scarf. "Love you, Mom," he said as he opened the door for her. "The roads will be slick, so drive carefully."

She gave him a jaunty wave and navigated her way carefully down the front walk to her sedan parked at the curb. The snow was beginning to stick, but there wasn't much on the walkway yet. Still, he watched until she was in her car, the doors safely locked.

Michael crouched down, his face in Scooter's fur, but he was already wearing his coat and knit cap. He straightened as David approached and, uncharacteristically for Michael, pulled David into a firm hug. David returned it with a smile.

"You did good," Michael said against David's ear. "I think they're going to go for it."

"I think they are too." David leaned back, looking into Michael's gray eyes. "Can I ask you a question?"

"Sure." Michael took his gloves from his pocket and began to pull them on.

"When are you going to cut Gil a break?"

Michael went still. "What?"

"Seriously, Michael. What makes you think it couldn't work with you two?"

Michael made a face. "The fact I don't think of him like that." But he was blushing again. David chose not to piss him off by mentioning it. "Look, just because you're all neatly paired off doesn't mean the rest of us want that."

"Okay." David gave him a slight smile, and Michael scowled as he turned to go. At the last minute, he kissed David on the cheek, then left the house in a rush, closing the door firmly behind him.

"You know you're taking your life in your hands every time you do that."

Jackson slipped his arms around David from behind, kissing him beneath his ear. David tilted his head to give him better access.

"Michael doesn't scare me." He covered Jackson's hands with his and leaned back into his strength. "And he says he doesn't have feelings for Gil, but he's lying."

"Yeah, well, he's not the only one. Gil keeps telling me Michael is too *snotty* for him." Jackson chuckled. "But he likes it." He nipped the lobe of David's ear briefly, and a shiver worked its way down David's spine, detoured between his legs, and slithered its way right into his cock.

"Okay, enough talking about other people." David broke from Jackson's embrace and grabbed his hand, backing toward the bedroom.

Jackson grinned. "What about cleaning up?"

"The mess isn't going anywhere," David said. "I'll get to it later."

"Works for me."

The sly smile on Jackson's face made David's dick even harder, but there was a shiver of nerves in the mix too. What was Jackson going to think of what he'd done? Would he like it, or would he feel like David had gone too far, assumed too much?

When they got to the bedroom, Jackson yanked his dark blue sweater off over his head, then reached for the hem of David's. Pausing for just a second with David's arms caught over his head, Jackson leaned forward and licked David's nipple. He shivered as gooseflesh broke out over his chest in response, and his nipples contracted into hard points. Jackson tossed the sweater aside and David backed up a step or two, his hands going to his belt. Jackson watched him avidly, his hands making short work of his own jeans and underwear. He straightened from kicking them off, and David took in the toned, bronze body, the muscled legs, the heavy, thick cock that hung between his legs. Want rolled through him, and he marveled again that anyone who looked like Jackson was standing naked, waiting for him. He kicked off his shoes and shoved down his slacks and briefs, but when Jackson reached for him, David held out his hand, stopping him.

"What…?"

David smiled tremulously, then turned, his head lowered. He was still half-hard, but scared enough that his erection was fading fast.

There was no sound from behind him, and that made his nerves ratchet higher, his trembling increased. He was afraid to look over his shoulder, and Jackson wasn't saying anything. David's heart was hammering like it wanted to escape through his sternum. Finally, when he thought he might expire from the tension, David felt a hand slide delicately down his spine, from his neck to the crease in his ass, and then over to the plastic-covered tattoo that now graced his hip, just beneath his waistline.

"David."

Jackson's voice sounded suffocated and unsteady. He cleared his throat. "David. My God, babe." His hands came to rest on David's hips and he turned him. David sought his eyes, startled by the tears rimming his dark lashes.

"Oh," David whispered. "I didn't mean to make you sad."

Jackson shook his head. "That's not it. I'm not sad. I'm just so… fucking touched, David." He put his arms around David and pulled him in, holding him tight.

David wrapped his arms around Jackson's neck, pressing his cheek to Jackson's, allowing the feel of his warm skin and his own relief to take the tension from his body.

After David had first seen Jackson's tattoo, he'd asked Shirley to show him the pictures of Jackson's great-uncle Erich, the one who had inspired the pink triangle on Jackson's hip. The one who vanished in the middle of the Nazi Holocaust. Jackson's grandmother had been right; he did look like Erich. Erich's face had been slender, his skin paler, his features more delicate, but the eyes were the same, obviously pale blue even in the old sepia-toned photos, and his dark hair and his hairline were identical. Just seeing the face of the doomed young man made David almost unbearably sad. So much had changed in the world and yet so much was still the same. So much hatred remained, and he knew it was silly, but he wanted to wrap Jackson up and protect him.

That was the day the idea for the matching tattoo entered his mind, and he hadn't been able to shake it. Hoping Jackson wouldn't find it silly, he'd made an appointment for ten o'clock, knowing Jackson would be with his mom by then. Two hours later he bore the mirror image of Jackson's tattoo on his hip. It had hurt like a bitch, and it looked so much darker on David's pale hip, especially with the red, swollen skin around it. But David was proud he'd made it through, and proud that now he and Jackson shared something important, something significant. Something permanent.

"You know this means forever, right?" Jackson asked, his voice rough.

"God, I hope so."

Jackson's response was a short, raw laugh, and he lifted David off his feet, turning and falling onto the bed on his back with David sprawled on top of him. Jackson slid his hands into David's hair, anchoring his head in place, and kissed him with more unfettered passion than David had ever been kissed with in his life. It made his body feel weak, his hip joints loose, and he tried to give back as good as he got. Jackson's tongue was in his mouth and David sucked on it, pressing it against his soft palate.

Jackson groaned, easing David's lips even farther apart, running his fingers down his back and into the crease in his ass. David teased Jackson that he was obsessed with his asshole, but when they were in bed like this and David could feel every inch of Jackson's smooth, softly furred skin against him, all David wanted was to feel Jackson's cock breaching him, filling him. If Jackson was obsessed, then David was too.

They hadn't been on the bed long when Jackson carefully slipped from beneath David to come around behind him. He pressed David's hands to the headboard and whispered next to his ear, "Don't move."

Jackson's hands went to David's asscheeks and, avoiding the skin that was still red and sensitive, he massaged the plump mounds of David's ass. His hand spread between David's shoulder blades as he eased him farther forward, then returned to his ass, pulling his cheeks apart. David felt really exposed until he felt Jackson's lips softly brush the freshly inked skin, then slid lower, kissing his exposed hole. Then his tongue swirled around the dusky, furled flesh.

David cried out, arching his back at a more pronounced angle. He loved when Jackson did this, loved the feel of his tongue against the hypersensitive flesh, loved when he pushed against his hole, trying to slip inside. David bore down slightly and pushed back, and Jackson's tongue was right there, pressing against him, searching for admittance. Then his tongue was replaced with long, lubed fingers, pressing inside, stretching him, finding the spot that made his cock flex and his balls feel tight.

"You ready, babe?" Jackson murmured against his ear.

Feeling shaky and weak, David still managed to shake his head. "Not like this. I want to see your face."

"This skin is raw back here, David. It'll hurt."

"Not if you lie on your back and I ride you."

Jackson didn't speak for a moment. "We can do that," he said finally, and slid under David to his back. David lifted one knee and straddled him, then positioned himself over Jackson's groin. He reached down and curled his fingers around the base of Jackson's thick cock, positioned the head at his opening and, bearing down, slowly began to lower himself. They'd waited until two sets of tests had cleared them both before having sex unprotected, and that bare skin beneath his fingers was something more that felt like a promise, an unspoken vow. It took a moment for him to be able to ease enough to accept the rounded head, but once it was past the tight sphincter muscles, David was able to lower himself slowly, feeling the stretch, the slow burn that caught his breath and made his eyes roll up. He lifted slightly and allowed himself to sink down again, and Jackson slid his hands up his thighs.

"Babe, you feel so amazing. So hot, so tight…."

David heard him as if from a distance; what was going on inside of his body had all his attention. The thick, beautiful arc of Jackson's flesh was filling him, so full it felt like he was touching the back of David's throat. Especially when he managed to lower himself all the way down until his ass was on Jackson's groin. David let out a ragged sigh and Jackson reached between them, curling his slick hand around David's cock, stroking the sensitive flesh with a delicate touch, base to tip, then down again. David fought to catch his breath and opened his eyes and looked into Jackson's, only to find him watching him carefully.

"You ready for more, baby?" Jackson asked, the fingers around David's cock tightening, his next stroke firm. "You ready for me?"

David gasped at the dual sensation of Jackson's cock pressing against his prostate and his hand stroking David's rigid length. He nodded raggedly. "Whatever you want," he managed.

"Go up onto your knees," Jackson urged. David did it, allowing the hot thickness of Jackson's prick to slide nearly out of him. Jackson's hands on his hips stopped him before he was completely off and held him in place. "Stroke yourself." David fumbled for his cock. He was so overstimulated, he could scarcely function, but he finally managed to wrap his fingers around his prick and began to pull gracelessly. "Perfect," Jackson said, his voice a low rumble. "Perfect."

Jackson planted his feet on the bed and began to thrust up, driving his cock into the tight heat of David's body. Pleasure washed over Jackson's face; his eyes went half-lidded and his mouth relaxed into a soft O. David leaned forward slightly, the one hand still stroking his prick, the other leaning against Jackson's chest, and the change of angle brought Jackson's cock into direct contact with David's prostate. He shuddered, needy sounds he was too far gone to be embarrassed about spilling from his mouth. Jackson began to move faster, driving up harder, and their skin was slapping together, the sound of the creaking bed and the ragged breathing the only accompaniment. Then Jackson grabbed David's hand from around his cock, linking their slippery fingers, taking David's swollen prick in his own hand and gripping him hard around the base. David made a frustrated noise and rocked into each upward thrust, searching for the perfect angle. When he found it, he cried out, his body shuddering.

"There?" Jackson asked, pushing up harder, stroking David faster. "There, babe?"

David nodded raggedly, rocking back into each thrust and forward into Jackson's hand. The skin of his prick was so tight it ached, and each time Jackson's cock nudged the bundle of nerves inside of him, David came closer and closer to falling completely apart. Then it was all too much, the pounding on his prostate, the feeling of Jackson moving thick and hard inside of him, and David cried out, every muscle in his body clamping down and going rigid as he spilled thick ropes of opalescent white over Jackson's fingers and onto the tanned skin and black hair of Jackson's belly. He hung there, shuddering, everything tight; then everything relaxed and he collapsed onto Jackson's chest, smearing the mess between them, his face pressed to Jackson's throat.

Jackson wrapped his arms around David, holding tight and pumping up into him until he finished with a choked groan. Then his arms eased and he held him tenderly to his chest.

They lay catching their breath for several minutes before Jackson rolled them to their sides, careful not to lay David on the new ink on his hip, as he withdrew from his body. He left the bed, and David remained where he'd been put, so limp and loose-jointed he doubted he could move if he wanted to. Jackson was back moments later with a warm washcloth, and David lay there with his eyes closed as Jackson tenderly cleaned him up.

"Feels good," he managed to say, his voice hoarse. He didn't remember yelling, but it felt as if he had.

"Good." Jackson rubbed the cloth over David's stomach and chest, then tenderly cleaned his ass. When he was done, he took the cloth back to the bathroom and came back to the bed, pulling the blankets up before sliding in beside David. He slipped his arms around him and pulled David's limp body in close, and David ducked his head under Jackson's chin, resting his cheek against his chest. Jackson's heart thumped calmly, even as his own was still trying to slow into a normal rhythm.

"That was amazing," Jackson said finally. His voice was a deep rumbling under David's ear. He curled his fingers as far as they would go around Jackson's bicep and squeezed.

"Yes."

"Are you okay?"

"Still coming down."

"Okay."

Jackson stroked David's sides and his back until he was breathing slowly and steadily and right on the edge of sleep.

"Babe?"

"Hmm?"

"I've never loved anyone as much as I love you."

Heart overflowing, David placed a kiss right over Jackson's heart. "I love you too."

They went peacefully to sleep as the snow continued to fall.

JACKSON WAS already up and in the shower when David's cell phone buzzed the next morning. He pulled it from its charging cable and squinted to read the text, then gave up and grabbed his glasses. Once he'd read it, he was out of bed and putting on clean underwear when Jackson wandered back in.

"Morning, sleeping beauty," he said with a smile, kissing David quickly. "I thought you might want to sleep in while I shoveled the driveway."

"I just got a text from Mom." David stepped into a pair of Levi's. "They want us to come to your mom's as soon as we can get there."

Jackson stilled, his brow furrowing. "What's wrong?"

"They didn't say anything was wrong. They just want us there."

That was all it took to get Jackson hurrying into his clothes too. David did manage to get himself dressed and his teeth brushed, but the rest of the grooming would have to wait until he got back. They bundled up in several layers, let Scooter out to do her business, then put her back in the house before climbing into Jackson's truck. Sitting wasn't particularly comfortable, and David grimaced as he tried to find a comfortable position. Jackson reached across the cab once he had the engine running and the heater on, and gripped David's hand.

"I'm sorry. I didn't mean to hurt you."

David gave him a smile and a small shake of his head. "You didn't hurt me."

"But when you sat down, the look on your face…."

"Oh, I'm sore. But I participated enthusiastically." He settled on one hip with a soft sigh. That would work. "And to be honest with you, I don't mind it. It reminds me you've been there. I can feel you for hours after, and I kind of like that."

"I'll take your word for it." Jackson navigated the heavy truck through the snowy streets with expert skill.

"Have you ever bottomed?" David had wondered, but he liked it so much and Jackson seemed satisfied with their current arrangement, so it had never come up.

"Once, a long time ago," Jackson admitted softly. "The other guy didn't know what he was doing and I tore." David wanted to find whoever had hurt him and wring his neck. "And I was a kid, determined to try everything. I'm damned lucky I didn't catch something."

"Aren't we all?" David looked out through the windshield at the snow.

"So, in answer to your question," Jackson said after clearing his throat, "I haven't got much experience bottoming, but if you wanted me to…." He hesitated. "I'd try it for you."

David looked over at him. "Maybe, at some point. I like what we're doing right now."

Jackson shot him a smile. "Me too." He squeezed David's hand and drove the rest of the way to his mother's with their fingers linked.

When they turned the corner onto the street where Shirley lived, even from the corner David saw his mother's car parked in the driveway. There was also a Coldwell Banker for sale sign in the middle of the snowy front yard. When Jackson saw it, his brow furrowed.

"What's that all about?"

"I don't know." David shrugged. "There's your mom. Why don't we ask her?"

Jackson parked and they climbed down out of the truck as Shirley and Beverley came out onto the front porch. David had seen Shirley just a couple of days before when they'd all had lunch, and she was so much stronger than she'd been. She didn't even have the walker with her today. Her hair was styled and her face was bright and alert. Jackson strode through the snow on the front yard and paused near the steps.

"Mom, what's up with the for sale sign?"

She pulled on her gloves, a smile on her face. "Oh, I've decided to sell the house, honey."

"Did you plan to tell me?" he asked, sounding faintly confused. "And if you sell the house, where are you going?"

David noticed with satisfaction that he didn't ask where *he* would be going.

"Well." Shirley crossed her arms. "Initially I'd thought to move in to an assisted living facility. One where if my MS progressed, there would be people to take care of me. But my dear friend here"—she gestured to Beverley—"has convinced me I could get the same and perhaps even a better level of care by moving in with her, and I wouldn't have doctors and nurses hovering around unless I needed them."

"You're going to move in with Beverley and sell Grandma and Grandpa's house?" Jackson still appeared faintly mystified.

"Honey," Shirley said softly, "this is no more my home than that monstrosity your father insisted on. This is my mother's house, and I don't want to live here anymore. By moving in with Bev, I can have my own room and my own bathroom, and the two of us get on well together. The only thing I'll regret leaving are the roses. But we can plant roses in Bev's backyard. You would help us, wouldn't you, Jackson?"

"I… sure, Mom. If that's what you wanted."

"It is." She held out one hand and he stepped up on the porch and took it. "Honey, you know how much I love you. But this isn't the right time in your life to be living with your mother. You need to be living your life, just as I need to be living mine."

"I haven't minded, Mom."

"I know, sweetheart. But wouldn't you really rather live with David?"

Jackson looked back at David. He was still standing in the yard, snowflakes drifting softly down around him. Their eyes met and held. "Well, of course. If that would be okay with him."

Then they were all looking at David, and his heart was beyond full. "I can't imagine anything that would make me happier."

One corner of Jackson's lips quirked. "Yeah?"

"Oh, yeah."

"I have an idea," Beverley said brightly. "Why don't we all go to Perkins for breakfast and we can sort out the details." She looked between the two men. "Have you boys eaten?"

"No, actually," Jackson answered. "We got your text and came right over."

"Well, good. I'd really like some pancakes. Shall we meet you there? We'll order for you."

"Mom, we can order our own breakfast," David protested.

"You don't want pancakes?" She smiled at Jackson. "You don't want pancakes, Jackson?"

He held up his hands. "Go ahead and order for me, Bev. I love pancakes."

"Kiss-ass," David muttered. Jackson shrugged, but he didn't look repentant.

"Come along, boys," Beverley all but sang as she headed for her sedan, a bemused Shirley in tow. "Pancakes are waiting."

"I want an omelet, Mom," David said, exchanging an amused glance with Jackson. "A Denver omelette."

"I can't hear you," she replied, getting in her car.

"A Denver omelette?" Jackson reached out and David took his hand as they walked to the truck.

"Oh, I'll be eating pancakes. That was just my attempt to assert my masculinity." Jackson shot him an amused look, and David smacked his shoulder. "Shut up."

They walked past the sign in the yard and Jackson gestured toward it. "This is a surprise."

"It is," David agreed, opening the truck door and climbing up into the cab. Jackson walked around the hood, taking his seat behind the wheel. He fastened his seat belt, his eyes on David. "Why do I get the feeling this is less a surprise to you than it is to me?"

David wasn't going to lie to him. "Shirley has been talking to Mom about it for a while, the thought of going into assisted living. It upset my mom quite a bit."

"Why?"

"Because Mom doesn't feel Shirley is ready for one of those places, and the expense is astronomical. She's afraid it would wipe out your mom's savings."

"Which it probably would." Jackson looked thoughtful. He fell into one of his trademark silences until the truck was running and David was belted in. "And it doesn't bother you, my mom and her health issues moving in with your mom?"

David shook his head. "No, not at all. My mom knows what she's doing. She took care of Dad, and she was amazing. And honestly, I think she's lonely without him. They're young enough that maybe they can travel a little, and they both love working in the garden." David shrugged. "Frankly I'm glad Mom won't be in the house alone."

"And me moving in with you? Is that a step you're ready to take?"

David studied his strong profile. "Absolutely."

"You sound pretty sure."

"I've never been more sure of anything." David paused. "Unless you aren't....."

Before David could say another word, Jackson grabbed his hand and held it firmly. He let the truck idle at the curb even after Beverley pulled out of the drive and disappeared around the corner. Finally, Jackson turned to David, his gaze level.

"I'm sure, David. I've been sure for a long time. I just didn't know what I was supposed to do about my mom. But between the two of them, they seem to have that problem solved."

David bit his lip to keep a smile from spreading over his lips. "You know they'll be living just down the street now." He tried to look dour. "That means barbeques with my sister and Sunday breakfasts at the house."

Jackson smirked. "If you're trying to convince me this is a bad idea, your mother's cooking isn't the way to do it."

David grinned. "We'll have to lock the doors and turn off our phones if we want to have sex uninterrupted."

"That's not much of a hardship." Jackson cocked his head to one side. "So, what do you say, Mr. Snyder? You interested in making me a kept man?"

David couldn't stop his smile now if he tried. "Sounds like a plan to me."

"Excellent. And we'd better go before our mothers send the state patrol out looking for us."

David agreed; knowing his mother, he found the scenario uncomfortably likely.

Jackson drove through the snowy streets, and David felt safe, cocooned in the warmth of the cab with the man who was about to share his house, his bed, his life.

He hadn't wanted Jackson to feel pressured to move in with him, and he didn't appear to. They would discuss it more later, but for now it was enough that he seemed happy about it. After everything David had been through with Trevor, he hadn't been sure he could ever make that sort of commitment again. Then Jackson walked into his life, and his heart hadn't asked his permission. It opened up to let Jackson in, and David did the only thing he could do: he followed.

David glanced across the cab and saw a smile tugging at the corner of Jackson's lips.

"What's that smile about?"

Jackson's blue eyes were shining. "It's just exciting, you know? A new beginning, for all of us."

"Yeah," David agreed. "It is."

A new beginning, and pancakes waiting.

It didn't get much better than that.

DIANA COPLAND began writing in the seventh grade, when she shamelessly combined elements of Jane Eyre and Dark Shadows to produce an overwrought Gothic tale that earned her an A- in creative writing, thanks entirely to the generosity of her teacher.

Born and raised in southern California, Diana moved to the Pacific Northwest after losing a beloved spouse to AIDS in 1995.

She lives in eastern Washington with four obnoxious cats, near her two wonderful adult children.

Don't Twunk With My Heart

Renae Kaye

His **RIGHT CHOICE**

MEN OF FALCON POINTE

THIANNA DURSTON

www.ingramcontent.com/pod-product-compliance
Lightning Source LLC
Chambersburg PA
CBHW070058260626
47160CB00004B/1249